THE LIGHTHOUSE
KEEPER'S WIFE

by

JC Restorick

ISBN-13: 978-1-3999-9225-1

For my long suffering Dad

Prologue

Christmas Eve 1854

The rigging was slapping against the yardarms from the ships moored in the harbour when Caleb, the Under-Keeper, descended the stairs into the snug at the foot of the lighthouse. A well-built lantern-jawed figure he had to ascend and descend the stairs sideways to accommodate the width of his shoulders, his heavy sea boots marking every step. The door to the quayside was propped open as the little stove threw out enough heat as though to boil a man alive.

"That's the lamps all filled Willie. We're all set to the

morn." Caleb moved to the outside door and glanced out across the harbour into the dusk, his breath frosting in the cold night air.

A giant Christmas wreath hung from the sign for the Downshire Hotel at the end of the pier, and festival lanterns from its windows painted the glass grey water with glowing warm streaks of colour, as the sounds of revellers drifted across the bay.

Willie the Head-Keeper rose from his chair and joined Caleb outside. He had an empty clay pipe clenched in his teeth. He studied Caleb for a moment then said, "What's the hurry? Sure we've all night to get the place squared away?"

"I see the Clancy is in," Caleb offered.

"Aye, she is."

"An' the Bright Girl."

"All berthed up and snug." Willie scouted around for his tobacco.

"You're pals with their Masters are you not?"

"Man and boy. Have you seen my tobacco pouch?"

Caleb was now hopping from foot to foot as he wrung his cap in his hands. In a burst of inspiration, he dragged a small package out of his pocket and thrust it towards Willie, "Happy Christmas, Willie!"

"Here wot's this?" Willie muttered.

"Just a wee present from me. I thought you'd like to share a pouch with them," he nodded in the vague direction of the door.

Grinning Willie said, "But leave you all alone here? On

Christmas Eve? That doesn't seem fair?"

"Oh Willie, I thought if I could just nip home and see
—"

"Go on then ye big lummox ye. Go and see the bairn then."

Caleb seized a nicely wrapped parcel from the table. "This is for Becky. This's her first wee Christmas, the bairn God love her."

Willie indicated a small parcel on the windowsill by the foot of the stairs. "An' that's —" but Caleb was gone, "from Mrs McKee and me," Willie finished.

She'd lain with half the town and her belly beginning to swell afore young Caleb had wed her, Willie thought to himself as he spat on the stove and banged his pipe against his knee. *A good lad young Caleb, but a bloody fool all the same.*

Caleb hurried along the shore towards the row of red-brick cottages. The windows were all aglow and throwing out light as a cheerful scene revealed itself. Children were playing in the yard, hunting out the sparse piles of snow hiding under the hedges and shrieking with glee as the muddy snowballs hit their targets. Bidding a Happy Christmas to a knot of his neighbours gossiping in the falling gloom he passed them by. Tied up outside his door was a big Chestnut mare. Caleb paused to stroke her neck. She craned round to nuzzle his shoulder in greeting. The horse was cold to the touch. "That's not fair," Caleb thought, "it's too cool of an evening for her to be standing out here."

Dazzled after the dark of the night Caleb took a moment to focus when he stepped into his kitchen. A pleasant room with a lit fire under a mantelpiece, well stocked with Caleb's pipes and assorted bric-a-brac, was completed by three stockings hanging from it. A large Welsh dresser laden with crockery and a cheerful paraffin lamp burning was against one wall, with doors on each side, and a table with high-backed chairs took centre place.

Standing alone by the mantelpiece, with his coat off, toasting his arse by the fire, was an Excise man he recognised from about the town. "Johnson what are!" Caleb paused, "Your horse is cold…what…what are you doing —"

Johnson started back from the mantelpiece. "This isn't —"

The two men stood looking puzzled at one another for an instant when Liz, Caleb's new bride, backed out of Becky's bedroom bedroom door. "That's her off." She turned and froze as she saw Caleb. "What are you doing here?"

Caleb swung back to Johnston with sudden fury, "What are you…no By God! Do you take me for a fool!" Caleb seized a heavy walking stick by the door, "I'll teach you both such a lesson."

Johnston paled, grabbed his hat and coat, and dashed around the table for the front door. Caleb almost had him when his wife ran in front of him. Scratching at his face she cried, "You leave him alone. He's —"

With one arm Caleb swept Liz aside sending her flying

against the wall, jarring the dresser and upsetting the lit paraffin lamp. As she slumped stunned to the floor the paraffin lamp bled blue flame. The fire puddled and leaked down and across the flags to the threshold of Becky's bedroom where it quickly caught the raw timbers.

"I'll have you!" roared Caleb as he followed Johnston into the night. The fleeing suitor had one one hand on the saddle and a foot in the stirrup trying to mount the frightened horse which was circling away from him. Caleb grabbed at his coattails, pulling him to the ground, and then the mare broke free and was off with flailing reins, scattering the onlookers who were thoroughly enjoying the unexpected entertainment. Johnston darted down onto the dunes that ran in front of the cottages pursued by Caleb.

Behind them, the cottage started to burn bright.

"Come out of there you coward," shouted Caleb as he stumbled through the whin bushes beating them with his stick.

The roof caught alight.

I'll find you," screamed Caleb as he thrashed around randomly. "You show yourself now. If I have to find you, you'll be sorry."

As the roof collapsed into the flames. The sound penetrated Caleb's fury and he quickly retraced his steps pushing his way through the crowd his anger replaced by fear. The crowd parted for him and he heard muttering, *He's back*! mingled with, *He's killed Johnson!* Their anger suddenly grew and cries of *Call the Police!* started to ring out.

Becky's Christmas present lay in the mud beside Johnston's hat and Caleb picked it up turning over and over in his hands as he stared dumbly at the inferno. Some of the Cottagers attempted halfheartedly to seize him but he shrugged them off. *Stay there! And the Peelers are coming!* stabbed through Caleb's pain. He looked down in shame as he bulled his way through the crowd and then ran.

Willie McKee was dozing by the fire when the door flew open and Caleb swept in jolting him awake, "What's that Caleb? You're back already?"

Caleb slammed the door shut behind him and then cried out, "You'll have to go Willie." He stood there looking wild-eyed about the small room.

"What are you talking about lad? What ails ye?"

"Oh Willie I've done a terrible thing and they'll hang me for it! My lovely Becky and…" Caleb stepped forward and took a firm grip on Willie's shoulder. "I'm sorry! I… I've done something terrible!" Willie was pulled out of his chair and bundled outside before he knew what was happening. Standing in the cold night air Willie felt his hand seized. "Goodbye, Willie. You've been a good friend." Caleb shook Willie's hand then, with a desperate glance, retreated back inside the lighthouse closing the door behind him.

The sound of shouting grew in the darkness and Willie spied a crowd coming up the pier towards him. In the lead was the Sergeant and two Constables from the barracks.

"What's going on?" Willie appealed to the crowd.

The Sergeant Restrick spoke, "Willie, is young Caleb in there?"

"Aye John, sure he's just got back this minute and put me out the door by God. My pipe's still...here what's…?"

"Excuse me." The Sergeant pushed past Willie and hammered the door. "Caleb! Caleb! Open this door! No nonsense now." He listened.

The Sergeant addressed the two Constables, "Get your shoulders to it, lads."

As the two Constables started applying their shoulders to the door a cry went up from the crowd, *He's up there!* and, *There's the murderer!*

The police drew back and saw Caleb on the observation deck at the summit of the lighthouse staring back at them. "Come on now Caleb," the Sergeant cried. "Don't be silly. We can talk about this."

Caleb started to pace the deck, round and round like a hunted animal pausing only to look down at the mounting fury of the crowd.

"Caleb come down lad. We'll try and sort this," Willie shouted.

Caleb stopped his mad circling and came to the railings. "There's no fixing this, Willie. I've murdered poor wee Becky and I deserve what's coming to me."

"Don't be a fool, Caleb," shouted the Sergeant. "We know you'd never —"

Caleb grasped the signal mast and hoisted himself up onto the guard rail that ran around the upper deck. He stood there, balancing in his heavy sea boots for a moment and staring down at the crowd, as though desperately searching for a friendly face before he fell, some say slipped, out and forward towards the ground with his arms windmilling the whole way down.

He struck the spiked railings that encircled the base of the lighthouse and hung there for a moment gasping like a fish out of water, then a great flood of blood issued from his mouth and he was dead, just as the church clock rang to announce the end of Christmas Eve and the beginning of Christmas Day.

Chapter 1

February 1855

A cold Easterly wind struggled to push the Brig against the ebbing tide. As the ship smashed into the waves, great showers of ice-cold green water washed over the prow and drenched a young woman hanging precariously onto the foremast shrouds. She gasped when the spray hit her face and caused her to retch and heave. *Was it possible to drown in such circumstances* Emma wondered as she struggled to catch her breath.

A crewman approached her. "Would you not come in and take shelter with the other passengers Miss?"

Emma struggled to contain her shivering. Drawing on what little strength that pride would afford her she replied, "I am very fine here, thank you."

The crewman looked nonplussed for a moment then

shrugged. He pointed forward. "There, we're just past the islands now and you can just see the castle peeking above the clouds. We shall be alongside soon enough."

Ahead of them, the small port of Donaghadee was appearing through the morning mist. Directly ahead was a harbour busy with the masts of sailing ships, and, to the port side, was a snow-white lighthouse perched at the end of the pier. To starboard a great green mound of earth with a castle on top stood proud overlooking the town below and a row of painted houses that fronted the bay. At the foot of the pier stood a grand-looking hotel; but any place with a fire, a hot meal, and a bed would have met the definition of grand at that point in the journey. Between the houses and the pier a wide prosperous-looking street bustling with miniature figures led away from the harbour up a short hill.

Emma shifted unsteadily on her feet. Her left shoe was leaking and she was feeling both slightly bilious from the stink of the cattle, that was the more usual cargo on board, and oh so tired for she had remained on her feet all night clutching onto the rigging rather than join the common fug and hard benches in the Second Class cabin below deck. Unfortunately, an invitation to the rather more comfortable looking First Class cabin on the main deck, with its warm blankets and soft chairs had not been forthcoming.

As the vessel manoeuvred into the crowded harbour a gangplank was quickly thrust aboard and Emma moved to the head of the rapidly forming queue. "Charlie," she caught herself, *people were looking!* "Charles, Charles, leave those boys alone and come here," she called. In response, her young son slowly walked to her side. Emma took out a handkerchief. "Spit," she commanded then rubbed the child's fat little cheeks. "What will the Doctor think? Look at you! Why you're just like one of those corner boys he'll think. And then where will we be? He'll not want the likes of us in his house, that's what he'll think."

Charlie grimaced, as his eyes quickly filled with tears. "I want to go home. I don't like it here," he whined.

"Well here you are and here I am, and we must make the best of it. Did you sleep well?"

Charlie, who had no such inhibitions about tickets, had slept well, curled up on the floor by the stove in the First Class cabin with the children of the Gentry. Indeed by standing in line with them and looking sad, he had also breakfasted on cold porridge cakes and mutton.

"Stand back there," barked one of the sailors waving his arms at the mob and sweeping off his hat. "Back now, and let the people through," as the First Class passengers filed down the gangplank, dropping a tip in the proffered sailor's cap as they passed. Those who did not have a servant and carriages awaiting were expertly intercepted by porters from the hotel and, together with their luggage, were swiftly conveyed inside to a warm fire and a hot toddy.

Emma strained to watch her trunk, big and brass bound to show the quality, swung ashore in a net and then roughly deposited on the quayside. A horde of loafers had poured out from a public house on the ferry's arrival and were quickly taking charge of the luggage, clearly seeking to guard it in exchange for a consideration.

"All ashore," the sailor announced as the last of the

quality left and the Second Class passengers surged forward. The hat was no longer proffered but clamped to his head. As Emma and Charlie were swept past she tried to press a penny into his hand but he was too busy.

A young man dressed in rough working clothes approached. He doffed his cap and asked, "Emma Hawthorne?"

"Mrs Hawthorne," Emma replied firmly, "Are you from Doctor Leslie's household?"

"I am. I'm Cob down to collect you," Cob indicated a waiting jaunting cart, with a shaggy-coated grey pony that was trying to bite or kick one of the crowd of small boys that had collected like flies around the cart. "Your baggage?"

Emma indicated her trunk now with its attendant never-do-well defending it fiercely from the other hangers-on.

Cob aimed a few half hearted blows at the youths. "Leave poor Jimbo alone now lads!" then nodded to the defender of Emma's case. "Here Quinn, here with it, here now!" Cob strode over and together they both seized an end of Emma's trunk, then staggered the short distance before bundling it onto the cart, "Hop on now."

Emma pushed Charlie towards the cart and turned towards Quinn who had appeared at her elbow. She opened her purse: a sixpence, a penny, and two farthings. Emma stole a furtive glance at the other travellers to see what the going rate was, but it was too late. The crowd had almost cleared and the loafers were returning to the public house to celebrate their good fortune, or not. Emma hesitated then placed the sixpence in Quinn's hand before quickly turning and allowing Cob to hand her onto the waiting cart.

Cob climbed aboard and clucked the pony forward. He laughed, "Auld Quinn'll happy with that."

"Should I have given him less?" Emma asked.

"Twice as much as he deserved. Sure he'll only spend it on drink anyway," Cob said as he encouraged the pony forward.

"Is that a Castle?" Charlie interjected pointing at a building on a hill overlooking the village.

"Ach no. They built that to hold the gun-powder for the new harbour." The pony turned into a gateway leading around the back of a good-looking house. "And that's us here."

"Oh, we're going to the back door?" Emma asked. "I thought we'd…"

"We're going where I was told to bring you," Cob nodded to the pony, "anyway Jimbo wants his breakfast, and so do I mind."

Chapter 2

Jimbo, now going hell-for-leather as his breakfast grew nearer, swung the cart into a gateway and up a pot-holed gravel lane. Steep banks rose on either side, with overgrown hedges atop whose branches whipped and grabbed at both Emma and Charlie.

The end of the short lane opened onto the cobbled backyard of an ivy-clad, two-story house; handsome rather than grand it looked kindly at its new visitors. Standing on the other side of the yard was a small stable block with a hayloft above it, and an open barn adjoining, in which a few stalls could be barely discerned.

To the far side of the yard was a paddock, with a covered well between it and the barn. Contained in the paddock lay a small orchard populated by an elderly donkey, who brayed a wild welcome to them, or probably Jimbo, and who hobbled towards the fence separating them. Opposite the paddock and closest to the lane were the remains of an old formal garden, now sadly neglected. The house itself was more comfortable than grand-looking and had a single-storied rectangular block tacked on the end closest to the entrance.

At the back door of the block a tall, grey-haired woman, with a white apron and draped in a shawl, stood watching them arrive. Her face softened when she saw how tired the travellers were.

"Cob! You and Henry lift that trunk up the stairs now, then get your breakfast! You pair," indicating Emma and Charlie, "get the both of you in here now."

Emma and Charlie alighted and hand-in-hand advanced together. The lady smiled at them and then bent lower to examine Charlie. "You must be Charlie. I'm Mrs McKee," straightening up, "and you must be Mrs Hawthorne?" She offered Emma her hand. "Why child you look exhausted and you're frozen. Get into the kitchen now the pair of you."

Emma and Charlie allowed themselves to be bundled through the door into the kitchen. It was a large flagged room with a range at one end with pots and kettles bubbling away. Charlie ran ahead and clasped the heated rail of the stove.

In the centre of the room stood an old wooden table. Scared and battered it was surrounded by a motley selection of chairs and cushions arranged around it, hinting at its role as the centre of the house. A bench seat along one wall hinted at good times and warm winter nights. An elderly Jack Russell was curled up on a chair beside the stove. It opened one eye and regarded them for a brief moment, before gently breaking wind and returning to its nap.

"You're wet through, and look at your boots." Sure enough, water dripped out from Emma's left boot onto the flags leaving an odd-looking row of footprints as though she had hopped into the room.

"I'm sorry," Emma said weakly.

"Nonsense child, get those boots and stockings off this instant, and I'll get you a basin of hot water." Mrs McKee tipped the chair expelling the terrier and settling Emma in its place. In a few seconds, a basin appeared before Emma's feet and shortly thereafter it was provisioned with hot water from a steaming kettle. "Mind now that's hot!" as she filled an enamel jug from a hand pump by the sink and poured some cold water into the basin. "That's better," as she tested it with a finger, "that's just right now."

Mrs McKee unbuttoned Emma's boots and peeled the sodden stockings off. "Child they're like blocks of ice!" then eased her feet into the basin; the warmth flowed in and the tension flowed out. Emma began to quietly cry.

"Why no child, don't cry. Everything's all right now, you're safe now." Mrs McKee busied herself at the stove, "A cup of tea will do us both good. Now hush, hush now."

A cup of tea was handed over.

"Now child what ails ye? Was the voyage so rough?"

"It was horrible. I didn't have the money for the First Class cabin, and the Second Class was full of men, and they were smoking, and such noise, and I had to stand on the deck all night, and my shoe was…" Emma gasped.

"Pride won't keep your feet warm Lass," commented

Mrs McKee. "What brings a little thing like you into service at your age? Where's Charlie's Father?"

"He's dead. He died in Sevastopol last winter." Emma swallowed. "And his family wouldn't help, and we had so few savings. It took the last of our money to get here. I don't know what I would have done if —"

"Hush child you're here now and that's all that matters. We'll soon get you sorted."

A door burst open and a smiling man in his shirt-sleeves, with a blue woollen waistcoat, somewhat strained riding breeches, and red satin slippers bound in, propelling Charlie in front of him.

"Caught him, Betsy! Young Apache scouting for a raiding party I'll be…" he paused at the sight of Emma, "Oh hello. I didn't know."

"Oh stop your nonsense. Apaches indeed. This Doctor is the new housekeeper. Mrs Hawthorne, and her son Charlie."

Emma stood up in the basin of hot water. "Emma, Emma Hawthorne. Nice to meet you at last Doctor Leslie." Emma gestured at the figure she made, "I'm so sorry I —"

"Oh, stuff. Sit down, sit down. We don't stand on ceremony round here much." He nodded as Emma sat down again. "In the wars Eh? Rough voyage. Never mind, welcome to Rosebank. Betsy will soon square you away. Best nurse, best cook, best damn everything. Looks after me —"

"But not well enough to look after the house no more," sniffed Mrs McKee.

"Betsy! We've been all through this. You're too stubborn to ask for a bit of help," retorted the Doctor. "Anyway this young Brave will add a bit of life to the old place. Eh?" Ruffling a panicked-looking Charlie's hair the Doctor turned to Emma. "You're both very welcome, welcome indeed. I'd only ask you to keep this young ruffian out of my study. There's dangerous chemicals in there and," the Doctor laughed. "We don't want him poisoning himself," looking at an open-mouthed Charlie, "do we?"

Mrs McKee handed the Doctor a cup of tea. He looked around and then sat at the kitchen table smiling at the company. Then Mrs McKee poured a cup for herself before sitting down opposite Emma in a comfortable-looking old chair.

"Capital, the cup that cheereth Eh Betsy?"

"Emma's husband was killed by those nasty old Turks," sniffed Mrs McKee.

"Betsy, I've told you before how many times? The Turks are our gallant allies."

Cob and Henry entered by the back door. Seeing the Doctor they removed their caps and placed a package on the table. Mrs McKee stood up. "Don't stand there like fools. Ye'll be ready for some breakfast now." Cob and Henry quickly sat down as Mrs McKee doled out bowls of porridge and a dish of boiled eggs before them. Silently the boys started into their task of reducing the steaming piles to naught.

"Ah! The mails! And our little family is almost complete," beamed the Doctor. "Betsy, where is Sarah?"

"I sent her out to get some fish for the dinner."

"Never mind. Emma these two young rapscallions are Cob, whom I think you've met? And Henry his partner in crime who…I'm not actually sure what his duties are. Betsy?"

"Neither am I sometimes," replied Mrs McKee.

"Ah well never mind. Mrs McKee is Henry's Mother for her sins. Say hello to Mrs Hawthorne lads. She'll be joining us as the new housekeeper. And you've met young Charlie?"

Both Cob and Henry half-rose, half-bowed to Emma, then returned their attention to the important task before them.

The Doctor turned to Emma. "So Emma tell us about yourself? How have you ended up here? You lost your husband in the Crimea I believe you said in your letter?"

"Indeed. Charlie's Father fell at the siege and —"

"Forgive the professional curiosity but was it in battle?"

"No. Of the flux but —"

"None the less gallant for that I'm sure. Forgive me. Do carry on," interrupted the Doctor.

"Well Charlie and I were in Aldershot at the time so we had some small savings to tide us over and —"

"Your husband's family? Would you not have applied to them?"

"My husband's family were…somewhat distant. I myself have no family left, so Charles and I are quite alone."

The Doctor picked up the mails and riffled through them. "Good-oh! The Times! A capital dispatch. Messrs Russell and Chenery are doing a most excellent job in exposing the incompetence that has," nodding to Emma, "cost such men as your husband their very lives." Turning to Charlie, "Do you know where the Crimea is Charlie? Could you find it on a map?"

Charlie looked towards Emma for reassurance. She pushed him. "Speak up Charles when the Doctor asks you a question."

Quaking Charlie muttered a sullen "Yes" before burying his face in Emma's arms.

"Capital then Charlie! I have a large map in my study where I am tracking the progress of the war. You and I will keep it updated from the latest dispatches and we shall present our findings to the ladies." Nodding towards Emma and Mrs McKee. "That they may be informed and encouraged."

Charlie started crying which then set Emma off again. Baffled the Doctor looked at them then to Mrs McKee, "Oh Dear me. What have we here? Now, now I'll…"

Mrs McKee came to Emma's rescue, "I'll be packing them off to bed is what I'll be doing. Can't you see the poor things are exhausted and you blethering on about your maps and the Turks and the whatnots? Henry, you get some coal for Mrs Hawthorne and Charlie's rooms and light the fires, and you Cob light the boiler and carry some water up so that poor Mrs Hawthorne may get a hot bath." She turned to the Doctor. "Don't you be worrying yourself, they'll be fine after a wee nap."

Chapter 3

Emma woke as the light streamed through a gap in the heavy drapes. The bedroom was small but comfortably furnished, with the remains of a fire smouldering in the grate. For a moment Emma allowed herself to lie there and enjoy the sensation of stretching out to find cool spots under the sheets. *Enough, what will they think of me lying abed* she forced herself out of the warm bed and sat there for a moment gathering her thoughts before venturing to the window, wiping the condensation aside, and looking out. The room was at the back of the house and overlooked the yard where she could see Cob brushing down a horse and Charlie carrying a bucket of water towards him.

This, better or worse, is home for Charlie and me. Rousing herself Emma quickly washed and dressed, then followed her nose to the kitchen. Mrs McKee was busy dressing some fowl. She nodded to Emma "Get yourself some tea from the pot," she nodded to the sideboard. "And there's some eggs under that cloth."

"What time is it?"

"Time we were at our work." Mrs McKee relented. "But enough time for us to have a wee sit-down. Pour a cup for me while you're at it."

Mrs McKee sat down as Emma placed two cups of tea on the kitchen table.

"How long have I been asleep?"

"Bless! We put you to bed yesterday morn."

"I've slept all night?"

"All day and all night," Mrs McKee chuckled. "But you must have needed it. Charlie woke up looking his dinner, that's going to be a big boy, so we gave him some bread and butter and a glass of warm milk and put him back to sleep."

"I saw him in the yard."

"Aye well, Cob's given him wee jobs. He'll keep an eye on him."

Emma brushed the crumbs of her breakfast from the kitchen table into her cupped hand and dusted them onto the plate. "So what do I do?"

"I run the kitchen and Sarah cleans the house. Henry chops the wood and lays the fires, and any odd jobs I give him," Mrs McKee paused. "They work for me."

The finality of that last remark sat there, heavy and seemingly immutable. Not a hostile remark, not a declaration of ill-intent, but a simple statement of fact.

"There doesn't seem a lot for left me?"

"I don't know what was going on in the Doctor's head when he engaged your services, I really don't. And I told him so. But there we are and here we are, and I wish neither you nor the child any harm. We'll work things out and all's well as long as you mind your place."

"Which is?"

"You work for me." Mrs McKee finished her cup of tea. "Come, I'll show you round the house."

Mrs McKee stood and indicated the far end of the kitchen. "Pantry, scullery, a little bedroom for Sarah, boot room, and back door to the yard. "Follow me."

Emma followed Mrs McKee out through the door the Doctor had entered from. It led directly to a short flight of steps at the top of which was another door with a fanlight. Mrs McKee climbed the steps and pushed it open and Emma scrambled to follow. They entered behind a grand stairway which faced a wide double porch with leaded windows flooding the area with light. Mrs McKee clattered across the black and white floor tiles and indicated a corridor to the right running along the back of the house. "Through there is the Doctor's study and consulting rooms, with the ballroom at the end. It would be best if we kept Charlie clear of them I think. Through here," Mrs McKee crossed the hallway to throw open a door "we have the dining room, and through there," waving at a door to the left "we have a door to the Drawing Room." She sniffed. "It's never used. The Doctor uses his study as his lounge, you should see how many books he has, and we tend to keep to the kitchen. I suppose you…"

"I'm sure the kitchen will be fine for Charles and I."

"Good. Come and I'll show you the Doctor's study." Mrs

McKee led Emma back into the hallway. She rapped on the door and paused. "He must be away down the town, or annoying Cob with some idea." Opening the door they passed into a large airy room with windows to the front, a large desk piled with papers and bric-a-brac, and a wall lined with laden bookshelves. Behind the desk was a large map pinned to the wall showing the progress in the Crimean War.

Mrs McKee approached it. "I don't like the look of them Turks at all. I think we're very foolish to allow them behind us."

Emma had moved over to survey some glass-topped cabinets in front of the bookshelves. They displayed curiosities of various types, mostly medical; a skeleton of a two-headed cat. Emma gasped, a dissected human hand with six fingers.

"Nasty old things them. He won't let me throw them out," said Mrs McKee.

"What's there?" Emma pointed to a heavy green curtain behind the desk to one side of the map.

"That's where the Doctor does his real work. It's locked and only the Doctor and I have keys. You don't need to concern yourself with that."

"But if I'm to keep house don't —"

"As far as you, or anybody else other than the Doctor and me, that room doesn't exist."

Mrs McKee scanned the carpet surrounding and in front of the desk.

"What are you looking for?"

"Mud. Sarah is always complaining about mud being tramped through the house all over the good carpets. I'm always at him to take his boots off when he comes in," Mrs McKee glanced at Emma. "Mind young Charlie does the same if you please. Now you and I have work to do."

"Work?"

"The Doctor is hosting a little dinner for some of the Quality tonight. You and I are not going to let them crow over us, indeed they'll not get the chance. Where's that Sarah got to now?"

Back in the kitchen, Mrs McKee handed Emma an apron. "Here. Now what dishes do you suggest?"

Emma hesitated. "I don't really know how. I never had to when…"

"Well, now you do and the man that marries you will be thankful for it."

"But I thought as housekeeper I'd…"

"You thought wrong then. In this house, we turn our hand to whatever needs doing." Mrs McKee pointed to a basin of fish. "Right for starters clean those herring."

"I…I don't."

Mrs McKee grunted. "You'll be a catch for any man when I've finished with you m'girl. Henry!"

Mrs McKee's command was sufficient to spring Henry from his sitting position in the yard and in through the back door before she turned around.

"Yes, mum?"

"Henry take Miss Emma outside and show her how to clean those herring." Henry and Emma hastened to obey. "And keep those blessed cats away Henry! D'ye hear me?"

It was pleasant in the late-morning sunshine as Henry led Emma over to a low wall on which he placed the basin. A small gang of cats gathered at a respectful distance and pretended indifference. Henry selected a herring which he laid on top of a piece of cloth, that he had placed on the wall in readiness.

"Watch me, Miss Emma. It's easy."

Henry picked up a thin knife. "Here behind the gills and slide down until you touch the backbone." He demonstrated, "Now turn the knife and follow the backbone along to the tail like this. Now we just go back along the backbone from the head until the fillet pulls off. There! That's the way she likes 'em." Henry rotated the fish onto its other side. "Now you try."

"Ugh! It's all slimy."

"That's 'as may be Miss but they're grand when Mum fries them in breadcrumbs. Fit for the Queen they are with a bit of salt."

Struggling Emma proffered a fillet. "How's that?"

Henry looked at it. "A grand start that." He gathered together the carcass and Emma's effort and flung them to the waiting cats. Reaching for another fish he placed it on the cloth. "And the next one will be fit to show to herself."

The kitchen was now swathed in steam. Bones were boiling, pots were bubbling, herring were breadcrumbed and ready for frying, and Cob was slicing venison for the pie. In the middle stood Mrs McKee. "Sarah! Once you've finished there strain those bones out!"

"What'll I do with the bones?"

"Give 'em to Cob," Cob looked up with a grin, "for his blessed dogs. Henry get those candied fruits out from the pantry and give them to Emma."

Emma looked askance.

"Emma cut those pieces of fruit up for me, please. About a half-inch square will do nicely thank you."

Henry emerged from the pantry his lips bulging and clutching four heavy earthenware pots.

"If you drop those Henry I'll skin you. Put them down and don't think I don't know you've been raiding my pantry.

Chastened Henry unloaded the crocks onto the kitchen table with exaggerated care. Emma stood over them and looked slightly lost.

"About half a dozen pieces from each pot girl and cut them into half-inch cubes."

"What'll I do with them then?"

"Put them in a basin and cover them. We'll not need them awhile. You can separate me out two dozen eggs next."

The kitchen was now wreathed in stream and good smells. Mrs McKee, Sarah and Emma were sitting at the table with the satisfaction that only comes to those for whom the hard work is over.

"You'll do girl," said Mrs McKee. "See if you don't."

Emma wasn't too sure at what exactly she'd "do at", as a Housekeeper, as Mrs McKee's general assistant.

"What did you mean I'd be a catch for any man when you'd finished with me?"

"I meant that you can't go through life without a husband, nor Charlie no father."

Emma thought for a while. "But in this modern age surely…"

"Nonsense. This age is just like the one afore it, and the one coming after it as well." Mrs McKee stirred her teacup.

"You'll need to catch a husband. I'm sorry girl but there it is."

Emma could hear Charlie outside playing with the dogs. "You don't seem to miss one?"

Mrs McKee laughed. "Bless girl I'm not sure what Mr. McKee would say to that."

"But you live here?"

"Freddie and I," she indicated the sleeping Jack Russell "goes home at night to our own wee house."

"And Mr. McKee?"

"Oh he's got his own wee job now he's off the boats. No, he looks after the new light in the harbour and sleeps…"

Henry entered. "Please Mum. The Doctor asks if Miss Emma…"

"Mrs. Hawthorne to you Henry. I'll not tell you again."

"Sorry Mum. The Doctor…"

"We heard you, Henry!" Mrs McKee nodded to Emma. "You'd better go girl."

Emma stood, removed her apron and started tidying herself up.

"You're fine as you are. He doesn't bite. Now off you go."

Preceded by Henry and Freddie, Emma made her way up the stairs into the hallway. Her breath came in short and shallow gasps and she felt an emptiness in the pit of her stomach. This place was the last best chance for Charlie and herself, there was nowhere else other than that terrible place that was used to scare children. Back in Aldershot she'd often walked past the workhouse and seen the poor inmates shuffling along in silent circles, clad only in coarse grey smocks. Their eyes darting hither for a stray morsel or, more likely, the threat of a casual blow. It was either that or join those poor fallen women outside the Barrack gates.

Emma drew a deep breath to steady herself and tapped the study door. *Too soft!* She tapped again this time more firmly and was rewarded by hearing a command to enter.

"Come in, come in Mrs Hawthorne. We don't stand much on ceremony here." Freddie darted ahead and leapt on the Doctor's lap. "Steady boy, yes I see you." He settled the excited dog in his arms as he stood for Emma. "Please sit down. Are you feeling recovered from your journey?"

Emma sat down and took some time to study her new employer. A kindly looking, barrel-chested, broad-shouldered man of middle age with mutton-chop whiskers who looked as though he could bend the poker by the fire in two if he chose.

"Doctor. Thank you I am much recovered. Charles and I thank you for taking us in and…"

"Stuff! We'll soon get you fattened up. When Mrs McKee and I put you to bed I couldn't but notice how little meat was on the bone."

Emma blushed furiously. She had wondered how she'd woken up in her nightgown and now she didn't know what to think; he was a Doctor but still!

The Doctor laughed. "Oh never fear. Mrs McKee undressed you and put you to bed. I was merely the hired help to get you up the stairs. She's the finest nurse in the district and, don't tell her if you please, a Midwife far in excess of my own poor skills." The Doctor paused. "Has Mrs McKee instructed you as to your duties yet?"

"She has. But I was under the impression I was to be Housekeeper rather…"

"Good, good then. She'll keep you right. She keeps us all on the straight and narrow. Now young Charlie…"

"I hope he has been no trouble to you, Sir."

"No. A…a watchful lad. I have instructed Cob to introduce him to Miss Wiley's schoolhouse for now. What age d'ye say he was?"

"He'll turn ten this year Sir."

"Ten you say. He looks bigger. Later this year we must sit down and plan out his future."

"So I…we are to stay?"

"I think so. One big happy family. Eh?"

Below stairs, Mrs McKee was marshalling her troops. Henry looked shocked and somewhat chastised, after having had his head held under the outside pump whilst Sarah scrubbed his face with a rough flannel, now had a firm grasp of a large tureen as he followed Emma around the table whilst she ladled imaginary soup into imaginary plates.

"You look very smart Henry," commented Mrs McKee. "Only try not to drip on the guests please Dear." Henry basked in the pale praise.

The doors to the Dining Room stood open to reveal the room decorated with fir boughs, a blazing fire that snapped and crackled good cheer, and a table laden with the best accouterments the house could furnish. That some were cracked or otherwise mismatched none were so churlish as to mention. Mrs McKee, Emma, and Henry stood at the sideboard ready to serve.

The Ladies were escorted to their seats with the Doctor at the head of the table, Mr Delacherois on his right and Miss Delacherois to his left. Lieutenant Nelson beside her and his wife opposite, to Mr. Delacherois' right.

Henry circled the table filling glasses. Mr. Delacherois pronounced "To our host!" and the assembled company drank as the Doctor smiled and bowed to his guests. Then, on Mrs McKee's signal, Emma and Henry began offering the soup as they had practised before.

"Mulligatawny" Capital! My favourite" cried the Doctor and the guests showed their appreciation by their appetite.

Miss Delacherois, perhaps not as used to the wine as the others, neglected poor Lieutenant Nelson and addressed the company at large. "Have you heard what Willie McKee's saying?" Aware she was on dangerous ground she glanced at Mrs McKee but on receiving no adverse signal she ploughed on. "The new lighthouse is haunted! Oh no I swear! Willie says he sees a dark figure at the top and he says…"

Mrs McKee approached Miss Delacherois from the side. She looked at the half-eaten soup in her dish. "Have you finished with your soup Miss Jane?"

"Oh no Mrs McKee."

"Then perhaps it's not to your taste?"

"Oh no Mrs McKee. It's very nice." as Jane picked up her spoon and took a lady-like mouthful.

"Well, then I'll leave it there whilst you talk to the gentleman on your left."

Mr Delacherois could barely hide his pleasure that a lesson in manners amongst polite company had been so deftly delivered. He raised his glass to Mrs McKee. "I thank you Mrs McKee. This soup is most fine indeed."

Chastened by her rough handling Jane sat and seethed for awhile, but she was careful to avoid Mrs McKee's eye and returned to torturing Lieutenant Nelson.

Emma and Henry cleared the dishes away to the kitchen, then Henry entered bearing a giant Venison Pie with Emma close behind staggering under the weight of a large tray laden with potatoes, both boiled and creamed, carrots, parsnips, early peas, and a giant jug of gravy. The scents and smells flooded the room as the pie was cut on the sideboard and served to the guests, whilst Emma and Henry placed the bowls of vegetables in the centre of the table.

It came to be Miss Delacherois' turn to be served by Emma when Miss Delacherois spied her chance to take out her humiliation on another. She was not a bad girl, nor a spiteful one merely embarrassed and seeking someone to distract the company from her shame.

"Hello you're new?"

Glancing at Mrs McKee Emma replied, "Yes Miss."

"You're a bit old for service are you not?" Miss Delacherois enquired looking at Emma.

The Doctor, who was now Miss Delacherois' conversation partner for this course, and well knew this high-spirited girl could create chaos if she chose, attempted to divert her. "Ah yes, this is Mrs Hawthorne. A new member of our family, who has consented to act as housekeeper in our little home. So…"

"And where's Mr Hawthorne," said Miss Delacherois looking at Emma.

Startled Emma replied, "He's dead Miss."

"Dead? Do tell?"

"Nothing to tell Miss. He died at the Siege of Sevastopol last Christmas…"

Spotting a fellow military man, even second-hand, Lieutenant Nelson interrupted. "Worst luck. I should be there but my duties keep me tied up here. What Regiment was he?"

"The Commissariat Sir. He was an Officer in the Commissariat."

Lieutenant Nelson guffawed.

Miss Delacherois tugged his sleeve. "Fatty Nelson! What are you sniggering at?"

"Here don't you call me Fatty or…"

"Or what?" cried Miss Delacherois.

"Jane!" cried her Father.

"Miss Delacherois!" echoed the Doctor.

"She started it." pleaded Lieutenant Nelson. "Anyway they ain't Officers. They're shopkeepers sent round the Army to hawk their wares. That's all!"

Mrs McKee threw a bucket of coal on the fire sending sparks soaring up the chimney.

Clearly irritated on Emma's behalf the Doctor snapped. "That's most unkind Nelson. Mrs Hawthorne's husband died in the service of his country. You shall apologise for that remark," as Emma fled the room closely followed by Mrs McKee.

Chapter 4

Emma returned to the kitchen and flung down the tray onto the table. The loud noise caused Sarah to nearly drop the icing bag which she was using to decorate some fancies.

"What's wrong Miss Emma, has something happened?" she said.

Emma gasped for breath. Her head swirled with what had just occurred. How a world of safety and warmth and welcome had suddenly turned on her.

Mrs McKee entered. "Are you all right child?"

"Why did they say those things?" Emma pleaded.

The Doctor entered and took Emma's hands in his own. Emma had never seen him angry before. "Mrs. Hawthorne," he said "I'm so sorry about that. It was inexcusable and I've told Nelson so. The man's a bloody fool!"

Feeling slightly annoyed at this Emma said "Surely it was Miss Delacherois who put him up to it Doctor?"

The Doctor dropped Emma's hands and stood back. "Miss Delacherois is a guest in my house. It…"

"Ach! She's a silly wee girl who doesn't think!" Mrs McKee interjected. "But she's got a good heart and she'll be mortified with how things turned out, and he's just a fool. The cut of him turning up dressed as a soldier." Mrs McKee started to put on her coat. "Sarah when you finish that dessert you an' Henry clear the table then serve pudding, and tell Cob to stoke the fire in the Drawing Room now. Miss Emma and I are going for a wee walk to clear our heads." Mrs McKee turned to look at her employer. "And you'll want to be getting back to your guests Doctor. Emma get your hat and coat now, there's a good girl."

It was dark when Emma and Mrs McKee stepped out into the backyard. Charlie who had been playing with Nero the donkey rushed up. "Can I come please?" he paused have you been crying, Mummy?"

Mrs McKee asked, "Have you finished your chores then boy?"

"Yes. I've mucked out Jimbo and Sultan and filled their buckets and put the feed out for them all just like Cob showed me."

Mrs McKee turned to Emma "It may do you and the boy good to be together for a wee while?"

Emma looked a Charlie then back to Mrs McKee "Yes. I think a walk would do us all good." She looked down at Charlie "Where do you want to go?"

Charlie bounced. "I want to go and see the ships." He looked back and forth between Emma and Mrs McKee, unsure where to address his appeals.

"We'll go to the dunes first, then down to the harbour," stated Mrs McKee. "My wee Freddie's gone for another walk and I want to see if he's got himself stuck down a rabbit hole again."

They walked awhile North towards the Castle. A sea mist had drawn in and the fog horns bellowed their warnings into the night as Charlie disappeared into the gloom ahead.

"Hear you! Mind you don't hurt yerself!" ordered Mrs McKee. "Down here." She indicated a lane that led directly to the shore. "We'll get to the dunes best this way." She looked at Emma. "Are you feeling better now girl?"

Emma considered her reply. "I think so. I was just so disappointed. I thought," she nodded towards Charlie, "he and I had found somewhere we could be safe. It was just so sudden realising how fragile it all is."

The lane opened out with the dunes to the north and the town about a mile to the southern end of the bay. The lighthouses had now lit their lanterns. The one on the Copeland Islands signalling *Danger*, *Keep Clear* and the lighthouse on the pier, Willie's light, signalling *Safety*, *Safe home and a warm bed*. Mrs McKee counted. "One, two, three, four, and light, one, two, three, four, and light. Well done man." She turned to Emma. "You mind tonight's lesson well. The likes of us aren't friends with the likes of them, not really no matter how they get on. Never have been, never will be no matter how sweet they talk to you."

Charlie had found what looked to be an old well and was

throwing stones down it. "Be careful darling! Don't…" Emma called.

"You get him away from that. Don't ever let him alone there," said Mrs McKee.

Emma furrowed her brow. "He's only playing. What's wrong?"

"That's the old Murder Hole. Bad things happened there. A bad place for a child, for anybody."

"A Murder Hole? What on Earth's that?"

"There used to be a river there but they covered it over. Oh years ago. Before my time, or my Father's Father's time for that. It's where the well in the backyard of the house drew its water from."

"But the name? Why call it such a horrid name?" queried Emma.

Mrs McKee tightened her lips. "It's where they used to kill them. In the old days."

"Kill who? Mrs McKee are you all right?"

"The women. In those days if a woman was sentenced to death they didn't hold it was decent to hang them, what with skirts and whatnot. So they'd bring them down here at high tide, tie them up, and put them down there head first to drown."

Emma shuddered. *To be bound. To know what was happening; was going to happen. To be raised up, then plunged headfirst into the dark. To choke on the cold water as the tide slowly rose. To be so very cold and alone as you waited.*

They continued on along the path that skirted the seaside of the dunes in silence for a while, the rush of the surf interrupted only by the squabbling of gulls as they settled for the night, and Mrs McKee's calls "Freddie, here boy Freddie."

Mrs McKee looked at the gathering dusk. "Well, there's no sign of Freddie here. I do hope he's all right."

Emma squeezed her arm. "I'm sure he'll turn up."

"Keep the boy out of these dunes as well if you can."

"Here?"

"Hmm…they finds animals in here sometimes. Dogs, cats with all their puddings out, all cut up and torn. Horrible things. Such cruelty." She stopped. "We'd better go back. Show the boy the ships."

Together they turned around and started to slowly trudge to the other end of the bay where the lighthouse shone out…one, two, three, four, and light.

A sea mist had rolled in by the time they reached the harbour. Ships were dozing at the quayside, their ropes dipping in and out of the water as they rose and fell with the swell. The noise of people laughing, quarrelling, being people, spilled out from The Downshire Arms hotel into the night.

Quietly Mrs McKee broached a subject that had been troubling her. "Tell me, if you will why can you and Charlie not return to your husband's family?"

"I'm not good enough for them," Emma replied "I was a shop-girl in their shop and they always said my husband married beneath him. I'd used Charlie, for he was an early baby, to trap him. They want nothing to do with either of us."

"And your own parents?"

"I fear that things were said…I said…they also were

against the match."

After a while, Mrs McKee responded, almost as a spoken thought "Never forget it was women like us they thrust down into the darkness to drown. Not women like them, women like us."

Charlie had run ahead into the gloom to inspect the sailing ships tied up by the lighthouse. The women paused at Kelly's Steps and looked down into the black swell rising out of the sea, the wave climbing up the pier wall then falling back and disappearing into the slow oily mass of water as if it had never existed.

"Mum, mum!" Charlie returned. "I saw a man," he pointed into the sea mist with the top of the lighthouse rising above it. "Back there on top."

"It was the mist child," said Mrs McKee glancing upwards. "It makes funny shapes in people's heads."

Emma bent to adjust Charlie better to her satisfaction. A quick pull here, a tug there and she stood up. "You're imagining things sleepy-head. I think it's time for someone's bed," but as they turned to go back to the house she glanced back and for a moment she couldn't be sure.

Chapter 5

It was morning when Emma and Mrs McKee sat down together. Freddie had returned and was having a nap by the stove. Breakfast had been served and cleared, the Doctor out on his rounds with Cob, Charlie at school at last, and Sarah was with Henry dusting the rooms and resetting the fires. The back door was open and weak sunshine was throwing a light, but little heat, into some dusty corners of the kitchen that had been hidden in winter's gloom.

Mrs McKee broke the mood, "It'll soon be time for a Spring clean."

Emma sipped at her tea. She was in a reflective mood after the tour of the town last night. "That place…last night. When was it last used?"

Mrs McKee chortled. "Oh long before our time lassie. But

it still does upset me. The thought of those poor women."

Emma indicated the old well outside by nodding her head. "And it's connected to that?"

"Worse. That old pump in the cellar is fed from the outside well. First thing the Doctor did when he came back home from Dublin was to condemn any property that drew their water from that river; nasty old thing. All the people in the town…well they throw anything in it if you catch my meaning."

Emma shuddered. "Back? So the Doctor is from here?"

"Born and bred. His father, the Admiral, was the old Magistrate here, an' a nasty cruel old creature he was too."

So you've known him a long time? What's he like?"

"He's a man like any other." Mrs McKee smiled. "Like all men, he has his faults."

"Tell me? What happened to the last Housekeeper?"

Mrs McKee paused, then took a breath. "Some didn't suit him, maybe some felt that what was expected of them wasn't what they wanted."

Emma settled back in her chair and took a sip of her tea. There was something more here but she wasn't sure what it was. "Expected?" Emma queried.

Again Mrs McKee hesitated. "The Doctor always found the girls himself. I was never asked. They turned up just like you but…you're the first with a child to be held responsible for. Normally they're younger lassies…and prettier but no children."

Emma considered this for a while. "Do you mean to say that it's harder for me to leave the Doctor's employ as I've got Charlie to consider?"

Mrs McKee rose to her feet. "Come on now. We've the beds to turn afore lunch."

That evening the chores were complete and peace held throughout the Doctor's small realm; Sarah was away visiting her family in the town, and both Cob and Henry were, allegedly, fishing off the rocks by the gravel pit when, with an almighty yelping, Freddie tore through the door from the yard and leapt on Mrs McKee's lap where he buried his face in her lap and lay trembling.

Startled Mrs McKee slopped tea from her cup down the front of her dress. "Bless me! What's the matter boy?" She reached across to place her cup on the stovetop and turned to examine the shaking dog. Patting him over her hand came away covered with bright red blood. "Oh Freddie what have you done? Emma, would you call the Doctor down with his bag, please? I think I heard him in his study."

As Emma rushed to obey Charlie came in without saying anything and stood at the back of the kitchen in the shadows watching.

The Doctor entered followed by Emma. "What's the matter, Betsy? Emma here gave me quite a start."

Mrs McKee rolled Freddie onto his side. "It's Freddie Doctor. He's cut himself bad like."

The Doctor looked closely. "Oh dear poor old Freddie. Been in the wars have you?" The Doctor placed his bag on the kitchen table. "Bring him across here please? Emma, would you reach over the lamp?"

Gently Freddie was laid on a towel and Mrs McKee held his head soothing him. The Doctor picked up the light and

45

examined the cut on Freddie's right haunch. "That's a deep one, Freddie. I'm afraid you'll need a few stitches there." The Doctor extracted a small glass bottle and a cotton pad from his bag. The Doctor looked at Mrs McKee. "Betsy you'll have to manage the chloroform. Mind now the merest drop. Just enough to calm him whilst I work on the wound. He glanced at Emma. "A basin of hot water please, then hold this lantern." Shaking his head he muttered, "I'm afraid of the effects on such a little fellow."

Once things were arranged to his satisfaction he gently touched the wound and was rewarded by a low growl. "Another drop if you please," and Mrs McKee allowed the smallest amount of the clear liquid to fall from the bottle onto the cotton pad enclosing Freddie's muzzle.

The Doctor withdrew a straight razor from his bag and touched the injury again but this time Freddie remained silent. "That'll have to do us. We must work quickly now," as he drew the razor along both edges of the cut, shaving off tufts of Freddie's fur and leaving the pale pink skin beneath exposed. He turned back to his bag. "Enough, that'll do. Emma wipe the wound clean if you please? Betsy maybe another drop for this bit and we'll soon be finished?"

The Doctor threaded a fine curved needle with some catgut and rapidly closed the wound. "That's that Betsy. You can let him breathe now. Emma, what about a cup of tea for the workers?"

Freddie was settled on Mrs McKee's lap and was subject to a tap on the nose every time he tried to lick his stitches. "Leave those alone this instant you silly wee fool," she commanded the unfortunate Freddie, as he slowly woke.

"So what happened?" queried the Doctor.

There was a silence then Mrs McKee broke it. "You're very quiet young Master Charles. Cat got your tongue?"

Shocked Emma looked up from washing down the kitchen table and addressed Charlie still hiding in the gloom at the back of the kitchen. "Charles! What do you know of Freddie's accident?"

Charlie remained silent and then ran to Emma burying his face in her apron sobbing. Emma knelt and held Charlie away from her. "Stop that now!" She shook him. "What happened Charlie?"

He sobbed, "I was just playing...Freddie and me. I was throwing stones for him to fetch an' he ran in front of one."

The Doctor pursed his lips and glanced at Mrs McKee. "That must have been quite a big stone, and a sharp one at that, to cut poor old Freddie so."

Mrs McKee looked back at the Doctor and shook her head.

"He's your child Emma. You're responsible for him," said the Doctor. "It's not up to Mrs McKee or myself."

Angered Mrs McKee spoke. "If he was mine then I'd have Cob cut a switch and have him given a good thrashing in the yard!"

Alarmed Emma pulled Charlie to her as he started sobbing. "I'm sure he didn't mean it." She looked at Mrs McKee and then to the Doctor. "Please, he's so little. I'm sure he didn't mean to."

The Doctor sucked his teeth. "He's a townie but —"

Emma suddenly clipped Charlie across the head. Stunned he stopped crying and looked at her. "Go to bed,"

Emma snapped, "go to bed this instant, or I'll have Cob whip you myself!"

A frightened Charlie stared at this new Emma. "But supper. I haven't —"

Furious Emma shook him. "This instant!" She shook him again. "Now!"

Sobbing the shocked Charlie tore himself free from Emma and ran up the kitchen stairs ignoring the Doctor's parting advice, "Next time sticks only eh old man. No throwing stones for the doggies…breaks their teeth…eh?"

Chapter 6

The next morning Emma was alone laying the fire in the Doctor's study when he entered. He threw his bag onto a table and pulled off his boots.

Flustered Emma gathered her things together. "I can finish this later Doctor."

The Doctor sat down behind his desk and looked at her for a moment, "So how are things today Emma? Recovered from that nonsense about your husband last night?"

Emma flushed. "They were very mean to me," she said quietly.

"Miss Delacherois meant no harm by it." The Doctor turned over some papers on his desk and then looked up at Emma. "How's Charlie doing at school?"

"Oh, he's doing well Sir. He likes it and says Miss Wilkes

is very nice."

The Doctor smiled, "All the children go to that school. We all did, at the beginning anyway. That's why we all know one another. Of course, the likes of Miss Delacherois and myself are withdrawn after a suitable period to be tutored at home or sent to boarding school but still, it's most egalitarian."

Uncertain Emma dropped a curtsy, "Will that be all Sir?"

The Doctor frowned, "Oh don't be like that Emma. May I call you Emma? The Doctor indicated the chair in front of his desk. "Please sit…we'll have a little chat. Eh?"

Emma paused. Weighing up the possible consequences if she said *No*, to this man who had such control over her, and Charlie's future. She sat.

"That's better," the Doctor smiled. "All friends together, all one big happy family here."

The fire had started to take and was now crackling away. The Doctor stood and rubbed his hands in front of the grate, "You can't beat a good fire." The Doctor turned his back to the heat and held his coat-tails apart linking his hands behind his back, "It's still cold out there. So have you given any thought as to what we'll do with Charlie next year?"

Emma felt there was something important here, something that she didn't fully understand. The Doctor was building up to something—something about Charlie and herself.

"I know that a school of Navigation and Mathematics is due to open not far from here. Perhaps Charlie would like to go to sea?" offered the Doctor.

"To be a sailor? An Officer?"

"Or he could finish school after this coming Summer term and I could find him an apprenticeship here in town?" the Doctor replied. He shifted in his breeches as his buttocks had become slightly overdone. "But that's as may. The money for the school wouldn't be easy for you to find I fear."

"We have no savings, nothing but the clothes we stand in, and this position," Emma sighed.

The Doctor moved away from the fire and picked a book from one of the shelves of his library. He stood there, leafing through it. "Maybe you and I could work something out," he murmured without looking at Emma. "You know," he started turning the pages without really looking at them, "between ourselves?"

There was a long pause. Emma suddenly understood what Mrs McKee had been saying to her. "You mean…we… us?"

The Doctor put the book away and turned to look at Emma. "Oh come on now. You're a married…were a married woman. I'm a man. Surely it's only natural…under the same roof so to say?"

The Doctor was looking straight into Emma's eyes. *He's not unattractive she thought and Charlie would have a chance to become a gentleman.* "And what would become of me? I mean after Charlie left school? Would I be cast out?"

"My dear Emma. No one is being cast out. I'm merely trying to do the best for our little family. You do know I'm very fond of the little chap? Want what's best for him, for us, for all of us."

"May I have time to consider your offer Sir?" countered Emma.

"Of course Emma," the Doctor picked up a newspaper on his desk and examined it. "But I would just point out there are a great many young women seeking positions here in the *News Letter*. Times are hard out there and many would go to any lengths to avoid the Workhouse."

It was afternoon and Charlie had finished school. It was, Emma felt, a good opportunity to find out what Charlie thought of their life here. Beside she, herself, found the Doctor's suggestion turning over and over in her head.

The morning's work done and too soon to start readying dinner Emma found Mrs McKee napping by the stove with a cup of tea on the arm of the chair. Emma disengaged Mrs McKee's fingers from the cup and carried it over to the sink. Mrs McKee started awake. "Emma! I didn't hear you. I must just have had a wee doze."

Emma smiled. "You look tired." Since Emma and Charlie had arrived it was always Mrs McKee who had stood up for them and looked after their interests. At first, Emma had been scared of her but as they'd gotten to know each other she'd become almost a maternal figure in their lives, as she was for the other members of the household.

Emma reached out and patted Mrs McKee's hand. "Would you like another cup of tea? That last one was cold." Emma was worried but she didn't know why. Mrs McKee was the one point everyone moved around, like a star that held a constant position in the sky. What would happen to them if that star moved, or even worse was extinguished?

"That would be nice dear. You're a good girl," said Mrs McKee.

Unsure that she would meet Mrs McKee's definition of a *good girl* if she took up the Doctor's offer Emma decided that, somehow, she would seek advice from Mrs McKee.

Emma settled them both with a fresh cup of tea. They sat in the chairs by the stove with the boy's potatoes gently boiling.

"Mrs McKee," Emma started, "the Doctor spoke to me earlier today. About Charlie and me."

Mrs McKee sat up in her chair and looked at Emma. She took a sip of the hot tea. Emma had her attention now.

With feigned casualness, Mrs McKee asked, "Oh Aye. And what'd he say?"

"Well, he said that he could get Charlie an apprenticeship here in town."

"Likely he could at that," acknowledged Mrs McKee.

"Or even, maybe, that he could put Charlie through the new navigation school in Bangor to go for being an officer."

Mrs McKee thought for a while. "Well he could afford it the prices he charges some of them. What about you…could you afford it?"

Emma studied the cup in her hand. Small spider cracks ran across the glaze. *Good enough for downstairs, but not good enough for up there, up the stairs.*

"I thought you'd no money girl?" Mrs McKee prompted.

Emma lifted her chin and returned Mrs McKee's gaze. "I think the Doctor was planning I pay him back a different way."

For a moment anger sparked in Mrs McKee's eyes…then it died back. "And what do you think to that?"

Emma considered her words, "I think…I think that it

may be Charlie and me's best chance." Emma rushed, "I mean he's not so bad and it's the only way Charlie will get a chance. And me, where would we go? The Workhouse?"

Mrs McKee spoke quietly, "There's Widow-women down the town make their living at the Tambour. It's not —"

"Tambour?"

"Piece work, the embroidery. But it's long hours and little reward, and most of 'em are half blind at it…and end up in the Workhouse anyway."

Mrs McKee got up and stuck a fork into the potatoes boiling away on the stove. "Done. Them boys'll be ready for their lunch soon." She drained them in the sink before she set the pot to one side. "I don't know what to say to you! I don't! I know what I'd like to say to you but I won't! In your position, at your age, I don't know what I'd do!"

Emma got up and set out three plates with knives on the kitchen table. Then she fetched a dish of salt and a large slab of yellow butter from the pantry. A tablecloth was placed on the table and all was ready.

Mrs McKee stood by the window looking out into the yard. "Them boys, Cob and the like. They don't know, they'll never know what…it's your decision girl and I'll not blame you one bit whichever you decide."

Emma got up and stood beside Mrs McKee. Arm in arm they looked out the window as Charlie, Cob, and Henry threw straw at each other. "I'll have to talk to Charlie. See if he's happy here."

Mrs McKee nodded then patted Emma's hand.

Chapter 7

It was a typical Irish day with rain alternating with weak sunshine. The sort of day that would encourage people to say it's turned out well while standing under an umbrella. Jimbo and Sultan, the Doctor's Hunter, stamped and nickered while pulling at their hay racks and ignoring the boys as they darted between them.

"Cave! Cave!" cried Henry.

"What you on about?" said Cob.

Diving behind some straw bales Henry warned, "They're watching and —"

"Who's watching?" Charlie whispered.

"Yer Ma and mine."

"Quick! Follow me!" ordered Cob and the boys scrambled up the ladder into the hay loft after him then wiggled forward to keep the watchers under observation.

Charlie considered Mrs McKee for a while. She was a bit too all-seeing for his taste. "Is she a witch?" he ventured.

Cob scoffed, "There ain't no such things as witches."

"Oh yes, there are. Mrs McKee showed Mum and me the place where they put them into the water upside down," defended Charlie.

Despite himself, Cob was impressed. "Why upside down?" he queried.

"It stops them flying away."

Charlie's evident expertise in witches silenced Cob and Henry for a moment, and then Henry said, "Well I don't *think* my Mum's a witch."

"She scares me," muttered Cob, "when she looks at you angry like."

"Well I like her," defended Henry. "An' she sometimes shouts but she's never smacked me… well hardly ever"

Charlie rolled onto his back and dug around in his pockets until he found a sticky paper bag. "Who wants a sweet?"

Henry and Cob turned their heads towards Charlie between them. "What sort?" demanded Henry.

"Who cares," said Cob, "I'll take one."

Charlie extracted a sweet each for Cob, Henry and himself and handed them over. The boys rolled on their backs furiously sucking.

"They're nice. Where'd you get them?" asked Cob.

"I stole them from the sweetie shop down the town," Charlie informed them.

There was a bit of a pause while Cob and Henry thought

about this news. "That's old Mrs McHenry's shop," said Cob.

Charlie thought. "Mmmm… I think so."

"What'd you mean you stole them?" asked Henry.

"I was in and someone else came in so I got a handful out of a big jar when she wasn't looking."

Cob looked across at Henry, then at Charlie. "That's all she has that wee shop."

"She used to slip me a barley sugar when Mum and me went in and Mum'd no money and got things put in the book," Cob said.

He took the sweet out of his mouth and handed it back to Charlie. "I think I've had enough. Save it back in the bag for later." Henry looked disappointed but did the same.

"But we used to steal sweets all the time in Aldershot," Charlie defended himself.

Cob frowned. "That's across the water, not here."

Henry nodded in agreement. "Not here."

Charlie was offended. He'd shared his sweets with them and, in return, they'd been nasty to him about some silly old woman; if she didn't want her sweets stolen then she should look after them better. It was hardly his fault if she didn't.

The boys lay in silence for a while. "Are you going to stay here?" asked Cob.

"Hope not. Don't like it here," said Charlie.

"Why not?" asked Henry.

"Nothing to do, nothing to see. All my friends are back home," Charlie replied.

"What about school? Have you made any friends there?" Henry enquired.

"No, they don't like me. They say I talk funny an' Miss

Wilkes she said she'd beat me 'coz I took Jane's pencil an' I didn't know she'd lost it."

"Doctor's sweet on your Mum," offered Henry.

Shocked Charlie considered this. If the Doctor became his new Daddy then they'd have to live here forever. Charlie resolved he'd find some way to make his Mummy not love the Doctor; to show her that he was not worthy to replace his real father. "No, he isn't! My Mummy loves Daddy," retorted Charlie.

Cob thought about this. "But your Dad is dead," he commented, "you can't stay married to a dead person."

"Why not?" countered Charlie.

"I think you can remember them…sort of," Cob said. "But not forever —"

"Otherwise you'd be sad all the time," Henry offered, "and you can't have everybody always sad."

Cob suddenly sat up. "Have you seen Freddie?"

"He was in here yesterday looking for rats," said Henry.

"Maybe he's sleeping in the kitchen?" Charlie contributed.

Cob considered this. "She'll go mad if that wee dog's run away again."

The next morning Charlie got up before dawn and quickly washed and dressed before walking across the yard and pushed open the kitchen door. Freddie stirred on his chair by the stove then raised his head and studied the unwelcome interruption.

"C'on boy rabbits…rabbits eh?" Charlie whispered. Interest piqued Freddie stood and stretched. "Rabbits

Freddie! C'on boy!"

With tail wagging, Freddie jumped from the chair onto the rug in front of the stove and carefully stretched, before he walked over to Charlie who reached down and rubbed the dog's head. "Good boy…rabbits!" Charlie picked up a heavy blackthorn walking stick from the pile behind the door and turned back into the yard, with Freddie eagerly trotting in his footsteps.

It was early yet, with a pale sun rising over the Scottish coast, and Charlie had done his best to avoid being seen on the way. He'd had a brief scare when a drover had appeared from the Cotton direction herding before him half a dozen little black cows down to the Bullock Quay, but Charlie had whistled Freddie back and they'd cut down behind the motte to the coast.

Now Freddie ran ahead searching as they entered the dunes under the castle. "That's it boy! Rabbits…rabbits, Charlie cried driving Freddie into a frenzy of blood lust.

As they crested a dune together they spied half a dozen rabbits standing stock-still in the dew-darkened sand by their burrows. With a frantic yapping, Freddie charged towards them as Charlie urged him on. "Get 'em boy, get 'em Freddie!"

As the rabbits disappeared back underground Freddie bounded up and started digging at the burrows, first one then another. A puffing Charlie arrived and Freddie paused looking up at Charlie for inspiration.

"That's it boy…rabbits," gasped Charlie as he took the end of the walking stick in both hands and then brought the heavy handle crashing down on the digging Freddie shattering his pelvis.

Freddie howled in pain and collapsed on his side whimpering. "That'll learn you, you…you witch dog!" Charlie swung the stick again striking Freddie a blow to the side of his head and dislodging an eye, and again hitting the dog on the flank shattering ribs.

"You deserve that for getting me in trouble you do."

Charlie stood there looking down at Freddie lying motionless with his breath coming in little wet gasps. "I hope the rats gets you first," spat Charlie.

That evening Mrs McKee entered the kitchen, "Freddie, Freddie where are you? Emma, have you seen that dratted dog?"

"No, I don't think I've seen him all day."

"He hasn't been at his bowl," said Sarah, pointing at a small bowl on the floor beside the stove with *Freddie* written on it.

Mrs McKee frowned. "I've never seen him shy from his grub before."

Sarah turned from the sink. "He'll turn up. Sure the wee dote knows the whole town inside out."

"Aye well likely he's cadged his rations elsewhere," grumbled Mrs McKee, as she bustled out the back door. "I'll just ask the boys to keep an eye out for him on their travels."

The next afternoon after school Emma took Charlie shopping. Passing the butcher's window paused and looked at the dead rabbits and other birds hanging on display. He studied them closely then turned to Emma and said, "Is Daddy like them?" The copper smell of blood permeated the atmosphere.

Startled Emma gasped, "No! No Pet. Daddy's with God now."

Charlie looked into Emma's eyes and considered this for a while. Then he appeared to lose interest and looked back at the dead animals. "I expect you're right," he responded, "they look more like Freddie does."

A horrible thought came to Emma, "Do you know where Freddie is?"

Charlie shrugged his shoulders engrossed in the study of the carcasses.

"Darling, where is Freddie? Do you know?"

Charlie had lost interest and had moved away to examine the next corpse. Alarmed Emma seized him by the shoulder and shook him, "Charlie! Where is Freddie!"

Frightened Charlie burst into tears.

Emma hugged him, "I'm not cross with you. I just need to know where Freddie is. We're all so worried about him."

Snot-stained and tear-streaked Charlie considered this. "Am I in trouble?" he asked.

"Of course not Sweetheart."

Charlie pointed to a jar of sweets, "Can I have one of those?" he inquired.

After a pause, Emma sighed. She moved to the counter and indicated a stick of rock.

"Not that Mum," Charlie intervened, alarm in his voice, he pointed. "That one."

Emma returned with the prize, "Now what happened?"

Charlie's attention was on the sweet. He reached out for it but Emma held it away.

"Charlie, you have to tell me what happened."

Charlie considered this his eyes fixed on the prize, "We went rabbiting in the dunes, Freddie an' me. Early in the morning coz Cob says that's when them come out. Mum, did you know rabbits have lots an' lots of babies?"

"I did," replied Emma, "lots and lots."

"If you were a rabbit then   —"

"Darling. Where is Freddie now?"

"I couldn't find him. He went into a hole looking for rabbits and I waited an' waited but he didn't come out and I had to go to Miss Wilkes coz I'm not allowed to be late an' Mum do I have to go back there?"

Emma handed Charlie the sweet and he greedily crammed it in his mouth.

Emma considered what Charlie had said, "so how do you know he's out there now?"

Muffled now by the sweet Charlie replied, "Coz I went back looking for him this morning before school 'n' he was there. Just where I last saw him."

"Where darling?" Emma asked.

He pointed, "Out there, in the sand hills. I poked him with a stick but he didn't move."

It was getting dull when Emma reached the dunes with the sound of a fresh swell stirring the rock-strewn beach beside her, and the sea mist growing closer as it rolled in obscuring the Copeland Islands. Between her and the town, she could see the Murder Hole; Emma shivered at the sight of it. What terror, what fear must that place have seen? She glanced back at the castle and imagined people looking down at the scene with cold dead eyes, indifferent.

Turning round Emma walked into the dunes, her feet slipping back into the sand as though it would pull her down if it could. Emma decided to skirt the outside of the hills first to try a spy some rabbits, or, better still a warren. Rabbits should indicate Freddie or so she hoped. Emma reached the end of the dunes without seeing any sign so she moved one line in and started to retrace her steps. It was getting darker now, and colder. Once or twice she lost her footing and was pitched back down the way she came. Emma could hear the church clock strike seven, enough she'd try again tomorrow and hope the foxes didn't find Freddie first, one more dune to climb then back onto the beach and mark her position. As she crested the sand hill a small dark shadow emerged to her left. Gingerly she made her way down and across and spied Freddie lying there. Emma approached him, "Freddie, Freddie boy, are you all right," although she knew he wasn't.

Closer now Emma got a better look in the growing dusk. On his belly with his puddings unwound behind him surrounded by tiny paw-prints. Emma puzzled *What sort of animal leaves such marks? Do foxes hunt in packs?* Emma didn't know; an eye missing, tongue bitten through, he had left marks in the sand as he had tried to drag himself across the sand hills. Emma looked up and a sob caught in her chest. He had been trying to crawl home as he died. She couldn't let Mrs McKee remember Freddie like that. It would break Mrs McKee's heart to see him thus mutilated. Emma thought for a while *Cob, I'll get Cob to come out here and quietly bury the little soul*. Emma took a last look at Freddie and then started up the dune leading to the shore.

About an hour later Cob appeared round the headland riding Jimbo bareback with a spade in one hand. "Hold on," he said, "we're here now." Cob dismounted and secured Jimbo's reins to an old post at the foot of the jetty and then took a section of hay from a bag tied to the saddle. "Now don't you be going nowhere," throwing the section at the pony's feet. He then turned to face the dunes and saw Emma's tracks leading in. *This must be the way she came* he thought. Cob shouldered the spade. "You stay here now," then started to follow the footprints. Sure enough, there was the small stiff body of Freddie at the foot of the first dune just as Emma had said. Cob stood awhile looking at Freddie pondering the seriousness of the matter *not so yappy now are ye?* was his conclusion. For a moment Cob studied the footprints then shrugged; they led off further into the dunes. Cob shivered, he'd not be following, *too cold*, and, looking at the sky, too dark soon to be tramping about in there looking for God knows what? He scooped Freddie's guts up with the shovel then bent down and picked up the carcass by the hind legs, before walking down to the seashore where he threw the body as far as he could into the receding tide. *Enjoy Scotland Freddie* Cob thought, then out loud, "Time for supper Jimbo." Emma had promised him an eggy cup for supper if he did this kindness for her and Cob was starting to think on that.

Mrs McKee was sitting in the kitchen staring into the fire.

The Doctor was dining out and the boys had been fed and were outside annoying Nero the donkey, while Sarah was washing up the last few pots and pans in the streaming Belfast sink. Emma finished stacking some plates away and then picked up the teapot from the kitchen table.

"Would you like that cup freshened?" Emma offered.

Mrs McKee roused herself and gave a wan smile. "That would be nice," she said.

Emma poured some fresh tea into both their cups and then added milk to hers. It clotted at the top. She sniffed it. "On the turn," she commented.

Mrs McKee nodded. "There's rain on the way." She looked out the window. "I hope he's alright."

Emma paused, unsure as to how to break the news. "I'm...I'm afraid I found Freddie on my walk. He was down the dunes hunting rabbits I think and...he was just lying there. Like he was sleeping."

Mrs McKee chortled. "Oh, he's a holy terror with those rabbits...I remember as a wee pup he caught one and he was so proud when he brought it over to me." Mrs McKee suddenly sat bolt upright. "Here where is he now? He can't stay out there —"

"Don't worry. Cob went out and buried him nicely... down by the rabbits," Emma soothed.

Mrs McKee sat back in her chair and considered this. "Yes... by the rabbits. He'll like that." Mrs McKee stood up. "That Cob's a good boy. I think I'll make him some ham and eggs for his breakfast tomorrow.

Emma stayed silent. Cob was a good sort and he deserved the occasional treat.

Mrs McKee threw on her old-fashioned cloak and gathered it about her. It seemed to have grown for she looked very small…small and lost in it. She hadn't appeared like that when they'd first met. "I think I'll be away home now…I may walk past the dunes and say goodnight to Freddie. If I'm a wee bit late tomorrow can you look after things please?"

Emma nodded. "Don't worry, goodnight."

Mrs McKee didn't look at Emma, she just nodded and then walked out into the night.

Chapter 8

It was early in the morning and the household was waking; the Doctor was still abed and Mrs McKee had not yet arrived, but Sarah was well on preparing the breakfasts and Henry had cleaned and relaid the fire in the Doctor's study already. The scent of toasted bread and boiling porridge filled the kitchen competing with the damp green smells of horse, hay and grass coming in the open back door from outside.

On Sarah's signal, Emma went outside to call the boys in. Charlie was sitting on the wall by the back door while Cob was at the barn brushing down the horses. Emma frowned, "Are you not going to help Cob?" she asked him.

"They don't want me," he answered.

Emma stood stock still for a moment. Any friction could, maybe would, threaten the new life that she was seeking to build for them. Cob was a servant but the Doctor valued him and enjoyed his company. Emma sat on the wall beside Charlie and put her arm around his shoulders. "Why Pet? What's happened?"

"Nothing. I just told the Doctor that Cob said the Doctor wanted to marry you an' the Doctor went mad an' beat Cob."

Emma felt her blood freeze. This was worse than the boyish squabble she had expected. Everything she had done, had hoped could be threatened by this. She shook Charlie by the shoulder…hard. "Go to your room," she hissed. "Go to your room this instant."

Charlie looked startled. This wasn't working out the way he had expected. "But I haven't —"

"You go to your room now or I'll get Cob to whip you!"

Charlie's eyes shot open. He glanced over at the grinning Cob. He shuddered to think what vengeance he would take now he knew that Charlie was on his own. "Mum," he wailed his eyes filling with tears.

Sarah came to the back door, "Miss Emma, boys… breakfast's ready."

Emma stood up and caught Charlie by the ear. "No breakfast for this one Sarah! No, nor lunch, nor supper either!" She dragged the sobbing Charlie to the house. "Get up those stairs to your room or I'll have Cob cut a switch right now!"

Emma rapped the Doctor's bedroom door, hesitated then walked in with his breakfast tray. The Doctor sat up in bed and gave Emma a broad smile. "And a Good Morning to you Emma. How are you this fine day?"

Emma smiled back. Emma placed the tray on the table at the foot of his bed and then carried the jug of hot water over to the shaving stand. She pulled the curtains open and the room flooded with light then turned and smiled. "It looks like a fine morning. Did you sleep well, Doctor?" The Doctor rose from his bed and pulled on a dressing gown. "It is indeed. I slept like a top. What reports from below decks?"

"Charlie's sent to his room for cheek, and Cob still sulking after that whipping you gave him. Otherwise, all is set fair."

"Whipping! Pah! I merely waved the switch in his direction. His dignity is affronted, that's all. The Doctor thought for a while. "I know I'll send the boys on some little errand and tell them to keep the change and take their time. That'll set them up again."

"But not Charlie," Emma responded.

"You are a stern Mistress so poor Charlie will remain in irons until you release him."

Later that day Emma came into the kitchen and saw Sarah working there. "Ah Sarah, I was just going to make a cup of tea. Shall I put your name in the pot?"

"Oh yes. That'd be lovely."

Emma filled the kettle and put it on to boil.

Sarah placed cups, saucers, and a jug of milk on the table and Emma poured the tea. They both settled back in their chairs.

Emma pointed to a small door set in a corner at the very back of the kitchen. "Where's that go?"

"That's down to the cellar," said Sarah.

"The cellar? I never thought of that. I've never even been down there."

"All these houses are built on sand. Our cellar's not flagged so the floor's sand."

"What do we use it for?" Emma asked.

"Mostly old rubbish but the Doctor keeps his wine down there and some of his doctoring stuff…chemicals and the like…for the coolness I expect."

"So you go down —" asked Emma.

"Oh no. I don't like it. When the Doctor wants his wine he goes himself mostly. Henry won't go down unless Cob's with him…and I have to stand on the steps with a lantern afore they'll go."

Emma stood. "Well, I must have a look. No time like the present. Where's that lantern?"

Emma descended the narrow staircase leading down to the cellar. The walls at this level were different to the ones that made up the house above. These were larger blocks; smoother and well-fitted.

Sarah called from the safety of the steps, "Are you all right? Can you see?"

It was cold and getting colder as Emma reached the door. Raising her lantern she saw a heavy iron-studded door but secured only by a small wooden latch. "Yes, I'm fine now Sarah. I'll be just a minute." Emma pushed the door and was surprised that it opened so easily, so welcoming to visitors. As Emma stepped into the cellar the lantern revealed a spacious room with broad stone pillars supporting massive arches that seemed to extend well beyond the boundaries of the existing cellar and a pair of heavy double doors that must led up the ramp to the stable yard outside.

The walls were constructed of the same well-finished blocks she had observed on the way down. *This isn't right*, Emma thought, *Not for the house above*. It reminded Emma of the interiors in the great Cathedrals that she had visited as a child.

To Emma's right, she was able to make out the racks of the Doctor's small store of wine and on the far wall another door, *again with heavy bars set on this side*. The light from the lantern showed the floor to be uneven, hummocks like miniature dunes casting small shadows which led the eye further into the darkness. Emma stooped down and ran her fingers along the floor. *Sand, the floor was made of the same fine sand that was found on the dunes*.

In the centre of the cellar on a small raised plinth, with steps leading up to it, was a large rectangular shape like a horse trough, *Or a coffin!* Emma approached gingerly, tripping a little on the uneven floor. It was about ten foot long and about half as much wide. Cut from fine stone and decorated with small carvings that seemed to move when she wasn't looking at them. The trough itself was full of water and radiated an icy cold.

Emma searched out a piece of flat surface and then set her lantern on the side. Putting both her hands on the edge of the trough she looked in. The surface reflected the light from the lantern and sent it dancing crazily against the walls creating strange shapes that took forms which seemed both unrecognisable and familiar at the same time.

Looking down into the water it seemed deeper; deeper

Emma could see no bottom. From the outside, the trough was about three foot deep, at the most. However when Emma looked down into the water it seemed without end. At the edges of her vision, forms seemed to come into focus and then slide away when she tried to look upon them.

There is, are, things in there, Emma thought. She reached down and touched the water with her fingertips. It was as though an electric shock had pulsed through her body and switched something on. Now, now she could see for the first time. A world seemed to be revealing itself. The shadows swirled in the water and she could feel them talking to her, calling to her. The cellar seemed to fill with the sound of babies crying, of screaming as the light spun more and more fantastical shapes on the walls.

Emma slipped her hand into the icy water. She could feel things quickly brushing past then they were gone back into the depths. A sharp pain made Emma shudder and quickly withdraw her hand. Four deep little cuts, parallel like claw marks, dripped blood back down into the water.

Emma felt she was standing in a drum of sound, of light, of memories, as the shapes called upon her to join them, to slip into their world, and to leave her world of cruelty, of sorrow, of despair behind. To dance with them in the water world, to sleep with them, and most of all to forget.

Chapter 9

It was a quiet morning in the household. Mrs McKee had not yet arrived so Emma had decided they all needed cheering up. She hadn't slept well herself thinking about the Doctor's offer and had dreamt fitfully for some reason about poor Freddie standing by the cellar door and barking at her. When dawn broke she got washed and dressed and started to make her way downstairs. Emma opened her bedroom door and stepped onto the landing. To the right at the far end stood the Doctor's room with a slight sound of snoring emanating from it. To the left and next door to her room was Charlie's. Quietly Emma opened it, the bed was empty with the sheets and blankets thrown aside in a heap. *He must be out with Cob and Henry* she thought.

Quietly Emma made her way down the stairs, avoiding

the two creaky steps at the very top, then across the hallway and down into the kitchen. The room was cold and the back door was lying open to the yard. She moved across and looked out spying Charlie grooming Nero the donkey, whilst Henry forked hay down from the loft into Cob's waiting wheelbarrow. *He's finding his place here* thought Emma.

Turning to the stove Emma riddled last night's ashes and then added fresh kindling before putting a match to it. Taking the kettle to the kitchen pump she filled it as quietly as she could; this sound was her normal alarm clock and she wished to give the household a little longer in bed; as much for her sake as theirs. Setting the kettle on the stove to boil she listened but no sound from the Doctor; *good let him lie in* and he'd wake up to a breakfast that would show them all what a good job she could do in Mrs McKee's absence.

The porridge bubbled away and the kettle boiled Emma made a pot of tea then, whilst it drew, she set the kitchen table with a separate tray for the Doctor. Pleased with her progress Emma thought *A cup of tea for me then the porridge will be ready*. She rapped Sarah's bedroom door. "Tea's in the pot Sarah!"

Then Emma went to the back door and shouted for the boys. In an avalanche, they all tumbled in and took their places. Flushed with their work, *or more likely their play* Emma thought, they sat there waiting as Emma ladled porridge into their bowls. Charlie used both hands to pour in some milk whereas Cob and Henry both took a pinch of salt and scattered it on their porridge. *It's little things like that that remind you you're away from home* thought Emma.

After a few moments, Sarah emerged sleepy-eyed and

wrapped in her heavy shawl. "These chilly mornings will be the death of me," she complained before picking up the cup. "Just the thing. Thank ye."

"Did you sleep well Sarah?" asked Emma.

"Indeed but it's hard to drag yerself out from a warm bed these dark morns. Mrs McKee not in yet?" Sarah asked looking around.

"Not yet," said Emma.

Sarah tutted. "She's still upset over Freddie."

"I saw her," offered Cob. He pointed to a dish of sliced ham and a bowl of eggs Emma had brought in from the pantry, "is that for us?"

"Maybe, if you're good," Emma replied. "Where did you see her?"

"Walking out past the castle."

"When?"

"Cob's got a girlfriend," teased Henry.

Cob flushed, "Last night. No, I don't!"

"Yes, you do. You're sweet on Henry Armstrong's sister," Henry replied.

Sarah burst into tears and they both stopped to look at her.

Emma quickly poured the Doctor's tea and filled a shaving jug with hot water then carried it upstairs leaving Cob and Henry quarrelling over Cob's surprisingly complicated love life.

The Doctor was still in bed but smiled when he saw Emma. "Ah, you ladies spoil me." He threw aside the blankets and stood up in his nightshirt. "Allow me," as he took the jug of hot water from the tray and over to his shaving stand. Pouring some water into a waiting basin he asked, "All's well Emma? I heard about poor old Freddie. Terrible business."

"Yes we're all very shocked," Emma replied. "Where would you like this?" Emma raised the tray with his cup of tea on it.

"Oh just put it anywhere. There on the table at the foot of the bed," he indicated. "Where's Betsy? Is she very upset?"

"I'm afraid she's not in yet," Emma said.

The Doctor studied Emma's reflection in the shaving mirror as he soaped his cheeks. "Still you seem to have the measure of things. Are you confident in all Betsy's duties?"

Emma nodded.

"And that other matter we discussed yesterday? Have you arrived at any conclusion?" queried the Doctor as he swathed a large path through the suds on his cheek.

"I spoke to Charlie yesterday. He…we are both very happy here."

"Capital news. Remind me I must write to the Navigation School," he paused as he carefully worked with the razor under his nose, "but you've seen a man shaving before Eh?"

Emma nodded again. "I used to shave my husband."

"Excellent! So please remind me tomorrow to write that letter."

"I was cooking some bacon and eggs for the boys. Would you like me to bring some on a tray for you?" asked Emma.

"No, no…I'll be down in a jiffy and I'll join you all at the kitchen table if I may? We'll all breakfast *en famille* shall we not?"

The scent of frying filled the kitchen and spread throughout the house. As fast as Emma could fill the skillet to supply the large plate in the middle of the table with ham, eggs, and fried breads the boys expertly hooked them onto their plates until Emma grew alarmed with the diminishing pile waiting to be cooked.

"Right finish your breakfast boys," she warned. "Leave some for the Doctor." Charlie slipped another piece of ham onto his plate while looking at her. Emma pursed her lips *That boy,* she thought, *is going to have to learn not to push things too far.* "Cob, when you've finished would you mind taking Charlie to school?"

Cob weighed up the merits of foregoing a nap in the hayloft with the potential for more breakfast feasts under a new regime. "Aye, I'll drag him over gladly." He threw a stray slice of ham onto some bread and stood up, "Come on you. Time for your lessons now."

Charlie pouted. "I don't want to go I —"

The Doctor entered clad in his breeches, stockings and shirt wearing his slippers, and a silk dressing gown over them, "Upon my soul, this smells good. What boys, is Miss Emma treating you scoundrels to ham 'n eggs without a day's work out of you?"

Emma smiled at the Doctor and dropped a quick curtsy. Inwardly she was furious at Charlie for striking the wrong note, "Charlie," she snapped, "get you down to that school this instant or I'll get Cob to cut a switch and give you a whipping in the yard!" Charlie was stunned at the sudden reversal, "This instant!"

Emma put down a fresh cup for the Doctor and filled it with tea. "Would you care for your porridge now Doctor?" she enquired, "and then I'll get your ham and eggs on the go?"

The Doctor nodded. "Capital, yes indeed. We could get used to this," he winked, "Eh boys?"

Emma placed a of bowl of porridge in front of the Doctor. "Are you pair still here?" she addressed Cob and Charlie.

Cob seized a still-outraged Charlie and propelled him out the back door. "Come on you. I'll cut a nice switch on the way past and give it a wee test on yer arse."

Emma placed a small jug beside the Doctor's porridge, "The cream of the milk," then started frying his breakfast. "Sarah, if you've finished you could start upstairs now? And Henry the fires? Make sure you do the Doctor's room first."

Sarah hesitated then said, "Mrs McKee usually —"

Emma looked round at Sarah, *I have to take this opportunity to show them I'm the housekeeper now* Emma thought. "Mrs McKee not here. I am now…let's be about our work."

Henry rose from his chair but Sarah remained sitting and looked at the Doctor. He paused raising a fork to his lips. "You heard what Miss Emma said, now hop to it you pair."

Happily, the Doctor spread some butter on his toast. "You seem to be finding your feet here Emma," he remarked. "Any word about Mrs McKee?"

"Cob said he saw her on the dunes last night."

"Upon my word. What would she be doing there?"

Emma paused for she was fond of Mrs McKee and didn't

want to get her in trouble. "Cob said he thought she went looking for Freddie."

"But didn't Cob bury the poor thing?"

"I expect she just wanted to see his grave."

"Ah!" The Doctor looked at Freddie's bowl still sitting on the floor. "I do miss the little fellow."

It was later when Emma had just cleared away the breakfast things when there was a knock at the back door. When Emma opened it she found Mrs McKee with a Constable. "Morning Missus," as he touched the brim of his hat. "I was patrolling the town when I saw Mrs McKee out by the castle. I thought I'd just walk her home."

Mrs McKee was standing there. She was wet still from the heavy morning dew and her hair had come out from under her bonnet.

Emma took her by the arm and nodded to the policeman who stood there with water dripping off his cape. "Would you like a cup of tea Constable?"

"Thank you no. I have my breakfast waiting for me at the barracks."

"Thank you then. I'll look after her from here." She guided Mrs McKee into the kitchen. "Look you're all wet." Emma helped her with her hat and cloak. "We'll just get these off and," leading her to the stove, "get you warmed up."

"I went out early to put some flowers on Freddie's grave and it started bucketing with rain." Mrs McKee settled in her chair and nodded at the teapot. "Is that fresh?"

"I'm sure it's cold by now. I'll put a fresh pot on." Emma

handed Mrs McKee a towel, "First we'll just get you sorted."

Henry entered with an empty coal bucket. "Henry, ask the Doctor if he would step down?"

Henry lifted up the bucket, "I need more coal."

"Henry! Now please!"

Henry looked at Mrs McKee, "Is Mum all right?"

"Henry! Stop dawdling and get up those stairs now!"

Henry looked alarmed, "Yes Miss," and disappeared up the stairs at a run.

The Doctor entered the kitchen closely followed by Henry.

"I was just…Betsy! Bless my soul!" exclaimed the Doctor. "Where on Earth have —"

Emma cut in. "Doctor she's been out looking for Freddie's grave. In this weather."

"Freddie! But I thought," he paused and looked first at Mrs McKee then to Emma, "we should make up the spare room I think. Henry some coals in the bed-warmer and warm the bed in the spare room for Mrs McKee," Henry hurried to comply, "and Henry! Then nip down the town and find Willie McKee. Tell him that Mrs McKee is found and we have put her to bed in my house."

The Doctor bent down and gathered Mrs McKee in his arms. "Emma, would you go ahead please and turn the bed down?

In the spare room the Doctor set Mrs McKee on the bed. "Perhaps you would help Betsy to bed Emma? I'll go down and fetch my bag." The Doctor exited the room shouting for Sarah.

Emma contemplated Mrs McKee. Now looking so old

80

and frail compared to when she had first greeted Charlie and herself into the house. Emma untied the patient from her dress then eased her back onto the pillows and tucked the blankets tight. Sarah entered with a hot water bottle wrapped in a towel and Emma lifted the blankets to allow it to be placed at Mrs McKee's feet. "Can you see to the fire please Sarah?" Emma asked then turned to Mrs McKee. "I'll just go down and get you a cup of tea. You'll —"

Mrs McKee seized her wrist as Emma turned to go. "The dead bairns. All the wee bairns. They've taken my Freddie to be with them!"

Emma winced. Mrs McKee had a firm grasp. "Now, now Mrs McKee. Nobody has Freddie he's —" but Mrs McKee relaxed her grip and lay back into the pillows and muttered to herself. Emma rubbed her wrist where fingermarks were starting to appear.

Chapter 10

Emma had just finished serving the boys their daily lunch of boiled potatoes when the Doctor poked his head around the kitchen door. "I've just checked our patient and she's sleeping —"

Startled Emma dropped the dishcloth and wiped her hands on her apron. "Oh my Lord Doctor! I forgot your lunch!"

The Doctor waved it off. "I do understand. You're busy with the invalid. Never fear I took the opportunity to call in at Lemon's Chop House when I collected the mails this morning. Half-a-dozen chops and a pint of claret was no hardship," he smiled, "and I have the latest dispatches! Fresh off the ferry" He waved the posts unsteadily. The Doctor addressed Charlie. "Are you ready to update the map young

Charlie? Plot the downfall of your Father's enemies?"

Charlie hesitated looking at Emma. She nodded. "Go on Charlie. Help the Doctor with his map."

Charlie remained seated avoiding eye contact.

Angry now Emma snapped. "Get up this instant Charles. I won't tell you again!"

Charlie slowly got to his feet and made his way across the kitchen towards the Doctor.

"Come along old chap. It's not as bad as all that," offered the Doctor. "Best foot forward and all that…eh?" And he turned back up the stairs with Charlie following.

Together they both entered the Doctor's study. The big map showing Crimea had a smaller map showing the city of Sevastopol in greater detail. The Doctor pointed to a small red one. "That old fellow is where I think your father fell in the service of his country."

Despite himself, Charlie was drawn to the map. He traced the space of Kalamita Bay with his finger. "Was there a big battle there?" he asked.

"Indeed there must have been," the Doctor pointed to the map. "Here," he traced out the Alma River, "here, a great battle was fought and the Highland Division saved the day!"

Charlie spanned the gap between the Bay and where the Doctor had placed the pin for the battle with his fingers then looked at them. He held them up to the Doctor. "How far's that?"

Picking up a ruler the Doctor held it to Charlie's hand. "How many inches Charlie?"

Charlie looked uncertain. "One and…six twelfths," he offered.

"Well done Charlie lad, well done. So at six inches to the mile, it would be about? Come on Charlie. Two times six is…?"

"Twelve?"

"And six-twelfths is what?"

Charlie remained silent.

"Twelve-twelfths is what of an inch?"

"One?"

"So half of that?… Charlie, what's half of twelve?"

"Half an inch? We haven't done fractions."

"Ah yes, Capital. Well done anyway Charlie. Yes, about ten miles." The Doctor paused. "Would you like to go to sea, to be a sailor then Charlie?" the Doctor asked.

Charlie considered the matter. He had seen sailors on board the ferry that had brought them to this place. They had their own little house on the ship where the passengers weren't allowed, but he had seen them climb into the rigging and pull on ropes which didn't look nice. "No," he replied.

"No? A life of adventure. Come now Charlie where's —"

"Cob says you want to see my Mum's knickers," commented Charlie.

"Does he by God? I'll have a word with Master Cob over that." The Doctor placed the tray of pins on his desk and then rushed out crying, "Cob, Cob! Where are you you rascal?"

Charlie stood there for a while looking at the map. He measured across different distances with his fingers. Things had gone well there. Cob may not realise it but he'd just been paid back for chasing him to school with a switch, but Charlie would make sure he told Cob when he was bigger. Charlie plucked out the pin on the map that the Doctor had said was where his Daddy had died; he held it in his fingers looking at it closely for a while then threw it on the fire.

That night Emma went to the Doctor's room.

It was still light the following evening before Emma was able to slip away for a walk. She needed time to clear her head and think about her position as *the Doctor's Mistress!* She gazed out onto the sea with the late sunshine painting shimmering stripes of silver on the water and Scotland low on the horizon. Emma felt this world was older than perhaps she had been used to; not the casual cruelty she had seen on the streets of London more…indifferent.

At the Promenade Emma looked to her left at the dunes that lay under the castle. No not tonight. Not with Willie McKee's story still echoing around in her head; those cries. How could they be? Children playing on the beach? No, not tonight and started walking towards the harbour and lighthouse.

The harbour was crowded tonight as the packet ship was tied up until the morning post, jostling for space amongst the other vessels. Together they rocked on the swell with the ropes alternatively slacking to dip into the tide, then tightening as the vessels rose on the swell shedding drops of silver as the water was squeezed out of them.

Emma passed what the locals called Kelly's Steps opposite the Downshire Hotel and paused to look down at them. This would have been the way the slavers had driven their prisoners. This place would have rung with their cries and lamentations. They would have had to whip their charges through the very streets. How could Willie claim that the people knew nothing, and did nothing? The whole place must have been guilty of silence at the very least. This was a place that had tipped their problems head down a well to drown from moral sensibilities, from notions of respectability. For the first time, Emma sensed danger in the atmosphere, from memories, from things done, and things left undone.

It was cooler now and a sea mist had rolled in adding a damp salty tang to the air. A single curlew called out and Emma shivered at the sound; how very lonely it sounded. She'd take a turn around the lighthouse and that would do.

Her footsteps rang out in the silence. The mist had suddenly deepened and the end of the pier was obscured but for the top of the lighthouse like an island. Emma stopped, she saw a figure on the top deck looking across the bay. *It must be Willie*, she waved, then stopped. She dropped her arm. *That's too big for Willie* she thought. Emma couldn't remember if *had he said he had an assistant or not?* The figure had now turned and was looking towards her. Emma raised her hand again to wave but something about the figure didn't seem right. She dropped her hand again then the mist rose and she could no longer see him, only the light which pulsed on and off.

By now the upheaval of Emma and Charlie's arrival had passed and the days had become, more often, fine and sunny compared to the more normal state of wet and windy. Windows were opened and allowed the airs to admit the scents of summer; life was good. When Emma lay with the

Doctor they would fall asleep with the drapes open and waken to the cawing of the crows as they prepared for another busy day in the fields. This was Emma's signal to quickly return to her own bed that it would not be found unslept in.

Most mornings Emma would slip downstairs and throw open the backdoor to allow the cool dawn air in before lighting the stove and putting water on to boil.

Often Emma would find Mrs McKee already there; dozing in her chair. Sometimes Mrs McKee would enter down the stairs from the hallway, or, more often, by the back door. Emma was never quite sure where Mrs McKee had spent the night, and every few days her husband Willie would call in for a cup of tea as though he too was looking for her, but never quite able to find what he was searching for.

Mrs McKee seemed to have recovered and was now as Emma had first seen her: tall, starched, brushed, and spotlessly clean; Freddie was rarely mentioned. Emma would sit and listen as Mrs McKee told her tales of her youth: of pikes in the thatch, and men marching in the night, armed with billhooks and home-forged spears, over to the Ards to fight the old King's army; of the Great Hunger when the walking dead had roamed the town begging for scraps; and older darker tales that she had heard from her parents, and they from theirs, of the people who had held this land from before time, and their fearsome priests.

A young girl from the town, Lizzie, had been recruited as scullery maid to replace Sarah who, in turn, had taken over most of Mrs McKee's duties with, to Cob's great satisfaction, a commensurate rise in her wages.

One hot June Saturday Cob, Henry, and Charlie had taken advantage of the good weather, and the Doctor's absence, to take the stables on holiday to the beach. Cob rode Sultan the Doctor's hunter, Henry was mounted on Jimbo, and Charlie brought up the rear on Nero the donkey. It was one of those rare days when the chill promise of the morning was rewarded with a blazing hot sun and a cooling sea breeze. The boys rode bareback, barefoot and loose reined as the animals squabbled for position in the surf.

"What are you doing," Cob addressed Charlie, "now schools over for summer?"

Charlie looked at Cob as though he was mad. "Doing? I'm not doing anything. I'm on holiday."

"No, but I mean on Monday?"

"Monday? Are you stupid I —"

Just in time, Charlie caught the flash of anger in Cob's eyes.

Henry intervened. "No, what he means is today is a wee holiday and tomorrow well it's Sunday but then it's Monday."

"What am I supposed to do then?" as Charlie held Nero back from getting into striking range of Cob.

"Well most children are helping their folks in their work," said Henry.

Charlie considered this for a while. "I help you two in the stables."

Cob snorted and Henry cut in, "I know you do but you're getting older. You'll be what eleven next year? You'll be getting too old for school soon. What'll you do then?"

The thought of work hadn't entered Charlie's mind. He'd seen people work, had seen people doing things that they didn't want, when what they really wanted was to do nothing, or maybe have a little nap. Charlie had seen all this and he hadn't liked what he'd seen.

"Ye'll be tatty-hoking soon enough anyway. See if you like that," Cob said in a tone of voice that suggested that Charlie really wouldn't. Charlie shot a wide-eyed glance at Henry.

"Picking the potatoes," Henry explained. "Every September Miss Wilkes takes the whole school out around the country to help the farmers pick the potatoes. It's great fun and you get to sleep in the barns"

Charlie didn't like the sound of that all. He resolved that, for him, school was over.

"Come on," shouted Cob. "Time for a swim!" as he steered Sultan into deeper water and slipped off his back. Henry and Jimbo followed their respective heroes into the tide, and Nero decided that he wanted nothing to do with this new venture, bucked Charlie off his back, and walked on in the shallows, leaving him gasping for breath in Nero's wake.

Chapter 11

The next morning was a Sunday and the rest of the house was going about the normal routine but Charlie didn't feel like helping Cob or Henry. Not after they'd laughed at him when Nero threw him off and he'd had to walk all the way home. He didn't want to have to go tatty-hoking and he just wanted to go home.

Bored Charlie moved through the house in stocking feet. He was too smart to go into the kitchen, too dangerous, and he didn't want to be accused of tramping mud through the house. He'd get a job if he was seen idling whilst everybody else was working so he decided to explore. He'd been through his Mum's room but there was nothing new there so he decided to try his luck downstairs. The Drawing room was empty; Henry or Sarah had laid the fire ready for a match. There was a flower display on the table near the window. Charlie pushed his nose into the middle and smelt a sweet sickly odour. He didn't much like that then he noticed that the vase was full of water. He picked it up and carried it over to the grate and held the flowers back while he slowly poured the water over the kindling, before returning it to the table. *Good luck getting that to light.* Charlie then moved to the back of the room where an oil painting was hanging. It was of some old Delacherois in hunting rig. Charlie carefully started scratching some paint off the corner blowing the dust off and working at the edges when he heard the doorbell ring. Charlie saw the Doctor answer and then leave the man standing there. Charlie studied the caller, a sailor by his garb, for a few minutes then the Doctor returned dressed with his boots and coat on, and carrying his bag. Cramming on his hat the Doctor walked rapidly towards the harbour with the sailor by his side.

This could be his chance decided Charlie. To see if he could find something so that Mummy wouldn't want to marry the Doctor and they could go home. Charlie took a furtive glance into the hallway but no one was to be seen. Silently Charlie skated across the tiles in his stocking feet to the door of the Doctor's study. He paused to look around, then knocked just in case someone was still in there. No answer so Charlie tried the handle, it turned and Charlie let himself in quietly closing the door behind him. It was warm from a small fire and the heat from the sun through the windows. Charlie moved to look out. The street was busy, a cart clattered past out the Millisle road then some drovers ushered their small black cattle into the town towards the

Bullock Slip. No sign of the Doctor.

Charlie moved over to the desk; it was littered with papers but Charlie couldn't read them. There was a big old book sitting there, bigger than any book Charlie had ever seen. He looked closely but he couldn't read the writing. He didn't recognise a single word and the letters weren't the ones Miss Wilkes showed them in class. Charlie decided that it must be doctor writing because, as he leafed through it, the pictures showed people being burnt on big fires, and some people being hanged, and on one was lots of ladies with no clothes dancing around a bonfire with a big goat sitting on a chair watching them; he liked the goat and the way it sometimes seemed to be looking back at him. Charlie turned to the very last page, tore a little bit off, and threw it on the fire; it burnt a strange colour and sparked a bit in the flame. Charlie sniffed. A barnyard smell had come of the burning paper and he hoped it would clear before the Doctor got back. Hurriedly Charlie restored the book to its previous position and then turned his attention to the other things on the desk.

There were some newspapers with drawings on them and Charlie recognised a group of soldiers trudging manfully through snow. He guessed it was from the Crimea where his Daddy had died. Looking at the picture again Charlie turned to the map on the wall behind the desk. The Doctor must have been updating it as a small box of coloured pins and some coloured wool was on the mantelpiece. Charlie studied the Doctor's work. In the corner nearest the window were some green ones linked together with green wool. Charlie pulled them out and threw them into the fire where the wool caught and flared. Drawn by the brief flame Charlie poked his head into the fireplace proper. The ember threw up a fierce heat that burnt Charlie's cheeks. He dribbled some saliva and heard it sizzle then turned his head to toast first the right cheek then the left one. The curtain over the door to the Doctor's laboratory was pulled slightly back and the door was ajar with a key still in the lock; the Doctor must have forgotten to lock it in his hurry.

Curiously Charlie glanced behind himself then put his head around the door and inspected the room. It was a surprisingly pleasant looking and welcoming sight: a desk with a blotter and some pens under the window along with a comfortable chair; a workbench against the far wall with flasks and bottles strewn about, and the third wall taken up with glass sample jars. After looking in the drawers of the desk and pocketing a shilling he found in one drawer Charlie moved to examine the contents of the sample jars. There was a head of a calf with another little head growing out of it, and there was a snake with a head at each end. The bulk of the collection was, to Charlie's horror, made up of infants curled up and floating in alcohol; little fists clenched tight in baby rage against the world. Fascinated Charlie moved along the shelf; he was particularly struck by several that seemed to have little tails growing from them. He moved closer to inspect them, he put out a diffident finger and tapped the glass but there was no response except for a little sediment that danced and swirled at the bottom of the jar. Emboldened Charlie took a firmer grip on the jar and shook it; an eye sprang open and fixed Charlie in its gaze.

Startled Charlie sprang back dropping the jar which

rocked back into place. The homunculus now used its hands to lever itself around inside the jar to face Charlie. The overlarge eyes set in a pink unformed face followed him as he backed away before his nerve went and he fled the room, running through the Doctor's study, across the hall, and down the kitchen stairs.

A few seconds passed then Mrs McKee entered the room. The jar Charlie had disturbed was sitting askew of the others. Mrs McKee checked the screw top was firmly in place then replaced it. "Now, now settle down. The nasty boy's gone," she said, "you stay in there nice and snug and I'll be back later to see you all in a wee while."

Chapter 12

It was late August when the crops were mostly in, with the going still soft, but not too soft, and when Sultan started earning his corn. For the Doctor was a keen huntsman and mixed with the cream of local society in the frantic pursuit of the fox. What harm this animal had done him neither he nor his fellows, could say other than it was part of the mating dance of the better sort. Sultan was the Doctor's hunter and for all his grand name, was not a fine, dainty, well-bred sort as would be found in the English Shires but a sturdy big-boned, hairy-toed Irish Draft. Strong enough to carry an increasingly tubby Doctor about the muddy fields all day, patient enough to carry him home in his cups, and mannerly enough to take him on his rounds the next morn.

One Tuesday morning silence reigned in the household,

the chores were done, the potatoes on the boil for the boys, and the Doctor away cubbing with the Gentry, not expected back till late. On these days the ladies of the household would take the opportunity for a little treat.

"Would you take a cup of tea Mrs McKee? Sarah?" Emma would offer.

"I'm obliged," they would respond.

"And a slice of this Ginger cake Mrs McKee? Emma?" Sarah would suggest.

"Oh I couldn't take another piece," and "I shall burst!" they would protest.

And they would all kick off their boots and sit by the stove for as long as they had peace.

The parish bell had just rung out eleven of the clock the noise of shouting, and the rattle of a cart from the yard broke into the quiet. The ladies were still holding their teacups and dainty plates when the Doctor burst in. He swept the table clear scattering all before him and deposited a recumbent Miss Delacherois amidst the wreckage of the meal.

Mrs McKee was the first to react. "Emma! Towels and a blanket quickly! Sarah! A basin of hot water!"

Emma and Sarah sat stunned. "Now," shouted Mrs McKee. "Don't dawdle!"

The Doctor and Mrs McKee expertly stripped off Miss Delacherois' coat and boots.

"She fell, Betsy." The Doctor was examining the patient. "Just coming up to a wall and her horse, the ill-bred brute, refused damn it." He looked up at Mrs McKee who was feeling for Miss Delacherois' pulse. "D'ye find anything Betsy?"

"It's weak but she's alive," said Mrs McKee.

Henry rushed in. "Cob's looking after the yard."

"Henry get up to my study and bring my bag down," ordered the Doctor. "Emma, Sarah help us wrap her in the blanket!"

This was quickly done. "Now Sarah your hot water on the blanket! We need to heat her up!" ordered Mrs McKee.

The patient was soon swaddled in a piping-hot blanket. The hot water flooded the kitchen and splashed over Miss Delacherois' attendants.

Henry returned with the bag and the Doctor extracted a spirit lamp which he placed on the table.

"Emma light the lamp quickly," instructed the Doctor rummaging in his bag, "where are those damn feathers?"

Mrs McKee reached over and extracted a small bunch of feathers from a tiny drawer in the bag. "Here." She handed them to the Doctor who touched them to the flame of the burning lamp then thrust the bundle under Miss Delacherois' nose, allowing the acrid fumes to rise into her nostrils. The stink of the burning feathers quickly filled the kitchen.

Mrs McKee had next extracted a small mirror and held it to Miss Delacherois' lips, "She's not breathing," Mrs McKee took the girl's wrist in her hand, "and the pulse is getting weaker!"

Mrs McKee looked up. "No pulse. She's gone Doctor."

"Damn it, stand back!" the Doctor hit the middle of Miss Delacherois' chest, once, Mrs McKee shook her head, twice, again Mrs McKee shook her head, and thrice.

"No I won't allow it!" he rummaged in his bag and extracted a long thin ivory pipe, bent at one end into a curve, with the other end attached to a long India rubber tube. Gently he inserted the curved end into Miss Delacherois's nostril and, "If I can just get past…Aha! Betsy, we're there!"

Mrs McKee had obtained a small set of hand bellows from the bag and quickly attached them to the tubing. She operated the bellows and…excitedly the Doctor exclaimed, "She's breathing Betsy, she's breathing!"

Steadily Mrs McKee pumped the little bellows. "We'll see, we'll see. Have you your watch there Doctor?"

The Doctor scrabbled in his waistcoat pocket. "Here Betsy, here" and placed it on the kitchen table. All eyes remained fixed on it as Mrs McKee pumped…two, three, pump, two, three, pump.

Sarah had another kettle of hot water in her hand. The Doctor nodded and it was poured over the sodden blanket flooding onto the floor and again drenching the ladies' stocking feet.

Pump, two, three, pump…and all watched the rise and fall of Miss Delacherois' chest as the time on the Doctor's pocket watch passed. Bright red blood bubbled at Miss Delacherois' other nostril with each stroke of the bellows.

After five minutes had elapsed Mrs McKee paused and all waited, waited but the rise and fall of the chest did not continue. "Here let me take over Betsy, rest yourself a moment." The Doctor and Mrs McKee exchanged places and the Doctor continued with the pump, two, three, pump whilst Mrs McKee monitored the patient.

Time passed slowly. Emma and Sarah stood frozen, willing the poor lady to gain the strength to breathe again of her own volition. The only sound was the wheeze of the bellows and the expulsion of air from poor Miss Delacherois' lungs.

Mrs McKee reached over and put her hand on the Doctor's. "She's gone. Let the poor girl be."

The Doctor flinched as though a blow had been struck. "No, I'll not allow that." He looked up at Mrs McKee. "We have one more card to play. Henry! Cob! Bring Jimbo round to the back door! Quick!"

The Doctor emerged into the yard with Miss Delacherois in his arms. Her head lolled back and her arms hung loosely waving gently with the Doctor's motion. "Here Cob, here. Hold him still Henry. Get her up on Jimbo!"

The Doctor hoisted Miss Delacherois up and across Jimbo's back. Cob caught her head and shoulders. "Henry hold him still! Cob…belly down!"

"That's it now Cob you hold her from that side! Henry trot on! Trot on!"

Baffled Henry started Jimbo into a trot whilst the Doctor and Cob ran along side holding Miss Delacherois in place. Angrily Jimbo tried to bite Henry but the bridle was in too firm a grasp for that nonsense. He tried to cow-kick Cob but received a mighty punch in return that put that idea out of his head. Resigned Jimbo trotted up and around the yard with this wretched bundle bouncing and jolting on his back, with a determined Henry dragging him forward, a vigilant Cob threatening him with blood-curdling oaths, and a puffing Doctor floundering in his rear.

The bundle stirred, once, twice, thrice, kicked feebly, and then vomited over Cob before it fell off. All stopped, all looked, all waited, all frozen. Even Jimbo ceased his attempts to murder Henry and paused to see what happened next. Miss Delacherois stood, arising from the blanket like a modern-day Venus, but clad only in her undershirt and long cotton drawers, and with an ivory and rubber tube dangling from her nostril.

She shook her head and fixed her gaze on the amazed Cob. "I'll have yer guts fer this Cob Nelson," she roared. Bemused she looked around at the onlookers, then screamed and attempted to cover herself before she ran into the house and a waiting blanket held in Mrs McKee's hands.

Miss Delacherois had been put protesting to bed by Mrs McKee, with the Doctor in close attendance.

The kitchen and yard were now crammed with the crowd that had assembled on hearing the fearful news of Miss Delacherois' demise. Her father, Mr Delacherois had arrived in response to the dreadful summons and had been present to witness her miraculous resurrection. In a fit of generosity, most unlike him, Mr Delacherois had sent his groom to Kelly's for a half dozen of Champagne, two dozen of claret, and six firkins of strong black beer. This precious cargo had quickly arrived in a commandeered cart, with Mr Kelly bringing up the rear and adding a half crate of his second-best brandy to the celebrations; these did however appear in the subsequent reckoning presented to the grateful father. A small cask of Poitín had been produced by some of the rougher elements and installed in the barn away from prying eyes much to Sultan's delight in the company, and Jimbo's ever-burning rage at the constant intrusion.

Emma and Lizzie circulated bearing great platters of

herring fried in oatmeal whilst poor Sarah, as is true for all cooks, spent her time working over an oil-spitting skillet.

At some point in the proceedings, Miss Delacherois herself had appeared in an upper window, draped somewhat inadequately in a sheet, and waved with her eyelids fluttering as though someone had blown a handful of hay-dust into them before Mrs McKee quickly materialised from behind and dragged the heroine of the hour away.

When the Doctor materialised the crowd carried him thrice around the yard calling out "Huzzah" and, for the common sort, "Hooray."

Mr Delacherois was placed upon a box and gave a speech which praised this, "Giant of Modern Medicine," and, "Master of the Scientific Arts," but went too far when he tried to share credit with someone called, "Aelius Galenus," or the like and was put down again being replaced by a fiddler.

All in all, everyone agreed it was a most excellent wake, albeit without a corpse, and was a credit to Miss Delacherois and she should do it more often.

The next morning the Doctor was found in Sultan's stall wearing a horse collar over his head and missing his boots.

Chapter 13

The days were starting to get shorter when the front door was hammered early one morning. It was one of the policemen from the barracks. "The Sergeant asks if you could attend to them on the beach if you please? Please hurry as there's a body and the tide will be turning soon."

"Cob! Cob harness the cart and follow me down to the beach!" The Doctor seized his bag and hurried down towards the shore.

When he got there a small crowd was on the promenade watching the activities of a party of police upon the sands. The tide was out and had left ripples in the sand full of water shining in the sun hanging high behind the castle. A stiff inshore breeze compelled the onlookers to keep a hand on their hats for fear of losing them.

The Doctor squeezed through them and stepped out upon the shore. A policeman gestured to the Doctor to make a wide detour and approach the scene from the north.

"Morning Doctor," growled the Sergeant in command of the Constabulary post in the town, "I've sent for the District Inspector but it'll be a while before he gets here." He nodded to the tide, "and we'll maybe be underwater here before he does."

"Morning yourself John," replied the Doctor. "Maybe if you told me what we have?"

The Sergeant indicated the body lying face down on the sand. "This here's Johnston one of the Custom's men from over there." He indicated a trim row of redbrick cottages by Bullocks' Wharf with the Luggers over on their side waiting for the cattle to be driven on board. "They say he left his lodgings when the tide started to ebb this morning to inspect a barque that put in late last night." The Sergeant pointed to a set of footprints that led to the body. "Ye see there Doctor? That's his footprints right enough."

The Doctor squinted in the reflected light. "And the second set? Following him? Whose are those? One of your men?"

"Indeed Doctor that's what I first thought but if you look closely they're sea-boots that made those footprints. None of my men wear them as," the Sergeant indicated the RIC men, "you can see."

The Doctor looked at the trail and then swung around. "But —"

"Precisely Doctor. Where is the owner of those boots now? For I can't see him here. Can you?"

Puzzled the Doctor offered, "The tide?"

"If the tide had washed away the boot prints leaving here then," the Sergeant nodded to the first set. "They would have washed away the ones arriving as well."

"That is a strange thing indeed. Perhaps I should examine the body?"

The Sergeant and the Doctor approached the remains which were clad in sea boots and a warm cloak. Some distance behind them was a three-cornered hat that lay on the sand.

"Here John, pray lend me a hand to roll him over."

The Sergeant and the Doctor gently rolled Johnston on his back. His mouth was open and his eyes showed their whites, or at least the one eye remaining did for the other was missing.

"Gulls?" offered the Sergeant.

"Doubtful unless they rolled him over afterwards," the Doctor held Johnston's chin and pulled the mouth open, "and stuffed his mouth full of sand."

"I don't need this Doctor I can tell you," moaned the Sergeant, "Thirty-four years this year since I left County Kerry. I was hoping to finish my time in peace and quiet."

"Not a bit of it John! We'll give you a good send-off!" He indicated the Downshire Arms. "I know our friend Kelly is laying in something special for you."

The Sergeant poked the side of the corpse with his boot. "At least there's one less of the Customs buggers snooping around." He smiled. "Well, you can't leave it like that. What's your verdict?"

"Never you mind. You'll find out soon enough." The

Doctor signalled Cob. "Get him up in the cart unless you want him to drown as well?"

The Sergeant sighed. "I wish the bugger would just float away."

Johnston was lying on a trestle table in the barn clad only in his drawers. The Doctor began the autopsy with the District Inspector, the Sergeant, a horrified Henry and Cob, and an appreciative Sultan, Jimbo and Nero.

Johnston's lungs, liver, and lights had been displayed for the admiration of all and were now sitting in a bucket on the ground, whilst the Doctor dissected out the heart.

Triumphantly he held it aloft. "There Gentlemen the seat of human passions! Behold the miracle that threw down the walls of mighty Troy!"

The Sergeant sniggered. "I don't know this Troy fellow but he certainly threw down the walls of poor Caleb's wife."

This coarse remark obviously appealed to Nero's sense of humour and he let out a great braying sound of approval, thus triggering the company, with the exception of Henry and Cob who were, thankfully, too young to understand the import.

Picking up a jug of small beer the Sergeant recharged both the Doctor's and the District Inspector's glasses, before addressing his own; alas the jug was empty so Henry was dispatched for a refill, and a bottle of whiskey to chase the beer down.

"Well Doctor, what are your thoughts?" queried the District Inspector.

The Doctor swept his hand over his trophies. "Well, so

far his hull is sound enough. Let me inspect the rigging." Drawing a sharp blade along the gullet the Doctor laid the wide pipe open. Leaving aside the blade he took a draft of small beer before wiping his hands on his waistcoat and inserting his fingers into the void. "Aha," as he hooked out a finger of sand, then another, then another. "This man choked to death...no wait! Lingua Amputo by God. Look here," commanded the Doctor. "Someone's stolen his tongue. His tongue has been cut out and the mouth filled with sand choking him." He indicated the lungs lying on the ground beside the bucket. "Hence the blood from ruptures in the bellows." The Doctor drained his glass. "Ah Henry, you've returned. Would you be good enough to refresh our guests?"

"So Doctor have you reached a conclusion?" asked the District Inspector.

"He was murdered by a one-legged man who smoked Burma cheroots!" announced the Doctor.

"This is good news!" exclaimed the Sergeant, "We can circulate —"

The Doctor smiled. "Forgive me John I couldn't resist playing the great detective Monsieur Dupin at last!"

The District Inspector laughed. "I fear the Doctor is taking a rise from us John. Seriously though this strikes me as a message...perhaps a warning to keep silent?"

"Oh very clever Doctor!" said the Sergeant, pouring out three whiskeys and handing the glasses around. He turned to the District Inspector. "To be frank Sir this smells of Mr Kerr's gang. He has long had a bone to pick with the Excisemen, and a desire that others do not inform to the authorities."

Late one afternoon Emma was about her duties when she reached the Doctor's bedroom, it was dark and, placing the pile of laundry on the bed, she moved across to open the drapes. The window was open and Emma glanced down into the yard and noticed that the cover was off the old disused well in the corner. *The well the children drown in!*

She saw Cob and Henry in the yard and called down, "Cob, would one of you put the cover back on the well?" Cob waved a reply and started walking over to the well.

Emma closed the window and snibbed it shut before she moved back to the bed and selected some undershirts to put away in the chest of drawers. That done, Emma picked up the remaining laundry from the bed and left the room closing the door behind her. From there she moved into Charlie's room. Again she placed the laundry on the bed and started picking up some of Charlie's clothes that were scattered on the floor: a dirty shirt, some underwear, and a single lonely sock lying exhausted by the foot of the bed. Emma bent over to pick it up and looked for its partner. *Where is the dratted thing? It must be under the bed!* Emma knelt and reached her arm under the bed feeling for the missing sock. Emma stretched her arm in deeper feeling around the floor for the missing sock. *Aha! That's it!* She grasped the sock and started to withdraw it towards herself. A faint pull on it away from her grasp caused her to hesitate before tugging at it more firmly. The resistance to Emma's efforts increased. Puzzled Emma put her head closer to the floor and looked under the bed. In the centre squatted an area of unformed blackness into which her hand disappeared. It was not black in the

107

sense of a colour but in the sense that it absorbed everything that touched it; it was a place where light went to die. Startled Emma pulled fiercely on the sock. There was a pause, then a steadily increasing pressure pulling her hand deeper and deeper into the void. Without thought Emma jerked the sock towards her with all her strength and was gratified to see her hand and, *Yes! It is the wretched sock!* appear out of the darkness.

Suddenly the force on the sock vanished and something seemed to grab her hand exerting a violent pull and dragging her head and upper body under the bed; her arm almost disappearing into the blackness waiting for her. Terrified Emma released her grip on the sock and tried to withdraw her hand. There was a resistance then a sharp pain and she was free leaving a long scratch mark along the back of the hand. Emma looked at the line of crimson bubbles as they appeared then screamed.

In seconds the Doctor burst into the room closely followed by Cob and Sarah.

"Something's in there! It had hold of Charlie's sock! Something tried to pull me in!" exclaimed Emma.

The Doctor shot a puzzled look at Cob. "Have a look there Cob. Emma come here that I may look at your hand."

Emma allowed herself to be seated on the bed with the Doctor holding her hand to the light whilst Cob wriggled under the bed to emerge triumphantly clutching the sock. "This auld sock was caught on one of the springs!" he declared waving it in his hand. "Boo!" he pretended to throw it at Sarah who screamed, then burst out laughing.

The Doctor looked at Emma. "Behave you two. Mrs

Hawthorne has had a nasty fright. Downstairs with us and I'll dress that hand eh? You must have caught it on one of those springs. Don't want you getting Lockjaw. Come on."

Cob and Sarah led the way with Cob occasionally waving the sock at Sarah who would give little shrieks. The Doctor indicated to Emma to lead on.

"Just a minute please," Emma said. She hugged her arms to herself and looked around. *The window!* The window was now open again. Emma moved to it and dragged her finger over the sill. *There were traces of damp mud on it, there had been none before. It rained last night. This was clean this morning.* She started, the cover on the well was now off again.

"Ready Emma?" queried the Doctor.

"Cob! Cob, did you put the cover back on the well as I asked you?"

Cob paused in teasing Sarah. "I did. Not ten minutes ago. Why?" he asked.

"Nothing. Nothing, it must have slipped off. That's all."

The room suddenly felt very cold to Emma as she snibbed the window shut again, and then pulled her shawl tighter around her shoulders.

The staff were sitting in their usual positions around the kitchen. The room was full of steam from a large rack of drying clothes pulled close to the stove which, together with the smell of roasting meats in the damp air, would have caused some old India hands to recall Sunday luncheon in a far-off hill station during monsoon season.

Mr Delacherois entered and they all stood. The ladies curtsied and the boys took their hands from their pockets and then didn't know where to put them.

"Sit please my friends, sit." Mr Delacherois waved them back into their seats. "I just wanted to thank you, thank you all from the bottom of my heart for what you did to save Miss Delacherois."

Mr Delacherois took a small purse from his coat pocket and approached Mrs McKee. "Please Betsy, your hand," He asked.

"Mr Delacherois Sir. This isn't —" she protested.

"Indeed it is Betsy McKee. I am in your debt, yet again." As he counted two Gold Sovereigns into her palm.

"And you Mrs Hawthorne."

"Oh no, I can't Sir. It's too —"

"It would be a kindness to me if you accept this, and Sarah of course." he pressed a Sovereign into each of their hands. He turned to the boys, "To Masters Henry and Cob I trust you'll accept this little token of my gratitude for all your help," and a Half-Sovereign to each was produced. "Master Cob here's an extra penny. If you would purchase Jimbo a bunch or so of carrots?"

Cob grinned. "He thanks you, Sir. It was a pleasure and anytime."

"Thank you all again. Now I must take my leave. I think I'll go for a walk." He doffed his hat. "I'll just slip out the back door if I may? No need to disturb upstairs again. Good day," and he took his leave.

The Doctor and Miss Delacherois were in the middle of one of those awkward silences. The fire had burnt lower, and the tea had grown colder, and both had been the subject of conversations about how much lower, and how much colder, they were. The weather had been discussed, and the need for Miss Delacherois to prevail upon her Father for a replacement Hunter after the last outing had been stretched out as far as was possible. Now they sat in companionable silence, taking turn about to throw a pine cone onto the embers, and listening to them crackle into life.

Miss Delacherois started. "Crikey, I nearly forgot," she said.

"Mmm," replied the Doctor who was very much enjoying stealing quick glances of her profile in the fading light, as she well knew.

"Here," Miss Delacherois offered the Doctor something from her bag wrapped in fine red tissue paper.

The Doctor took it and unwrapped it. It was a "George and the Dragon" Golden Sovereign from the time of the old King, set on a heavy gold watch chain. "I say this is handsome!" The Doctor held it back to Miss Delacherois. "But I can't take this!"

"Father insists. No, I insist!"

The Doctor protested, "It's really —"

Eyes flashing Miss Delacherois stamped her foot, "Do you think so little of me?" she demanded.

Shocked the Doctor said, "Oh No. You know I think the very world of you."

Miss Delacherois smiled and stood. She allowed the Doctor to place her cloak over her shoulders. "It is settled then." She curtsied to the Doctor who returned a bow. "I have no doubt I shall see you again Doctor?"

"I'm sure you will Miss Delacherois."

Miss Delacherois opened the door and stepped into the hallway then paused. A moment, then she turned and ran back into the room and kissed the Doctor on his cheek. "I know I will," then she ran out and down the front steps into the street.

Chapter 14

It was one of those cool crisp misty mornings that signal Autumn was around the corner. Emma strode into the yard and crossed over to the barn where Cob and Henry were feeding the animals. Nero nuzzled her and put his head on her shoulder in the hope that the broom she carried would change into a bunch of carrots.

Emma approached the boys. "Would you give me a hand with the old well for a moment please?"

"Surely, what d'ye want to do?" Cob said.

Emma considered her answer. "To be honest I'm not sure. Do you boys ever take the cover off?"

Henry rested against Jimbo's flank. "Not us. It's no use in the yard. The Doctor won't let us use the water from it."

"There's a funny smell to the water. This lot," Cob

indicated the animals. "Won't touch it."

"Come on then," gestured Emma. "Let's get a better look."

The boys shrugged then, accompanied by a curious Nero, followed Emma across the yard to the well. Emma lent her broom against the small stone surround. She grasped the wooden cover. "Help me lift this off the —"

"Let go there," Henry said, "We've got a grip of it." Cob and Henry took hold of the cover and lifted it clear placing it on the ground. As the cover came off Nero shied away and returned to the barn where he stood watching and stamping his foot.

They all looked down into the well. It radiated cold, with damp slime-covered walls, and released an underlying smell of decay. Deep down in the dark, they could discern a dim reflection of the light from above. Cob curled his lip in disgust and picked up a small stone dropping it down into the water. It fell for what seemed a long time then the sound of the splash coming back thicker and heavier than it should. Emma shivered.

"Aye, it's bad water right enough," Cob said. "Must be full of mud and weed."

Henry laughed. "Look at old Nero. He's not too keen on it at all."

Emma studied the cover. "How come this is always coming off?"

Cob furrowed his brow. stirred the cover with the toe of his boot. "Heavy enough. It's not the wind."

Henry returned from the barn with a lamp and a length of rope. He lit the candle with a brimstone and then lowered the lantern down into the well. Emma and Cob craned their necks to see as the lantern went deeper and deeper down until it was just above the surface of the eater.

Cob looked in disgust. "As I thought. That there's just mud soup I don't —"

"Hang on," Henry said pulling the lantern back up a bit.

"What?" said Cob.

Henry pointed down into the well. "Look at them bricks. No, the other side. Come round here and you'll get a see."

Cob and Emma moved beside Henry.

"Look there," said Henry. "Them bricks sticking out."

Two columns of bricks jutted out from the side of the well.

"What are those for?" asked Emma.

"Maybe they were used by the boys digging the well?" said Henry.

"Wouldn't have thought so." Cob craned his neck to see better. "There'd be the same on the other side so as you could put a plank across."

"They're not level with each other," Emma pointed out. "They're more like a ladder. Something for climbing."

"A hairy enough climb," said Henry. "I wouldn't fancy it. Not down there."

There was a sudden sound in the well echoing up into the daylight. Everyone started.

Henry smiled ruefully at the others. "Frogs?"

They laughed nervously.

"Henry, Bring that lantern round over here a minute," Cob commanded. "Aye, that's it! Hold it there now a minute."

Cob pointed to Emma's broom. "What's that for?"

"I thought I would brush the top of the wall."

Cob looked at Emma closely. "Naw I've a better idea...hang on." Cob went to the stables and returned with a barrow of straw.

"What's this for?" asked Henry.

Cob picked up a handful and scattered it on the parapet of the well. Henry watched him then shrugged and did the same.

With that done Cob went over to the cover. "Give us a hand here."

The cover was manhandled by the two boys back into place without dislodging the straw.

Emma had been watching Cob. "What did you see down there when you asked Henry to bring the lantern across?" She followed his gaze to the ivy-clad back of the house with the upstairs windows ajar to allow the weak heat from the sun to air the rooms.

Cob held his gaze on the house. "Nothing...nothing. I thought...a shadow. That's all."

The next morning Henry woke early. Cob was not in his cot. *He's away agin chasing that Sarah one,* he laughed. After getting a wash and dressed Henry climbed down the ladder into the warm cosy barn. Sultan snickered a welcome and Jimbo kicked the door of his stall. *Another grand morning.* Henry stretched and wandered out into the yard. Cob was standing by the well and the cover had been slid half off.

Henry approached Cob. "What'd you do that for?" he asked.

116

Cob didn't turn around. "I didn't. I never touched it. It was like that this morning."

Henry took in the straw that had been scattered off the well parapet and had fallen onto the ground. "Rats?"

Cob remained silent for a moment. "Aye, rats." He indicated the cover. "Come and give us a hand getting this back on."

The boys manhandled the heavy wooden cover back into position.

"What are you going to do?" asked Henry.

Cob gathered his thoughts. "I'll have a word with your Mum." He turned to Henry. "I wouldn't be saying anything to Mrs Hawthorne just yet."

Henry nodded his agreement and they stood there quietly awhile, in the early sunshine, considering the well.

The Doctor had been out playing cards with Mr Delacherois and some friends until late so Emma had spent the night alone. Normally Emma arose and performed her ablutions before dressing and then going and lighting the stove, but this morning she felt distinctly queasy and merely pulled a robe over her nightgown before going downstairs to start her day.

The house was quiet so Emma opened the back door and let it stand ajar whilst she put the kettle on to boil. The silence could not still a small, unwelcome thought in her mind. *Oh God no. Let it not be,* but she pushed it down down down and locked it away. Tea mashed Emma poured herself a cup and took it outside where some rough chairs and a table had been arranged by the back door.

Sultan, Jimbo, and Nero looked out from their stalls and started kicking the doors for attention. "Hush," Emma ordered them. "You'll wake the house." Realising that Emma wasn't going to give them an early breakfast they returned to dozing. Across the yard, in full view, was the old well. Emma shuddered and looked elsewhere. They were experiencing an Indian Summer and it was going to be another glorious day. A light dew had washed the leaves on the fruit trees, and the gentle offshore breeze gave an edge that refreshed the body and soul.

Deep inside her, Emma knew something had changed, something she remembered from the time she had carried Charlie. Emma didn't want to believe this, wouldn't believe it, but she knew that what she feared was happening, had happened, and didn't much care if she believed or not. *What would the Doctor think if she bore him a child? How would he greet an unwanted bastard? Would he publicly acknowledge the child as his? What would the consequences be for her, for Charlie? For their place here in Rosebank?*

The house was stirring now. *The boys must be up*, as bits of straw drifted down from their snug in the hayloft. The animals were catching the wisps and tasting them before spitting them out in disgust. Jimbo started kicking his door again and a muffled curse failed to silence him.

Inside from the kitchen came the sound of pots clattering. Sarah would be pleased and surprised to find the stove already lit, and a fresh pot of tea sitting ready for a restorative cup. *I must do this more often while the weather lasts*, Emma thought.

Behind her was the sound of footsteps on gravel. Emma

turned her head to see Mrs McKee walking up the path from the street. "Good morning," Emma offered. "There's tea in the pot."

"Morning Emma. I'll bring my cup out here and join you if I may?" replied Mrs McKee, entering the house by the back door.

After a few minutes, Mrs McKee rejoined Emma. She had brought the teapot with her. "Sarah is making a fresh pot for breakfast so I thought I'd bring this out in case you wanted a top-up?" Emma dashed the contents of her cup on the grass then held it out whilst Mrs McKee refilled it. "This is the best part of the day," said Mrs McKee. "It's like everything has been washed afresh ready for us to start again."

Emma gave a wry smile. "Is that enough?"

"Are ye going to tell him?" Mrs McKee replied.

Emma put her cup down on the table and, without looking at Mrs McKee, said, "Tell who, what?"

"The Doctor, about the bairn."

Emma's mind raced, *How did she know, this old woman?* In earlier times they would have put her down the Murder Hole as a witch. She turned to look at Mrs McKee. "Will you tell him?"

"Don't be a fool girl. He's a Doctor and a good one. He'll see your belly soon enough." Mrs McKee took a moment to stir her tea.

Cob and Henry exited the barn, throwing a few sections of hay into the stalls to keep the animals quiet before crossing the yard to the house. "Good Morning Mum, Mrs McKee, Mrs Hawthorne," they chorused.

"Morning you two. Go on now and Sarah has your

breakfasts. On with the pair of you and tell Sarah we'll be in, in a minute."

Mrs McKee put her empty cup on the table and stood up. "He'll not like it. Not one little bit."

Emma shaded her eyes from the morning glare to look at Mrs McKee." Please, Betsy, you know him best?"

"Aye that I do. From when his father came here as the Magistrate, and a rum old bird he was. He was an Admiral an' thought mighty highly of himself." She picked up the cup. "He wouldn't be doing with his son taking up with the likes of a shopkeeper's daughter."

Mrs McKee sighed. "The day's awake now. You'd better be up and get dressed."

Chapter 15

Emma and Sarah were in the kitchen. The weak autumnal sun streamed in the window and illuminated part of the kitchen table where Emma had set out the great ledger in which Mrs McKee, and now she, recorded the household accounts. Sarah was happily kneading bread at the other end, Lizzie was elbow-deep in hot soapy water at the sink, and all had cups of tea close by in case of fatigue.

Emma put the pen down and rubbed her eyes. "Mrs McKee had a very unusual way with managing the figures," she said.

Sarah chortled, "Oh she's her own way with most things she has." Sarah slapped the dough down and started kneading it.

"Speaking of mysteries Sarah, were you here when the

Lighthouse Keeper was killed?" Emma asked.

"Killed? Poor Caleb killed his self he did. That dirty scutter he took up with was the death of him." Sarah stretched out the dough and then slammed it on the table before taking a sip at her tea."

"Scutter?" asked Emma.

"The one he married. She'd walked out with half the lads in the town, and sure didn't he take pity on her and took her and the baby on," sniffed Sarah. "Too soft for his own good. But he was warned."

"What happened?" asked Sarah.

Sarah glanced around and then sat down at the table. "Well, he caught her on with that Excise agent, the one they found down the beach the other week. Caleb and him was fighting at the cottage and a lantern was upset. Sure wasn't she sent flying and didn't the Exciseman take to his heels and away like Flynn with Caleb coming after him and crying murder."

"So the cottage burnt down with her and the baby in it?" asked Emma.

"Well no. Didn't that scutter wake up, she was only dazed a wee moment. She knew she was in trouble if he found her when he got back so she grabbed up the bairn an' away across the fields and didn't stop running till she was at her sister's in Belfast."

"Oh, Dear Lord!" Emma exclaimed. "What did he do then?"

"Well Caleb thought he'd killed her, and the bairn. So away back to the lighthouse he goes and locks himself in then the police turn up and doesn't he go up and jump off the top."

"He killed himself? How horrible."

Sarah stood up and returned to rolling out the dough. "I suppose he thought it was better than hanging." She paused. "I knew him at school, he was a few years ahead of me, but he was a nice sort of a big lump."

Emma was dusting and Mrs McKee was stacking his books back onto their shelves when the Doctor rushed into his study. "Ladies, ladies!" he called, as he brandished the newspaper over his head. "We've won By God. Chased 'em right out!"

The ladies paused in their actions. "Won what Doctor?" asked Emma.

Mrs McKee, who read all the Doctor's newspapers to her husband in the evening and prided herself on her knowledge of Great Affairs said, "Have we chased those nasty old Turks away yet?"

Stunned for a moment the Doctor attempted to explain, for the umpteenth time, "Betsy, the Turks are our allies."

Unimpressed Mrs McKee remarked, "Indeed, that's where Lord Raglan and myself would differ."

There was a short silence whilst the Doctor pondered her remarks. "Nevertheless they are…Oh Damn it! We've taken Sevastopol at last. The fortress is ours! Emma your husband's great sacrifice is finally crowned in triumph!"

"I'm sure he'll be very happy Doctor," replied Emma.

Somewhat deflated the Doctor said, "Well I'm a tad taken aback by your reactions." He refolded the newspapers and tucked them under his arm. "If anybody is looking for me I shall be in Kelly's discussing the outcome with a more," here the Doctor raised his voice, "patriotic assembly!"

Emma was making her way back from her daily walk around the Commons when the sound of hooves approaching caused her to stand to one side and look behind.

A good-looking Gentleman, on the largest horse Emma had ever seen, was cantering up. As he came nearer he drew the animal to a halt and touched his cap to her.

Smiling he looked down at Emma. "You must be Leslie's new housekeeper?"

"I am Sir. And may I know whom I'm addressing?"

He removed his cap and swept it in an extravagant arc. "John Kerr of Portavoe, at your service. You have an English tongue I see."

Emma smiled. Mr Kerr was an unshaven, well-set man of some thirty-four years, with a heavy jaw and close-cropped brown hair. "And you have the Irish charm I see."

Mr Kerr swung himself down from his mount. "I'll walk awhile with you, if I may?" They walked in silence for a few minutes then Emma ventured, "Am I safe with you? You have the most fearsome reputation amongst polite company."

"Polite company! You mind them well now. Take my word for it a bunch of money-grubbing hypocrites I warn you. They'll steal the skin off your teeth on Monday and mither about in Kirk on the Sunday."

Emma felt that to say anything risked being disloyal to her new employer so she said nothing.

"I'm sorry. I didn't mean to upset you. How's that son of

yours doing."

"Very well Sir. He's doing his letters and sums with Miss Wilkes."

"Good God is she still going? Such thrashings she used to give me."

Emma laughed. "I'm sure they were richly deserved, Sir."

"They were indeed to be fair…richly." They walked on a few paces. "So what brings you here?"

"As I'm very sure you are already aware I lost my husband in the war, and the Doctor was kind enough to offer my son and me a situation here."

Mr Kerr broke into a broad smile. "I'm sorry to hear that…yet again." Mounting his horse he looked down at Emma. "I'll have to leave you here," indicating a lane leading up to the motte." He touched his cap. "Miss Emma, and my regards to Master Charles." Then he pulled the horse around and kicked it into a canter towards the Castle.

The next morning a somewhat subdued Doctor arrived in the kitchen. Offered his breakfast he declined and merely requested a cup of tea.

"Did you have a nice evening Doctor?" inquired Emma.

Mrs McKee cackled from her chair and the Doctor held up his hand. "Ladies please, please."

Mrs McKee left the room and returned a few moments later with a small paper slip. She filled a glass with some wine and stirred in a small amount of the contents. "Here Doctor, some willow-bark powder for you."

The Doctor took the glass from her and greedily drank it

down in one draft. "Thank you, Betsy. That is most kind."

"Did you have a pleasant evening Doctor?" asked Emma.

Ruefully the Doctor smiled. "A quiet evening amongst a few old friends." He brightened. "Mr Delacherois was there. We shared a bottle of Mr Kelly's finest brandy."

Mrs McKee started rearranging the condiments on the kitchen table, noisily putting them in their place.

Pained the Doctor looked up at her. "Please Betsy, please. Have a mercy."

"You're not supposed to be drinking brandy. I've no sympathy for ye."

The Doctor stood. "Emma I'm going to my study. I do not wish to be disturbed...apart from Henry. Tell him to bring me a fresh pot of tea...and light the fire please...and Sarah, would you be so kind as to send up a bacon sandwich, or two?"

The Doctor carried his cup over to the door leading back up to the house. He released the Parthian Shot. "By the way I may have offered to throw a party. Celebrate our victory and all that."

"Indeed Doctor, and when would that be do ye think?" asked Mrs McKee.

The Doctor shuffled his feet and paid great attention to the floor. "Ah well...er...tonight actually," and darted up the stairs.

Chapter 16

The unexpected late summer was continuing and the windows and doors of the house had been thrown open to let in the warm night air. The drawing room was ablaze with candles and the fire flickered merrily in the grate, drawing in the more elderly of the guests, who craved warmth as Varney the Vampire craved blood.

The very best of local society was gathered and, as is the way with the smaller sorts of places, all were already known to one another and very little formality existed between old friends. Mr Hugh Montgomery, the High Sheriff and Magistrate, had driven over from his seat in Greyabbey, and Mr Delacherois, together with his daughter, had strolled up to Rosebank from the Manor House. Lieutenant Nelson and Mrs Nelson from the military, and the Reverend Hill and his lady wife, who took upon themselves the burden of representing the ecclesiastical side of society.

Four barrels of porter beer and a fiddler had been provided in the backyard by the Gentry for the common sort.

The kitchen heaved and steamed with Sarah and Mrs McKee stirring and tasting and seasoning, with Emma taking charge of upstairs, aided by Henry and Cob both of whom cast an envious eye to the gathering crowd outside.

Charlie had meanwhile secreted himself in the hayloft and, after picking over Cob's meagre possessions and pocketing his prized folding knife, got comfortable waiting ready to swoop on the unsuspecting partygoers in the yard once the party was in full swing.

The Reverend Hill approached the Doctor. "This is very fine. A most pleasant gathering."

"You, and Mrs Hill, are both very welcome," the Doctor bowed.

"I believe you are studying the early inhabitants of this area? You must tell me more."

Warily the Doctor said, "I'm not sure it would be to your taste."

"You'd be surprised what my flock get up to. You were excavating around the old motte I believe?"

The Doctor laughed. "The all-seeing eye of the church."

"And have you found anything of note?" enquired the Reverend.

"Only some graves. We think they are connected with what people call the Murder Hole," responded the Doctor.

"Indeed. But I thought that was filled in?"

"Oh yes. With rubble, and it would take more resources

than a simple country Doctor to excavate that," the Doctor explained.

"Of course, I've heard the stories. Those poor women. What a dreadful end."

"Maybe," said the Doctor.

"Maybe? To be murdered in such a gruesome way. I shudder at the thought. Perhaps I should offer a prayer over the graves?"

"It may not be appropriate," the Doctor cautioned.

"Why not?"

"I doubt they were Christian graves," explained the Doctor. "Some of my research would indicate that they were sacrifices rather than executions. I have, in my study, a most interesting book that —"

Thankfully Miss Delacherois seized the Doctor's arm. "Do stop you two. It's a party! The rotten old Russians have been taught a lesson and we're having a celebration, not a wake!"

"May I charge your glass Miss Delacherois?" enquired the Reverend.

Miss Delacherois transferred her hold to the Reverend's arms and, with a wink at our Doctor, guided him towards the punch.

Mr Delacherois took the opportunity to call the Doctor over to his company. "Well Doctor, Mr Montgomery was telling me about these footprints found in Devon this Spring. Hoof marks By God. A hundred miles! What do you think of that?"

Perking up the Doctor replied, "Yes indeed. A Polish Doctor writes from Galicia that it is a regular occurrence."

"Good Grief, "exclaimed Mr Montgomery. "What would cause such a frightful manifestation?"

The Doctor reflected on the matter for a moment then pronounced. "Well as a Scientist, taking into mind the form, which is that of a hoof and the distance covered, some several hundred miles I believe, well I can only conclude that it is a supernatural phenomenon."

"Pon my Soul," remarked Mr Delacherois. "And do you think," with a glance at Miss Delacherois, "such a thing could happen here?"

"Certainly," replied the Doctor. "For I have observed the very same thing not half a league from this very spot."

The Doctor had now gained the attention of the whole party.

"Where Doctor? You have to tell us!" entreated Miss Delacherois.

"I would caution you that some matters are best left uninquired," the Reverend cautioned.

But Mr Montgomery and Mr Delacherois were not to be put off from their quest for knowledge. "I'll wager it's that damn old well on the foreshore," Mr Delacherois remarked.

"I don't want that sort of thing in the Ards upsetting my tenants," grumbled Mr Montgomery.

"No indeed it is in the dunes I have observed tracks. I have, several times, attempted to follow them to their lair but the sands are too fine and shift too readily."

"Are those the same tracks around poor Johnston the Sergeant reported?" asked Mr Montgomery sharply.

The Doctor glanced around the company then, weighing his words, replied, "Yes indeed. In my opinion the very same."

"Hmm...I'll still hang my hat on Kerr's gang at the root of it! Mark my words," grumbled the Magistrate.

A gong sounded and Henry opened the doors into the hallway. "Dinner is served," he announced and the party proceeded across the hallway into the Dining room.

The Doctor sat at the head of the table with the Reverend, Miss Delacherois, and Lieutenant Nelson all to his right. On his left was seated Mr Montgomery, the Reverend's lady wife, Mr Delacherois, and finally Mrs Nelson.

On a signal from Emma, Henry and Lizzie served the guests poached salmon with pickled samphire accompanied by a glass of German Hock.

The Reverend addressed the Doctor. "I was much interested in your remarks about the early inhabitants of this place. There are several very old gravestones in the Kirk."

The Doctor laughed. "I'm afraid the original inhabitants would predate your church by a thousand years."

"But Christianity has blessed this island since Roman times. How could you associate the early Christians with such practices?" said the Reverend.

"That's my very point!" cried the Doctor. "If we accept Saint Patrick converted the people to Christianity then they must have been pagans before then. My research shows that the old pagan beliefs were still held, or at least followed, much longer than we thought."

"For example?" asked the Reverend.

"For example what the common folk call the Murder Hole. According to local lore, it was used for executing witches, however, I hope to show they were, in fact, sacrifices made to the Pagan deities of water."

The Reverend put down his fork. "Very tasty. Of water?"

"Of water. It is well documented that, in antiquity, people would look at their reflections in still water and see another world reflected."

"And what of it?" the Reverend queried.

"And I suspect that still waters were seen as a pathway, a portal into the other world."

The Reverend raised his eyebrows in alarm. "But to murder…to sacrifice how —"

"My belief is that the victims were rather messengers to that *other* world." The Doctor finished his plate and cleared his pallet with another glass of Hock. "But the texts are unclear if they ever received a reply, a messenger in return. Some claim they have but —"

The Reverend was outraged at the nature of the Doctor's remarks. "It sounds to me as if you are attempting to communicate with the very Devil himself Doctor!"

Amused the Doctor said, "Oh I wouldn't worry about my soul too much Reverend. Mr Delacherois and I root about for old bones and read old books. That's about the height of it."

The Reverend was most unhappy. "Kerr, that madman out at Portavoe? The man's a maniac. He rode a horse into my Kirk whilst I was conducting a funeral!"

"Oh, I wouldn't be too hard on him Reverend. The next course is from his estate," the Doctor teased him.

Emma had relieved Mrs McKee from the burden of

decorating the Ballroom, which was now festooned with Crêpe banners of red, white, and blue. Henry and Lizzie proudly stood in their finest castoffs under a monstrous Union Flag which took up most of the back wall over the sideboard, which, in turn, was almost covered in a display of candied fruits and sweetmeats. Henry and Cob had cleared the floor and rolled up the carpet ready for dancing if any guests so desired.

The front door was in constant use as the better sort, together with their sons and daughters, arrived to join the celebrations. Cob, who greeted each and everyone, escorted them to Henry, who stood at the entrance to the Ballroom behind a trestle table where he freely handed out cups of punch. It should be noted that both boys were becoming increasingly animated; possibly with the heat for it was a warm night yet the fire blazed in the hearth, possibly with the effects of the punch.

After the meal, the company had moved back to the Drawing room. The noise from the party outside increased as the Doctor threw open the back windows, and the room soon filled with the laughter and song of those in the backyard. "Friends, friends!" the Doctor called raising his arms for attention. "Charge your glasses, charge your glasses please!" There was a great commotion as all quickly rushed to complete this task, for few needed to be bidden a second time. "A toast ladies and gentlemen! A toast to Her Majesty and her victorious armies! Ladies and gentlemen! Friends and neighbours! The Queen!" A great cheer went up and glasses drained. "The Queen! The Queen!" cried the assembled company, though more in sympathy for the

Doctor than in any rush of loyalty; for the memory of '98 still ran deep amongst the common sort.

The Doctor looked down and spied the fiddler who was lurking under the window. "Here!" The Doctor threw down a half crown. "Play your heart out tonight for we'll dance till we drop!" The fiddler caught the coin and soon The Scotch Reel echoed through the yard and bounced down the hill into the town.

Smiling the Doctor retired from the window and stood watching the young dancers flocking towards the Ballroom. Soon he was joined by Mr Delacherois. "I noticed your hand was empty my friend," as he offered the Doctor one of the two cups he was bearing.

"Ah thank you. Just the medicine," replied the Doctor.

Mr Delacherois nodded towards the dancers. "The young ones are enjoying themselves."

"Indeed. It does one's heart good to see it."

Mr Delacherois nodded to the door. "We should talk."

The Doctor glanced around the happy room and nodded. "We should. My study."

Settling down in the study they ruminated for a while listening to the sound of the music and dancing outside the room.

"The youngsters seem to be enjoying themselves," remarked Mr Delacherois. "Especially a certain Miss Delacherois."

The Doctor smiled. "The very belle of the ball. You must be very proud of her."

"Indeed aye. It's been difficult enough to bring her up

without her mother but she has turned out very well."

The Doctor raised his glass. "To Miss Delacherois."

Mr Delacherois returned the toast. "To Jane the apple of my eye."

The Doctor rose and recharged their glasses before returning to his seat.

"So what news of the work?" enquired Mr Delacherois.

"It progresses. I have only been able to obtain stillborn infants to date but, once we can get a suitable specimen then I see no harm in a trial. Betsy is in attendance on two cases in the town. I am hopeful one will come to term and Betsy will be able to...acquire it for our attention."

"How?" queried Mr Delacherois.

"To spirit it away before the mother realises that it lives."

"Please God. When Jane came off her horse I was terrified you'd not be able to revive her and you'd," Mr Delacherois shuddered, "end up sending her through."

The Doctor looked troubled. "I don't know if I'd dare. It's hard to tell with infants but when they look at me...I don't know. It's like something is missing."

"The soul. Do unbaptised infants have a soul, or maybe it has not yet formed?" asked Mr Delacherois.

The Doctor moistened his lips with some brandy. "You are fishing in deep waters, my friend. Here science is silent. We are on the edge of something...but we cannot judge how big it is...or where it goes. Only we must follow it.

Mr Delacherois laughed. "Maybe we should seek guidance from the Reverend Hill eh?"

The Doctor raised his glass again. "To my learned Reverend cousin."

"May his ignorance and superstition never meet!" returned Mr Delacherois.

The door of the study opened and Miss Delacherois burst into the room. "Daddy, Doctor come quickly! It's Charlie!"

Chapter 17

The kitchen was full of arguing people. A frightened Charlie was clinging to Emma, and the Sergeant was standing there looking grim-faced over a collection of purses, coins, and assorted nick-knacks displayed on the kitchen table.

Cob grabbed his pocket knife. "Here! Where'd ye get this?"

"Put that back on the table young Cob. That's evidence," cautioned the Sergeant.

"But it's mine!" challenged Cob.

The Sergeant looked gravely at Cob. "It's the Magistrate's now young Cob…put it back."

Cob reluctantly obeyed and stood glaring at Charlie. The Doctor and Mr Delacherois entered the room, closely followed by Miss Delacherois.

"What's happened?" The Doctor looked at the Sergeant. "John, what's wrong? Emma, is Charlie all right?"

Quickly Emma cut in. "Oh, Doctor they're accusing Charlie of the most horrible things!"

"It's all right Emma. John, what's happened?" said the Doctor.

Embarrassed the Sergeant gestured to the items on the table. "This lot was found on the youngster." He indicated Charlie. "All this lot here," indicating the crowd, "are saying he's been going through the coats and emptying the pockets."

Shocked the Doctor turned to Charlie. "Charlie, is this true?"

Charlie burrowed deeper into Emma's skirts. Emma gently shook him. "Charlie tell the Doctor that you didn't steal these things." Charlie's sobs merely increased. "Doctor you know Charlie," she appealed. The Doctor looked dubious. He looked at Cob who, grim-faced, merely nodded to his knife on the table. "John could there be some mistake?" he appealed.

Mr Montgomery, the Magistrate, entered the kitchen. "What's happening? Where is everybody? Ah! Sergeant someone told me you'd caught a thief?" he said.

Not looking at either Emma or the Doctor the Sergeant drew himself up straight and replied, "Sir. I was outside when members of the public," he indicated the company in the kitchen with a sweep of his arm, "reported that they had observed a young boy stealing items from unattended coat pockets. I approached the suspect and, on searching him, found some items alleged to be stolen in his possession."

Mr Montgomery looked at the pile on display. "What all this? How could he carry such an amount? Did he have a sack?"

The crowd tittered but was silenced by a glare from Mr Montgomery.

"Well Sir, I was told he'd been seen in the hay loft so when I searched that I recovered...well all this lot," the Sergeant replied.

Mr Montgomery turned to the Doctor. "This is most distasteful on such a night, but it does look like a case of Simple Larceny. Sergeant take —"

Emma burst out, "Doctor please help him. He's only little."

Stung into action the Doctor appealed to Mr Montgomery. "Surely we can forgive —"

Mr Delacherois interrupted. "Not another word. You're the Doctor but I'm the lawyer here." He put his hand on the Doctor's sleeve. "Leave this to me." He turned to the Sergeant. "John, did you have a warrant for this search?"

The Sergeant looked dumbfounded. "Such a thing! I —"

Mr Delacherois cast a glance at Mr Montgomery then back to the Sergeant. "Never mind eh? We'll leave that for now...tell me John did anybody see the boy place items or withdraw items from this alleged cache in the hay loft?" The Sergeant and the room looked at each other but remained silent. Mr Delacherois waited for a moment then asked the room, "Did anybody see this young boy in the hay loft this evening?" Silence reigned. "Well then John there seems to be no connection established between my client," he paused and addressed Emma, "Madam, is my son your client or not?"

Shocked and unsure Emma looked to the Doctor. "What shall —"

"Yes Mr Delacherois, indeed the boy is in your charge," confirmed the Doctor.

"In that case would the Magistrate," he bowed to Mr Montgomery, "allow me a moment to consult with the accused?"

With a grave nod of assent from the Magistrate Mr Delacherois drew Emma and Charlie to one side and, with Mr Delacherois kneeling, a whispered consultation took place between the three. Satisfied Mr Delacherois returned to his previous position. In the meantime, someone had found Mr Montgomery a seat at the head of the table.

Mr Delacherois bowed to the Magistrate, who hushed the room by striking the table with his pipe. "Continue please Mr Delacherois," he commanded.

"Well Sir if we may dismiss the second allegation for want of a warrant then we are left only to address the first allegation," quoted Mr Delacherois. "Sergeant who saw the boy steal? Bring him forward that we may hear the accuser."

The Sergeant looked at the Magistrate, waited, and then shrugged, before entering the crowd and drawing out an elderly man to the front. Realising he was now the centre of attention he swayed gently and grinned slyly at the mob before Mr Montgomery rapped the table again with his pipe. "Issac Armstrong isn't it? I know you from afore don't I?"

Beaming widely Issac replied, "Indeed so. It's good to see you again Your Honour, and I've been keeping the peace as much as you told me now."

Mr Montgomery smiled, "I'm glad to hear it, Issac. Now

hark to Mr Delacherois for he's something he wants to ask you."

"I will Sir, I will." Issac turned to face Mr Delacherois. "Ask away Sir, ask away."

"Tell me Mr Armstrong when did you detect the offence?" asked Mr Delacherois.

Issac's face fell as he looked blankly at Mr Delacherois.

"Never mind," said Mr Delacherois. "Are you enjoying the celebrations?"

Issac recovered his good humour. "Indeed Sir, indeed. It's a pity we don't beat those Russians every year!" The crowd cheered. "Or indeed Sir, indeed every month!" The crowd roared and Mr Montgomery beat his pipe against the table.

Mr Delacherois continued to examine the witness. "I am very glad to hear it. Now tell me Issac where did you see the boy picking your pocket?"

"Well to be truthful Sir I didn't see him as you say. I more sort of heard him."

"Heard him? Pray explain?" asked Mr Delacherois.

"Well Sir, well I was just coming out of the barn when I heard someone playing a wee tin whistle. Well Sir, well I looked round and it was the wee boy and I recognised the wee whistle as me own."

"Can you see the boy here today?" asked Mr Delacherois.

Issac pointed to Charlie. "That's the wee fellow there Sir."

"And you recognised it…how?"

"Well, I wasn't too sure at first and didn't want to say anything in case I was in the wrong; stealing being such a serious matter. So I went back and looked in my coat pocket first but it was empty. So that's when I went for the Sergeant and fetched him to see for hisself."

"So," Mr Delacherois asked, "when the Sergeant approached the boy what happened?"

"Well Sir, well I recognised the whistle so I told the Sergeant so and he took it off the wee boy."

"A few more questions if the Magistrate will so indulge me?" He bowed to Mr Montgomery.

The Magistrate, who was thoroughly enjoying this evening, refreshed his glass from his hip flask and nodded his consent. "The floor is yours Mr Delacherois," he said.

"Thank you Sir," replied Mr Delacherois bowing to Mr Montgomery. He then turned to address Issac. "Now Issac. May I ask you what you were doing in the barn?"

Issac glanced uncomfortably at the Magistrate and the Sergeant. "Well now indeed I'd been at the dancing and I was looking for a glass…a drink of water maybe to cool me down." He grinned. "To maybe whet me whistle like."

"Very droll," remarked Mr Delacherois. "And had you been wearing your coat, it's a greatcoat I believe?"

"Well indeed Sir, wasn't it too hot? So I put it away Sir."

"Hot work dancing, I know it Issac, hot work. Tell me did you make sure your whistle was in your coat pocket before you put it away?"

"Well indeed Sir, for I don't know where else it could have been for that's where I keeps it."

"Just to clear things up Issac, just when did you last see this whistle?"

"Indeed Sir, when I placed it in my pocket afore I went to

the dance."

"You are an honest man Issac. Your truthfulness do you great credit," said Mr Delacherois.

Issac beamed in the praise and the crowd murmured at this newfound status of their fellow citizen.

"So to sum up Issac," said Mr Delacherois. "You placed the whistle in your pocket, then you went dancing, you threw your greatcoat into a pile of others, you made a number of trips to the barn, which we need not enquire too deeply into, and then you saw your whistle in the possession of the accused."

Mr Delacherois swept his gaze over the silent crowd. "Is there one of you who saw the accused go through the coats?" He raised his hand and indicated the haul on the kitchen table. "Or who saw the accused in the hayloft?" He waited but none spoke up. "So none would gainsay this child," pointing to Charlie, "when he says he was playing with a whistle that he found on the dance floor, and that he rescued from certain destruction?" Mr Delacherois addressed directly the Sergeant whose mouth was hanging open, "John, I'm surprised at you in this matter." Mr Delacherois turned to the Magistrate, "Sir, the matter is in your hands," he bowed.

The crowd cheered.

Mr Montgomery smiled and returned the bow. "Judging by the acclamation your speech has generated I hardly think it worthwhile to put it to the jury." He gestured to Emma. "You madam, turn the boy to face me."

With difficulty, Emma managed to pry Charlie from her skirts and turn him to face Mr Montgomery.

"You have had an extremely fortunate escape young

man, for which you may largely thank Mr Delacherois. Be under no illusions that if you come before this bench again you may not be so lucky a second time. This court is dismissed," he thundered striking the table with his pipe. "Now on with the party!"

The crowd roared their approval and seizing Mr Delacherois hoisted him on their shoulders and then bore him outside under the sullen gaze of the Sergeant.

With the kitchen largely empty Mr Montgomery rose from his temporary throne and stretched his arms.

The Doctor hurried over. "Mr Montgomery, Dear Sir I must —"

Mr Montgomery raised his hand. "Not a word dear Doctor. I haven't enjoyed a party so much since…well, I don't rightly know, but a long time anyway. Shall we search out a glass for all that listening has made me damned thirsty?"

Relieved the Doctor gestured to the back door into the yard, then to the kitchen door leading upstairs. "And which party do you wish to attend?"

"Oh, I think upstairs. For we'd get no peace outside in that." He drew the Doctor closer to him by the arm. "Empiricus warns us, 'The mills of the gods grind slowly, but they grind small'. Mark my words that boy will come to a bad end someday." Mr Montgomery released the Doctor's arm. "Now you mentioned a party. Lead on, lead on dear Doctor."

In the aftermath of the party, Charlie found himself at the centre of unwelcome attention. The townsfolk had come to a somewhat more sober verdict on the matter, and not to Charlie's advantage. Several days later the Doctor asked Emma to attend him in his study. As Emma entered the Doctor was sitting behind his desk looking grave. Without rising he indicated a chair. "Please Emma sit."

Emma did so. "What troubles you Doctor? Have I done anything wrong that you look so serious?"

The Doctor hesitated then picked up a piece of paper from his desk. "This, it's from the Headmaster of the Navigation School."

"Is it about Charlie? Please, what does he say?" asked Emma.

The Doctor looked down at it and then back up to Emma. "Mm...he offers his regrets but it seems there is no longer any spare place for Charlie in the school next term."

"But does he give a reason?" Emma asked.

"Well he merely alludes to *recent occurrences* I'm afraid; that's all."

"But that was all a silly misunderstanding. Why Mr Montgomery himself —"

"Had decided on six months hard labour in the Belfast Gaol if the crowd hadn't been swung by Mr Delacherois. Much to his surprise I may add."

"No! The matter is closed! Charlie has been absolved and —"

The Doctor continued as though Emma had not spoken. "Stealing from your shipmates is a most grievous crime. Cob and Henry will have nothing to do with him." Picking up another letter from his desk. "Miss Wilkes does not want him back in her school, and you tell me his Father's family will

145

not take him in. So I'm afraid if he, and you, are to remain in this town then we must find Charlie a berth elsewhere as soon as we can; for his own sake."

Chapter 18

The next morning the Doctor had just returned from his rounds, after kicking off his boots and replacing them with slippers, he made his way up the kitchen stairs towards his study. He was crossing the hallway when the front doorbell rang.

"Botheration," muttered the Doctor as he opened it. "Reverend Hill…cousin, what a pleasant surprise. What brings you here?" The Doctor stood aside. "Please come in."

"I was wondering if I may have a word," the Reverend said.

"Of course. I've just finished my rounds so," the Doctor guided the Reverend into his study. "Please be seated," the Doctor pulled a bell chord. "I'll get us some tea?"

The Reverend Hill placed his hat on a table and seated

himself. "Thing is Doctor, well the thing is I've come to you with a few questions." He gestured, "Rumours y'know. Just so that I may set people's minds at rest."

Henry appeared at the door. "Doctor?"

"Ah yes Henry, tea for two, please. And maybe ask Sarah for a few rounds of ham sandwiches?" He glanced at the Reverend who shook his head. "That's the lot Henry if you please."

Henry nodded and disappeared closing the door after him.

"Questions you say. Well fire away then Reverend," said the Doctor.

"That castle thing Mr Delacherois caused to be built on top of the old motte. I was talking to Rennie and —"

Laughing the Doctor interrupted. "Rennie's got it back to front I'm afraid. Mr Delacherois had it raised for his own enjoyment. Felt the place could do with a castle. Don't know why really. Rich man's folly I suppose. Mr Delacherois offered Rennie the use of it for storage when the new harbour was being built, that's all."

"So it wasn't built for storing gun-powder then?"

"Not at all. Silly place to build it for that purpose. No pure folly. Anyway, you should ask him, not my bailiwick."

The Reverend sat back in his seat and smiled wanly. "I fear Mr Delacherois would have told me to mind my own business. Well, that explains that, thank you. These silly rumours need to be nipped in the bud."

Henry entered the room and set the tea tray on the Doctor's desk.

"That'll be all," the Doctor lifted one corner of a

sandwich. "Oh good, ham…and a spot of mustard. Thank Sarah and off you go then." He looked at the Reverend and smiled. "I'll play Mother." He poured two cups and handed one to the Reverend.

"Ah that's better, just the spot," said the Reverend.

"And the others?" queried the Doctor· through a mouthful of ham sandwich.

"Ah yes. In view of your explanation about Mr Rennie's misunderstanding. Well, I only have one other. Silly really but as I said rumours."

"And that is?" as he swallowed and reached for his cup.

"Well I'm embarrassed but well there," the Reverend pointed to the curtain behind the Doctor's desk. "That room. A…person came to me with allegations. A child's fantasy no doubt, but I thought I'd ask, in case anybody said anything."

The Doctor swung around and looked at the curtain then returned his gaze to the Reverend. He furrowed his brow. "A child? My smoking room you mean?"

"Smoking room?" said the Reverend.

"My refuge really. This room," he gestured with his chin. "There's too many people coming and going here. Patients, visitors, and the like." The Doctor quickly smiled, "Present company excepted of course. I go in there if I want to be alone with my pipe and maybe a book." The Doctor stood up. "Come, survey my inner sanctum. Put the rumours to rest."

"Oh no! I have pried too much. I —"

The Doctor laughed. "Come. Finish the job." He pushed the curtain aside and opened the door. He turned to the Reverend, "Come, come," and made a sweeping bow.

Amused the Reverend stood and set his cup on the table. "Since you ask so nicely. Maybe I will inspect this nest of daemons." He followed the Doctor into the room.

"Daemons?" queried the Doctor when they were inside.

"Baby Daemons," replied the Reverend. "As I said a fertile imagination."

The room revealed itself as a pleasant sitting room with a desk and chair by the window, and a leather wing chair beside an occasional table over by shelves which bore a collection of books, mostly classics, and some curiosities.

The Reverend picked up a fossil and turned it over in his hands to examine it.

The Doctor took it from him. "*Parioscorpio Venator*, the Sea Scorpion, Mr Delacherois and myself have found them in the rocks at the base of the motte." He placed it back on the shelf. "And also at Scrabo. We believe that in ancient times the sea was much higher."

"Pon my soul. The wonders of the Lord," exclaimed the Reverend. "And that," he pointed to a door at the back of the room. "Where does that lead to?"

"My cellars, do you also wish to inspect them also?"

Blushing the Reverend retreated to the outer study. "No, no. I have intruded enough." He picked up his hat and stood shifting from foot to foot. "I hope…embarrassed myself… rumours y'know." He placed his hat upon his head and fled.

The Doctor entered the kitchen and looked around. Emma was folding some laundry on the kitchen table, and Sarah was stirring and seasoning a large pot on the stove, under the supervision of Mrs McKee who had decided to pass on to

Sarah the Doctor's favourite recipes. Charlie was at the table digging into a plate of cold stir-about.

"Ladies, Betsy, all well," said the Doctor.

A chorus of reassurances greeted his enquiry.

The Doctor frowned at the sight of Charlie. "Good show. Emma, may I have a word?"

"Of course Doctor." Emma finished folding a sheet. "Now?"

"Please. In my study." Then the Doctor returned whence he came.

When Emma entered the study, a few steps behind the Doctor, he had already settled behind his desk. With his fingers steepled the Doctor asked Emma to be seated. He was silent, playing with a few items before him, settling their position to his satisfaction, then he spoke, "I've had a word with McGowan, the Postmaster, and he's willing to take Charlie on as an Apprentice."

Emma was doubtful. "Can we not ask the School of Navigation again?"

"I don't think so. Emma, we must be realistic about what is best for Charlie. He could go to the Navy as a boy entrant, which I think would be best, or —"

"Oh no! Not the Navy. He's too young," Emma cried.

"Well then," the Doctor continued, "it's an apprenticeship down the town for him with McGowan, and after the incident the other day most doors are already closed."

"That's not fair Doctor," Emma protested. "You know Charlie's a good boy. It was a mistake. Mr Montgomery was very cruel when he said those things."

"The boy was damned lucky Mr Montgomery was drunk," said the Doctor.

"But what would he do for McGowan? What —"

The Doctor was growing bored with the conversation. Sharply he said, "He would deliver messages, stack shelves, collect McGowan's piece work, whatever task McGowan —"

In tears, Emma said, "But his poor Father. An Officer who died —"

Exasperated the Doctor snapped, "Your husband wasn't an Officer, he was a shopkeeper in uniform, and unfortunately he shat himself to death in the Crimea!" The Doctor took his handkerchief from his sleeve and offered it to Emma. "Nevertheless Emma you must decide. McGowan's, or the Navy? But he cannot stay here much longer. For his own good as much as yours."

Chapter 19

Later that afternoon Emma went to Charlie's room bearing a tray of sandwiches and a glass of milk. Since his banishment from the company of Cob and Henry, he spent most of his time looking out the window overlooking the yard and pretending a complete lack of interest in the activities therein; he rarely attended meals in the kitchen any more preferring to scavenge when people were elsewhere. Emma knocked on his door. There was a scuffling noise then "Come in." The room itself was plain and airy. Simply furnished with an iron bed, a chest of drawers, and a wooden seat, nevertheless, it was clean and comfortable. Emma looked around, the first thing she noticed was the complete lack of decoration or ornamentation. There were some marks on the wallpaper where items had been hung and, with a sudden jolt Emma thought *Oh Dear God! Let him not have sold them*.

Charlie looked at her with a sulky face. "I don't like it here. Nobody will talk to me. I want to go home."

Her heart breaking Emma replied, "Where Charlie, where? Where do you want to go?"

Charlie sat quietly for a while then said, "I thought I was going to the Navigation School in Bangor?"

"No Dear, not this year. Maybe —"

"They all hate me here!" Charlie his lower lip trembled.

Emma sat on the bed and threw her arms around Charlie. "Oh no! The Doctor was telling me a very nice man in the town would like to offer you a job."

Charlie sniffed, then asked, "What job?"

"Very important work. Helping him in the Post Office, and making deliveries, and just anything that needs doing."

Charlie slowly digested this news. Looking around at his room he asked, "Would I still live here?"

"No Dear. You'd be so important that you'd have to live with Mr McGowan."

Charlie's lower lip started to tremble again. "Is the Doctor sending me away?"

Quickly Emma said, "No, no. But you'll have to come and visit us. We'd all like to see you."

Charlie's brow furrowed and he pointed towards the window. "They wouldn't. They all hate me here."

Emma hugged him tighter. "Of course they will. This silly mistake will blow over. You'll see."

Charlie pushed Emma away. "I told the Reverend about the monsters the Doctor keeps."

Emma instantly thought back to her experience in the

cellar, the strange noises and quick movements in the shadows, around the house that appeared in the corner of her eye and were gone before she could be certain. Unsure Emma held Charlie at arms length looking closely at him. "What monsters Dear?"

"In the room behind the Doctor's chair," he replied.

Startled Emma asked, "Where? In the study do you mean?"

Charlie nodded. "Behind the curtain. In the secret room."

"Why what did you see?"

"He had little monsters in jars. And they looked at me," Charlie said.

"Nonsense," Emma hugged him tight but inside her mind was thinking back *The staircase at the back of the cellar! It would lead up to the study! She had never been admitted there; Mrs McKee had said the key was missing!*

Emma hugged Charlie again. "There are no monsters. Now wash your face and I'll take you down the town tonight and you can just show them that you're your Father's son, a war hero, and you don't care what they think!"

Emma descended the stairs from Charlie's room bearing the empty tray. The house was quiet with the boys in the yard and the sound of Sarah rising from the kitchen. *I should check thought* Emma. *After all, it's my job to make sure the house is kept up, rooms dusted, and fires laid.* Emma put the tray down on the hall table and knocked at the door of the Doctor's study – no reply. Quietly letting herself in Emma took a minute to adjust to the darkness that greeted her. *I must remind Lizzie and Henry to open the drapes when they come in to lay the fire in the mornings.* Reassured now that she was merely performing her duties Emma moved to the windows and tugged the drapes open flooding the room with light. The curtain that habitually covered the door behind the Doctor's desk was pulled back exposing the entrance to the room behind. Emma had idly tried this door on a number of occasions before and found it locked but this time it opened easily. With a glance behind her Emma entered the room.

A simple sitting room with nothing untoward: a desk by the window with papers, pens, a pipe rack; a battered-looking winged armchair, and a few books, some lying open with scribbled notes in the margins. A wall of shelves was largely empty apart from some of the Doctor's collection of stones and the like. Emma moved to examine them, curious as to the attraction. Several seemed to have the imprint of strange animals or plants set upon them. Baffled Emma turned them over in her hands and then replaced them. She ran a finger along the shelves leaving a line in the dust until she came to several dark rings where some sort of fluid had spilled. She smelled her finger and detected a slight trace of something unpleasant. *It must have been jars of the Doctor's chemicals,* Emma decided. *I wonder where he stores them now?* Emma looked at the door leading down to the cellar. Emma shuddered at the memory *I was overwrought allowing my imagination to get the better of me,* Emma rationalised.

Casting a final glance around the room Emma thought *Why must the boy lie so? Does he not realise that he will drag us all down?* Reflecting on Charlie's diminished future, and her hopes for him, Emma left the room and closed the door behind her.

Later that evening after dinner had been served and the day's duties complete Emma announced, "I'm going to take Charlie down the town for a walk. Get him out of that room and get a bit of air about him, if anybody wants to join us?" Emma stood there expectantly but neither Sarah nor Mrs McKee, who were sitting in their chairs by the stove,   took up the offer.

"Well if you change your mind we'll be down at the pier," Emma said.

Mrs McKee paused at her embroidery and said, "Take your cloak. It looks like rain."

Sarah tutted and glanced at Emma. "I may see you down there. Cob has offered to take me to see Lemon's new mare." She laughed. "What a treat to look forward to."

Emma went upstairs to Charlie's room and, after knocking and receiving no reply, entered. The room was empty apart from some plates and a glass. Emma looked out the window over the yard but no sign of him there; Cob was brushing down Sultan whilst Nero and Jimbo looked on jealously, and there was no sign of Henry. *Maybe Charlie and Henry have gone for a walk together?* Emma thought, but her hopes were dashed when Henry came out of the barn carrying two tankards; he raised one to Cob and then sat on a bench waiting for Cob to finish his task.

Hating herself Emma turned back to Charlie's room. Emma quickly checked the drawers in the oak chest that stood to one side: underwear, socks, a spare nightgown; nothing. Pleased at Charlie's innocence so far, Emma examined his wardrobe. A couple of shirts were on hangers and his school shoes were on the bottom sitting beside a spare blanket. Pleased Emma started closing the door then paused. In her wardrobe the spare blanket was on the shelf at the top of the wardrobe, *why would Mrs McKee do it differently in this room?* Emma pulled out the blanket and a small wooden box tumbled out. Emma picked it up and opened it. Inside she found some small coins, a plug of tobacco, a flint and a tin box of brimstone matches, and a gold sovereign. Sarah had complained bitterly about mislaying her gift from Mr Delacherois! Emma rocked back on her heels stunned by what she had found. *If she removed the sovereign from the box, in order to restore it to Sarah, then Charlie would know that his room had been searched. On the other hand, failing to restore the item to Sarah would be as though she had stolen it herself!*

Now was not the time Emma decided. Charlie's place in the household was so tenuous that she dared not expose another of his mistakes. Thoughtfully Emma replaced all the items in the box and restored it to its hiding place.

After calling into her own room, and retrieving the sovereign that Mr Delacherois had gifted her, Emma descended back into the kitchen. "Sarah, didn't I hear you'd lost that sovereign Mr Delacherois gave you?" she asked.

Sarah who was still sitting with Mrs McKee looked up. "Indeed. I've searched for it everywhere. I don't understand it."

Emma smiled and held up a gold sovereign. "Is this it?"

Leaping to her feet Sarah eagerly took the coin in her hand. "Where did you find it?" she asked.

"I was just walking along the landing when I thought I

saw something glinting," Emma said.

Sarah looked puzzled. "That's very strange. I didn't take it upstairs. I just put in my wee box down here for safety."

"Well all's well that ends well," offered Emma. "Now I'm away out for that —"

"Not find Charlie upstairs then Emma?" Mrs McKee said with a tight smile.

Emma flushed. "Where's my boots?" as she rooted around in the rack by the back door.

Mortified Emma hurried out the door, pulling a shawl around her shoulders, into the yard where Cob and Henry were grooming the horses. They called out a greeting to her but she couldn't face them. Not knowing that what they thought of Charlie and herself was as thieves!

The cobbles at the corner were uneven nearly causing her to stumble. *Everything everyone said about Charlie was right. He was a thief!* Her mind raced. *If he was caught she had no doubt he'd go to gaol! Everything she'd hoped for him would be over. He was risking both his and her futures. Could she stop him, or was it too late?*

Emma did not doubt if the Doctor found out they'd be both on the street before the day ended, and she hadn't made much of an effort to make friends in the town, regarding the locals as a little below her. That sovereign had been put aside *– a little something in case of emergency, a little security in case the bad times came back.*

It was dark now with the street lights lit and casting a warm glow across the harbour. Noise and lights spilled out from Grace Neill's public house; Emma knew Mrs McKee and Sarah sometimes slipped in the back way to a discreet snug but she had never joined them feeling that was not the conduct of a respectable lady, the widow of an Officer no less, no matter what the Doctor had said.

Crossing the road, to avoid the loiterers gathered around the tap-room door, Emma walked along the pier with the ships tied up alongside. She glanced up at the top of the lighthouse but her mysterious friend could not be seen. Shivering now, for the Autumn was starting to show itself Emma wrapped her shawl tighter around her. The horror and despair of her position overwhelmed her. Great gobbing lumps of grief forced themselves up and out of her chest. Sobbing Emma tried to control herself, not by choice, but aware that if she couldn't then she and Charlie would soon be adrift with no safe harbour open to them. As she sobbed Emma felt a presence appear from behind and a pair of strong arms encircled her. Emma turned and put her head on his chest, and wept with all the sorrow of the helpless; broken and bereft of comfort or hope.

As Emma's cries subsided she realised that she was alone now. Quickly she looked around to spy her comforter but there were only a few men at the door to the public house looking at her strangely. Pulling herself together Emma withdrew her handkerchief from her sleeve and blew her nose. She glanced back at the lighthouse and the figure was back on the top deck looking down at her. *Friend?* she thought. *What sort of friend is this?*

Chapter 20

October 1855

It was a grey day with the Westerly wind sending the clouds flying helter-skelter over the town and out to sea, throwing the incoming waves aback and knocking their tops off to reveal their frothy centres. Henry had been scrubbed up again and his hair plastered with some of the Doctor's hair oil into a solid, smooth, shiny gloss.

Standing in the hallway of Rosebank he flung the door open admitting Mr Delacherois and his daughter together with a handful of dead leaves.

"Mister and Missus Delacherois," Henry announced and the Doctor advanced smiling to shake Mr Delacherois' hand, and cast the fondest glance at the young lady accompanying him.

"Sir," he greeted, and taking Miss Delacherois' hand he kissed it, whilst she, eyes cast down, dropped him a dainty cutesy. "And Miss Delacherois, my friends, it's good to see you. You are most welcome, both of you."

The Doctor invited his guests into the Drawing Room where the fire was blazing and snapping away and a table laden with dainties was already provisioned. Lizzie entered the room and dropped a bob before placing a teapot in front of the guests. "Thank you, Lizzie, that will be all," said the Doctor reaching for it when Miss Delacherois interjected, "Oh do let me Doctor," and, with a shy smile at the Doctor, took control of serving the Gentlemen.

Cup charged and plates heaped Mr Delacherois sat back in his chair and looked at the portrait of the Doctor's father which was in pride of place over the mantelpiece.

The picture was that of a stern-looking man, with mutton-chop whiskers, dressed in the uniform of a Rear Admiral of the Royal Navy, sitting with a pretty dark-haired woman standing behind him, her right hand on his shoulder. Mr Delacherois sighed, "Dear Sam, and Martha of course. I do miss them you know. Many's a night we'd sit here, your Father and I, and put the world to right."

The Doctor shifted uncomfortably in his chair.

Mr Delacherois continued, "Of course he wanted you to follow him into the Navy but," he nodded to his old friend the Admiral, "we old men have to give way to you youngsters...to admit this modern scientific age is best left to those who understand it."

"Oh come now Mr Delacherois you're not ready to be boxed up yet I hope," cried the Doctor who was quickly joined by the entreaties of his daughter.

"Mr Delacherois laughed. "I thank you both. But," turning to the Doctor, "In all seriousness, I have only one last duty to perform," indicating Miss Delacherois. "I have only one issue, the apple of my eye indeed, and the sole heir of an ancient line."

Mr Delacherois placed a hand on the Doctor's arm and took Miss Delacherois' hand in the other. "If I could know that my dear daughter was happy and secure it would, my friend, be of great comfort to me."

The Doctor and Miss Delacherois protested that he was still a young man, relatively speaking anyway. But Mr Delacherois waved their objections away, "That's as may be but these things must be approached, as your Father would say in a practical, seaman-like fashion. Now I know you young ones are all talking about love matches and all that but sometimes the old ways have something still to be said for them. For," he looked at them both "can you Doctor not say your Father and Mother did not love each other very much? And you Missie can you say that I did not love your Mother and she I?"

Miss Delacherois was close to tears as she and the Doctor protested that they were very very sure that everyone loved one and another very much.

"Well then," said Mr Delacherois. "I'll say no more on the matter for now." He took a sly look at them both, "and I'll let the cards fall where they may."

Mr Delacherois rose from his seat. "Now I must be away. No," he smiled at Miss Delacherois. "You and the Doctor finish your tea. I'm going to walk up to the Kirkyard and visit your Mother. It's been a while since we've had a gossip."

Late one evening Emma was awake in the Doctor's arms. The fire in his bedroom was casting a warm glow and softening the shadows in the corners. Feeling safe and content after their lovemaking she dared to hope that, at last, Charlie and her had found their positions in this world. Not the stations she would have particularly chosen had she been asked a year, or even six months, ago but a home nevertheless. Snuggling deeper into the warmth of his embrace she thought, *This is not a bad place, nor is this a bad-man. We can be safe here.*

Her half-awake reveries were broken into by the sound of running feet in the yard and a policeman's whistle. The Doctor stirred and Emma shook him. "There's something happening outside."

He stirred and then sat up. "What is it?" then the sounds from outside took his attention. He threw the bedclothes aside and went to the window. "Christ Almighty! The stables are alight!" Pausing only to pull on his britches and a shirt he opened the bedroom door and hopped out of the room.

Emma quickly went to Charlie's bedroom. "Charlie wake up! Wake up! There's a fire," but his room was empty, the bed unslept in. *Dear God! Let him be safe at McGowan's and not be sleeping in the stables with the boys!* Relations between Charlie, Cob and Henry had been frosty of late since the misunderstanding over Cob's knife but she had hoped things may have started to settle. Quickly Emma dressed and followed the Doctor down the stairs; she paused at the back

164

door to don her boots then dashed into the yard. The Doctor was on his knees holding Henry who was gasping for air.

Cob was just visible in the burning barn struggling to release the animals. The crowd called on him to save himself, that the beasts were lost and to abandon his attempts of rescue. The flames flared up at the entrance of the barn as a beam fell then Cob emerged triumphant leading a blindfolded Sultan through a wall of fire.

Nero burst out past them and disappeared kicking and bucking down the lane braying his outrage as smoke rose from his hindquarters

The crowd cheered Cob as Henry staggered to his feet. "Where's Jimbo? Cob, did ye get wee Jimbo?" He moved to the blazing barn and from inside the crowd heard Jimbo's screams of pain and terror. "Jimbo son! I'm coming!" Henry pushed the Doctor to the ground and barged through the crowd and into the inferno just as the roof collapsed throwing a cloud of bright sparks into the sky to join the night stars.

The next morning after the fire had the hint of autumn and a heavy dew had fallen overnight. A few silent remnants of the crowd remained, talking quietly amongst themselves, and cast occasional glances as the Sergeant and several Constables picked over the still smouldering remains of the stable. The smell of roast meat mingled with the damp morning air and permeated the yard before it drifted into the street and down to the town below. Henry's body, contorted by the heat, lay curled up and covered by a sheet, waiting for the Magistrate to view it.

After attending to Cob's burns, the Doctor had left him in the care of a distraught Mrs McKee, and gone to see to Sultan who had been led down to Mr Delacherois's stables. Nero had been caught and returned to the orchard, where he stood by the fence watching over Henry; tears tracing silver paths down his muzzle.

About noon the District Inspector rode up on his gelding. He dismounted and a Constable ran over to take the reins. The Sergeant wiped his hands and saluted.

The District Inspector returned the salute. "Well then John. Did you find much?"

The Sergeant indicated Henry. "We got the poor wee laddie out...but he's in a bad state."

"That's not good now. He was a grand young fellow." The District Inspector turned to survey the remains of the barn. "Any ideas?"

"Not a thing. It's burnt to the ground. A couple of lanterns lying in the ashes as you'd expect but Cob swears he checks them every night afore bed and they were all extinguished. Other than," the Sergeant dug into his pocket, "this tin. Cob says he's not seen it before."

The District Inspector took the small tin box from the Sergeant. He examined the outside, "I can't tell," then opened it to reveal thin black strips of carbon. "Sulphur?" He offered the open tin to the Sergeant who smelt it.

"Aye, that'd be it."

"Brimstones. Did you ask Cob where he got his light?"

The Sergeant indicated the house. "In there. I've been in the kitchen myself when he's come across to get a lantern lit.

166

He won't allow anyone to bring a naked flame into the barn. Very strict on that is Cob. I've even seen him chase the Doctor and his pipe out."

"Maybe somebody didn't like Cob's rules?" The District Inspector handed the tin back to the Sergeant.

Chapter 21

Emma had been in the yard to watch the search. She had managed to snatch a brief word with Cob and he had assured her that Charlie had not been staying in the barn that evening. Emma thanked him, and then Cob and Sultan had been collected and taken to the stables in the Manor House to lodge until other arrangements could be made.

Emma felt an icy chill steal across her heart. *What if! What if! Oh God let it not be so!* she thought. Reluctantly, knowing the answer deep down, she crept into Charlie's room and opened the wardrobe. Her heart raced as she reached into the folds of the blanket and withdrew the wooden box that she knew he had hidden there. Emma sat back on her heels. If she looked inside she would risk everything, would know too much. If she replaced it without looking inside she could try to push all her worst fears back down into the dark and attempt to keep them there. Her hand trembled as she opened the box; the flint and tin box of brimstone matches had gone.

Emma rushed down the town as soon as she was dressed in search of Charlie. Mr McGowan had been behind his counter when she entered his Post Office. He looked at Emma and then removed his eyeglasses to reveal a pair of twinkling blue eyes.

"I'm so sorry for the Doctor's troubles Mrs Hawthorne. Dreadful news about young Henry. If there's —" he said.

Ignoring Mr McGowan's greetings Emma interrupted. "Is Charlie here? Have you seen Charlie?"

Mr McGowan put down his pen. "He's out Mrs Hawthorne, and about his duties. I judged it better to keep him busy today."

"Did he sleep here?"

"No. I was given to understand you preferred to keep him at your side in the Doctor's though we have a perfectly good room over the kitchen for our apprentices."

"He'll have to sleep here from now on. I won't have him spend another night there."

Mr McGowan looked at Emma with some concern. "I'm sure that'll be possible. There will have to be a small adjustment to his wages to account for food and lodging of course, but I'll instruct Sally to make up his bed for this evening."

"Thank you, Mr McGowan. Thank you. If you'll tell Charlie to come up to the house tonight I'll pack his bag?"

Mr McGowan started to reply but Emma had already

fled.

A few days later the household gathered together in the Presbyterian graveyard at Ballycopeland, just outside the town, to bury Henry. The Reverend Skelly took the service on a blustery afternoon, which was well attended by both Low and High Church as the McKees were well respected in the town, and Henry himself liked by all.

The weather had turned now with grey skies and a taste of salt in the air. The stink of rotten seaweed from the rocks pervaded all, and a cold Easterly wind swept the spray from the waves and whipped it across the mourners hiding their tears.

The Doctor stood with Mr and Miss Delacherois, all looking stony-faced with anger. Cob, who was openly weeping, stood with Sarah, their arms linked.

Willie and Mrs McKee were at the graveside committing the only son they had, and one that they had whole-hardheartedly wished to have been entombing them at the proper time.

Emma remained at the back of the crowd closest to the road where the carts that had born Henry to his resting place remained ready to ferry the mourners home. Urgently she scanned the crowd searching for Charlie, *Surely he'd not be stupid enough to show his face here!* Mr McGowan was a little in front of her talking to fellow merchants from the town. Emma approached him and he touched his hat. "Sorry to see you in such circumstances, Mrs Hawthorne. Such a fine young man."

Emma nodded. "We were all very fond of him. His poor

parents." She touched his arm. "Is Charlie?…"

Mr McGowan looked at the crowd. "He's away doing messages for me in the Ards. I judged it…better."

Relieved Emma nodded. "He was very upset."

For a moment it looked as though Mr McGowan was going to say something then he just nodded.

Discombobulated Emma said, "I'm sure Charlie is very happy with you. He's such a good worker when he's given —" *I'm babbling*. Emma stopped.

Mr McGowan took off his eyeglasses to wipe the mist from them. Re-seating them he said, "He'll be alright with me for now." He looked sadly at Emma. "But he'll never find a life here. Maybe Belfast, maybe somewhere else but they've taken agin him here." He touched his hat to Emma. "Better you think on that rather than have him found floating in the tide one morn."

The service had finished now and the crowd was starting to make their way home. Emma made to join the Doctor's party in his new cart but a look from Mrs McKee convinced her that she would be intruding on private grief. Emma moved onto the road to join those walking when she glanced into the trees that lined the other side of the road from the cemetery. Emma thought she recognised her friend from the lighthouse. She waved but couldn't be certain that he'd seen her in the advancing gloom.

Late that evening when dusk had fallen Cob, officially classed now as walking-wounded, and Mrs McKee met in the yard. Mrs McKee had a straw doll in her hand around which she had tied a handkerchief that had belonged to Charlie.

Before that it had belonged to Charlie's father for it still had his initials on it, lovingly embroidered by Emma.

Mrs McKee nodded to the well cover. "Slide yon back a bit."

Cod pushed the cover to one side and a coldness rose to envelop them both. Mrs McKee approached the open mouth of the well. She raised the doll and spat on it then proffered it to Cob, who hesitated then also spat on it. "Are you sure about this?" he said.

Mrs McKee nodded her head, "That wee bastard murdered my Henry," then spoke a few words that Cob did not understand before throwing the doll into the well. Mrs McKee patted Cob's arm. "It's done now."

Cob pushed the cover back and then shivered. "Or maybe it's just started."

The following Sunday morning Emma arranged to meet Charlie down on The Parade. The household had split into their respective places of worship and Emma, being English, wasn't really expected at any of them. This gave her, and Charlie, the freedom afforded to strangers, since they were expected to know no better. The sea mist was still present and the flat oily swell merged almost imperceptibly into the horizon and cloaked any sight of the Copeland Islands.

She had now stood there for an hour and Charlie was late. *Slept in, please God, let him have slept in!* There was a nip in the air with the promise of another cold rainless day when Charlie appeared from behind some crates stacked nearby on the quayside. He glanced around before approaching Emma. As he got closer his face crumpled and he ran the last few yards into Emma's embrace.

"I'm sorry Mum! I'm so sorry! They all hate me here! I'm scared!" he cried.

Emma, her heart breaking, drew him to the steps running along the sea wall and hugged him tight. "I'm sorry Charlie. I should never have brought us here."

Charlie extracted himself from her arms and stood back looking at her. "Can we go?"

Go! Where can I go? Who would have me? Don't ask me that! Emma considered her reply. "I would only hold you back Charlie. I think you're right but you'll have to go first. Maybe you could send for me when you're established?"

She's not going to look after me. She's on their side. She wants to send me away! Charlie folded his arms. "Why can't we go to Granny and Granddad?" he asked.

"I can't my love. Granny and Gramps don't like me, but," she said hurriedly, "they still love you. Oh, they love you so very much. You should go to them!" Emma extracted a piece of paper from her handbag and scribbled on it. "Here's their address." She opened her purse and handed coins to Charlie. "There, that's all I have but it'll get you there safe."

Charlie pocketed the coins and looked at the note. "Do you want me to go?"

Her eyes filled with tears. "Oh no! Never! But I fear for you, fear you'll never find a home here."

"You want to stay here with the Doctor!"

"Charlie, you're young." Emma spun Charlie around to face her. "You have your whole life in front of you. Look at me. No! Look at me!"

Charlie spat. "You don't love me! You love the Doctor!"

He turned on his heels and started walking away. He weighed up the cash in his pocket and considered his relations with Big Tom the senior apprentice. *He'll like me if I take him to the tap room in Gracie's and stand him a few glasses.*

Emma heartbroken stood as to go after him – but didn't. "Wait Charlie, wait please." *Don't look back for I don't know what I would do if you made me choose.*

The Doctor and Jane Delacherois were sitting in the living room of the Manor House in front of a cheerful fire.

Jane studied the burning coals her cheeks blushing from the heat. "Look there! A Dragon!"

The Doctor leant forward in his chair until their heads almost touched. "D'ye know I think I can see that one…yes, I can!"

Jane laughed, "I don't believe you, Doctor. That's the first occasion you've agreed with me this evening."

"Maybe it's because I find the company so 'agreeable'," he offered, with a broad smile and a chuckle.

"Oh a weak sally Doctor," Jane giggled.

"Jane I did mean to say, rather ask you something tonight."

Jane turned her gaze back to the fire. "And what would that be Doctor?"

"Well I was going to ask you…rather ask your Father, with your permission of course…"

Jane squealed, "What is it you're trying to say!"

"What I'm trying to say." The Doctor levered himself from his chair and, clutching the mantelpiece for support lowered himself onto one knee. "Miss Delacherois, may I have the honour, the privilege, of asking your Father for your hand?"

"D'ye mean you're asking me to marry you?"

"Well yes…that was rather the gist of the matter," replied the Doctor, looking slightly put out. "What do you say?"

Miss Delacherois flung herself to her knees in front of the Doctor and threw her arms around him. "I say 'Yes' dear Doctor "Yes with all my heart'!"

The Doctor shuffled around on his knees the said, "You make me very happy. Now d'ye think you could haul me up agin?"

That afternoon Emma walked down the town to buy some provisions for that evening's dinner then called at Mr McGowan's to see how Charlie fared.

Mr McGowan was behind the counter working on one of his endless lists of figures. "Mrs Hawthorne. What news?"

"I beg your pardon. I just came in to see how Charlie has settled in with you?"

"You must have missed my messenger. I sent a boy up some ten minutes ago to enquire after the boy."

"I don't understand. Is he not here?"

"No indeed Mrs Hawthorne. He didn't appear for work today. I assumed he was delayed with you."

"But —"

"A moment please. Tom! Tom come here."

A burly youth of about fifteen summers emerged from the back room wearing a cap on the back of his head. His low brow indicated a general lack of intelligence, and he had the heavy rounded shoulders of a confirmed tap-room bully.

"Uncle?" he asked.

"I apologise. He's my wife's brother's son and a lazy ill-mannered brute for all that. Take your cap off this instant sir!" Mr McGowan commanded.

With ill grace, Tom removed his cap and stood there looking sullen.

"Now sir young Charlie. Where is he?"

"Dunno," Tom mumbled.

An increasingly irritated Mr McGowan asked, "When did you see him last then?"

Tom shuffled and remained silent.

Mr McGowan stamped his foot. "Damn it boy. I'll take the whip to you. See if I don't! When did you see Charlie last?"

Spying Mrs Hawthorne and an opportunity for mischief Tom said, "In Grace's uncle. He was in the back room buying drinks with Kerr's lot."

"Buying drinks! With what sir, with what?"

"Dunno."

"And what time did he come back from…buying drinks?"

"Didn't."

"Has his bed not been slept in?"

"No."

Mr McGowan turned to Emma. "Mrs Hawthorne I'm sorry but this is intolerable. Consorting with that lot. I cannot —"

Emma burst in, "Oh please sir. Give him —"

"I cannot Mrs Hawthorne. The boy's had more chances than many in the town would choose to afford him. No, I cannot. I'll have his things sent up to Rosebank."

"He's not a bad boy. Just easily —"

"Nevertheless he will have to find another place. Now if you'll excuse me I want to…now I have to balance my books post haste. Good Afternoon."

Chapter 22

The next evening Mr Delacherois was working on his accounts in his study when a knock on the door occurred. Frowning he put down his pen. "Come in," he called.

The door opened and the Doctor stood at the threshold. "Am I disturbing you?"

"Not at all." Mr Delacherois gestured to the desk littered with ledgers and receipts. "I'm heartily glad of the excuse. I thought you were with Miss Delacherois? A glass?"

The Doctor hesitated, then entered the room closing the door behind him. "No, no thank you...at least not yet."

Mr Delacherois rose and, taking the Doctor by the arm, escorted him to a seat. "What's wrong with you man? You look as though you've seen a ghost. Seat yourself."

"I think we'd be better standing for what I have to say to

you."

"Now you're alarming me…is Jane alright?"

"Oh yes, she's fine. I just…I mean I —"

"What is it man? Spit it out."

"Well I just…we just…no, I just…Miss Delacherois has… I have just spoken —"

"Damn it what —"

"She has given me her permission for me to approach you to —"

"If it is what I think it then yes, with my blessings." Mr Delacherois broke into a wide smile and offered his hand to the Doctor, which was eagerly taken.

"Oh thank the Lord." The Doctor visibly relaxed, he indicated the chair. "May I?"

Mr Delacherois relinquished his grip and steered the Doctor into a safe berth, then rang the bell. "Now a glass to celebrate I think."

It was a raw morning, a few days after the engagement had been announced, with a cold wind from the East when the Doctor gently knotted a scarf over Miss Delacherois' eyes and led her into the stable yard of the Manor House.

Cob was standing there looking pleased with himself and holding a handsome young Bay gelding about sixteen hands two: good big hairy feet, with a deep chest, and an inquisitive eye.

With the flourish of a showman, the Doctor removed the blindfold. "Miss Delacherois may I introduce you to young Master Jupiter?"

Jane gave an excited squeal, "He's lovely! Where did you

get him?" as she rushed forward to examine the horse.

"Cob found him. He's from Jamie Blackwood's stable in Ballyleidy."

Miss Delacherois looked up from lifting Jupiter's feet. "Are you planning to hunt him this year?" She stood back and looked the Doctor up and down. "Will he carry you? Would you not be better staying with Sultan? He's more your weight."

The Doctor and Cob grinned at each other. "D'ye know," the Doctor said. "I think you may be right."

Jane looked between them. "What are you two smiling about? Cat got your tongues?"

"Well Sir what were you thinking of?" the Doctor addressed the smirking Cob. "This beast is no use to me at all. What do you suggest I do with it? Straight to the knackers I suppose?"

Sometimes the Doctor's little jokes went over Cob's head as he looked alarmed. "But I thought we'd —"

The Doctor ignored Cob and turned to Miss Delacherois. "I say I don't expect you'd take him off my hands?"

The Doctor was sitting in his study with a good fire with a plate of ham sandwiches and a decanter of claret to hand when there came a knock on the door. "Enter," cried the Doctor who was in fine form, "Enter, and welcome to all!"

Mrs McKee entered.

"Betsy! Take a seat." He poured a glass and placed it on the table between the chairs. "Have a glass with me. Today we celebrate!"

Mrs McKee sat down. "We need to talk."

"We need to celebrate!" The Doctor held up his glass to her. "Come take —"

"Put the glass down. This is important. You know me I speak as I find. Well, she's pregnant. She's carrying your child."

"Betsy!" The Doctor put his glass on the table. "Miss Delacherois? I can —"

"Not her you fool. Mrs Hawthorne! Have you no eyes?"

"Emma! Pregnant? Are you sure?"

"Of course I'm sure."

"But mine?"

"For who else would it be? Sneaking into your room of a night. D'ye think we're all blind?"

Ashen faced the Doctor picked up his glass drained it, then took up the glass he had poured for Mrs McKee.

"Stop that at once," she said. "That'll not make things go away."

The Doctor looked at the glass and put it down. "You're right Betsy. This could ruin everything. Miss Delacherois won't tolerate my bastard running around the town, nor will her father."

"It would be the end of you here. You'd have to leave. Give up everything you've worked for, this, your home."

"Yes, my work. My research. It would all end...your place here."

"Aye, everything."

"I shall send her away. Give her enough to go away and start again. And take that little shit Charlie with her."

"No! Not yet! I will have my revenge on her and her's first."

"Betsy…she didn't know. How could she?"

"Her son murdered my Henry! And she'll pay for it! Both of them!"

That evening Sarah and Cob were walking out together, and Lizzie was visiting her family in the town. Only Mrs McKee and Emma were sitting in the kitchen.

Mrs McKee stirred her tea. "Emma dear, any news of young Charlie? Did you have any luck tracking him down?"

"No not a sign. I even went into the back room in Mrs Neill's."

"Upon my soul. You shouldn't be looking in such places."

"Oh, Betsy I've no choice."

"Next time ask Cob. But don't give him more than a shilling or you'll never get him out."

"Where else could he be?"

"Oh, there's worse around the town than Grace's wee place. He could be holed up in some low shebeen or the likes."

"What's a shebeen? I've never heard of such a thing."

"It's an unlicensed drinking den."

"Oh Lord! Are there many of them about?"

"More than a few. Some I've heard down Murder Lane but mostly just outside the town."

Emma started shaking. "But Charlie…he's so young." Emma burst into tears rocking back and forth. "Betsy, what will I do? What…where…I need to —"

Mrs McKee took Emma in her arms. "There, there child. It's only a wee place here. The Sergeant will find him soon enough."

Emma shot bolt upright her face white. "The Sergeant! Why is he looking for Charlie? What's wrong?"

Mrs McKee stood up and took a small packet from her apron. "Now, now child. I'll give you a wee something to help you sleep then Cob and I'll look for him in the morning." Mrs McKee poured the powder into a cup and added hot water. "Here drink this down and we'll put you to bed."

Emma took the cup. "What's this?"

"One of the old cures. It'll help you sleep. Now drink up."

Emma took a sip. "Oh, it's so bitter."

"Hush now. That means it's doing you good. All down? Good."

That night Emma went to bed early. She felt a strange pain deep down, and when she fell into a hot uneasy sleep her dreams were filled with fantastical figures, visions of babies, of children reaching out to her, calling for her, trying to pull her towards them. In the midst of this, she thought she could see Charlie lying motionless, but when she called out he did not answer.

Emma reached out in an attempt to embrace Charlie when she felt her hand gripped and being dragged deeper and deeper into the dream. She realised that she was losing contact with reality and becoming part of this new, terrifying world; if she allowed herself to cross over then she had no way back.

A sudden jerk and claws dug deep into her wrist and

Emma woke with a gasp. She withdrew her hand and held it up to the early dawn light. It was covered in blood; Emma screamed bringing Mrs McKee and the Doctor, somewhat the worse for drink, running in.

The Doctor stood at the foot of the bed. "What is it now Emma!"

Mrs McKee drew back the sheets revealing Emma lying in a bed of blood. "Never mind that Doctor. Go and wake Cob and tell him to boil water…plenty of it too. And get me some towels. I'll take care of this…and send Sarah up."

The Doctor hesitated looking at Mrs McKee.

Losing patience Mrs McKee repeated her order, "Come on man! Move!" and the Doctor scurried out to obey.

Emma dreamt that the demons had got her, had got her baby and were tearing them both apart. For a moment she thought she heard a baby cry, then she fell back into a troubled sleep where her newborn son was calling out to her but remained just outside her grasp.

Mrs McKee wrapped the infant in a towel and handed the Doctor his son. "The poor wee thing's stillborn I'm afraid."

"What a heartbreak for Emma," muttered Sarah. "May I get a look at the little one?" She moved as to draw the covering aside but Mrs McKee put her hand firmly over Sarah's.

"Best not I think. Bad luck and we don't want to jinx yourself and Cob do we?" Mrs McKee replaced the bottom sheet, rolling Emma from side to side. "Now take those dirty bedclothes down and steep them," she ordered. Sarah gathered the bloodied laundry together and took it away.

The Doctor felt the baby move in his arms. Startled he glanced at Mrs McKee. She returned his gaze. "Stillborn."

He hesitated for a moment. "I'll take it away then."

The Doctor left the room carrying the baby and Mrs McKee moved around the bed tucking it in. "Nice and tight now." Before moving to the head of the bed to plump up the pillows. "All done. You rest now Emma…and don't you be thinking I've even half finished with you." She brushed an errant lock of Emma's hair from her forehead. "Or yours."

Mr Delacherois was waiting on the landing when the Doctor backed out of Emma's room carrying his bundle.

"Well what is it?" he said.

The Doctor hesitated then pulled the sheet aside to look. "A…a boy. My —"

"My nothing!" spat Mr Delacherois. He paused. "What are you going to do with it? You can't keep it. Not if you hope to marry Jane."

"I could give the child away to —"

"Be sensible man. You can't have your bastard running around the town. Not a man in your position. You'd be a laughing stock. Jane would be humiliated."

The Doctor looked up smiling. He had his little finger in the baby's mouth. "Look, he's suckling."

Mr Delacherois pursed his lips and then held his hands out. "Give that to me."

The Doctor recoiled clasping the bundle to his breast.

"Damn it man, you'll be ruined, and my daughter will be disgraced. Now give the bloody thing to me!" Mr Delacherois insisted stepping closer to the Doctor.

The Doctor allowed Mr Delacherois to take possession of the bundle. "What…what will you do with him?"

"I'll put him downstairs in the cellar with the others."

Aghast the Doctor protested, "But wait! He's alive! You can't —"

"It's not baptised. It has no soul!"

"It's my son."

"Make your mind up man. Either you allow me to do this for you or you may pack your bags and go…I don't care where! And you'll not be marrying my Jane so put any thoughts of her dowry out of your head."

"But…I could —"

"It's for the best man. Look I'll deal with this then join you in your study for a nightcap eh?"

Carefully holding the bundle in his arms Mr Delacherois negotiated the steps down to the cellar. As the baby started to cry he proffered his finger for it to suck and rocked the infant to and fro. "There, there," he said. "It's all right. I'm here now." Pausing at the door he placed the child on the ground and struck a brimstone to light a candle. He stood there awhile looking at the dancing shadows on the walls, and listening for the reassuring sound of the stables from above. "Why not damn it? What's to be lost?" Leaving the child he returned upstairs for a few moments then returned with the Doctor's leather-bound book in his arms.

Moving quickly he placed the book on a small table by the water trough, then picked up the candle and lit the lanterns. "Now, where was I?" He spied the baby and extracted it from the swaddling blanket. Immediately it started to fuss. "Yes, now," he turned the pages in the book. "That's it now…I'll be with you momentarily." He dipped his hand in the water and traced some arcane signs upon the infant; shocked the child started to howl. "There, there!" Mr Delacherois plunged the baby into the ice-cold water and held it there, whilst studying the diagrams in the book.

"That should do it!" Mr Delacherois lifted the infant out of the water and placed it at the side of the trough where he could study it. He waited then, uncertain, he poked it with a finger. "Hey there you," he said. "Look lively there." The baby opened its eyes and started to howl again. "That's not right!" Mr Delacherois turned the pages searching for an answer while patting down his pockets. "Drat, where are my spectacles?"

The cries of the infant increased in volume. Mr Delacherois looked around in alarm. "Hush now. You'll bring the house down on us." He gave a start. "What am I doing? We're supposed to be reanimating the dead, not the living! How can I have been so —" He picked up the crying infant and, stifling its cries with his hand, returned the baby to the icy water.

Mr Delacherois felt it move in his hands. "Hush now, it'll be all right," he said as the struggles grew weaker. A final burst and the infant was still. "Better safe than sorry." He continued to submerge the baby until quite certain life had fled, and then he lifted the child out and placed it on the cold stone of the trough.

"All done, you're safe now. It's all over," he murmured then returned to the book. Leafing through the pages he made practice signs in the air, repeating several until he had the way of them. He glanced down at the dead infant. "I think that's that. We're ready now."

Tenderly lifting the remains he smoothed its sparse locks then kissed the infant on the forehead. "Such an adventure you shall have," then wet his fingers and traced the signs on the baby again before returning it to the water. The shadow from the lanterns danced on the walls, throwing grotesque shapes that merged, broke apart and reformed. A mist rose from the trough forming tendrils that threatened to choke Mr Delacherois and he could feel something, some things brushing past his hands in the rapidly warming waters.

Mr Delacherois shuddered as his wrists were grasped pulling him downwards towards the trough and its contents. He gasped, "By God, no!" as he tugged backwards. The grip on him tightened, a lantern flared and the shadows on the walls grew, twisting, writhing, growing. Small hands grasped at his legs and the present faded as he felt himself start to lose the will to resist.

A crash ran out from the stable yard and the sound of Cob cursing Nero for kicking over a bucket penetrated into the cellar. Mr Delacherois staggered back as he was released and the lantern returned to normal. "By God! What happened there?" He shook his head to clear it then, steadying himself against the trough he scrutinised the surface, the body of the infant was floating face down. Suddenly a twitch! Mr Delacherois looked on in horror as arms and legs started to move. Summoning his courage he reached back into the water and quickly lifted out the writhing infant and placed it on the edge of the trough than quickly stepped backwards wiping his hands on his coat.

Glancing around Mr Delacherois said to himself, "No-one must ever know about this."He glanced at the stairs leading up to the Doctor's study. "Especially him." Casting around he saw a spade sitting in the corner of the cellar. Quickly retrieving it he dug a small hole in the floor then, using the spade to keep the infant at a distance, he carried it across and deposited it in the pit, which he rapidly filled in and tamped down with several blows using the back of the spade. "He must never know."

The Doctor entered his study and flung himself in an armchair. He sat there momentarily, as though in a trance, then stood up and quickly strode to the fire. There he threw half a bucket of coals on the glowing embers then seized a poker and stirred it back into life.

Mr Delacherois entered from behind the curtain leading to the back room. He walked over to the fire and stared into it as he rubbed his hands as to clean them.

The Doctor coughed and then asked, "Is it done?"

Mr Delacherois remained silent.

The Doctor stirred the fire furiously. "I said is it done?"

Mr Delacherois looked up at the Doctor. "Yes…yes. It's done."

"No problems?"

"No, no…the business is finished." Mr Delacherois looked at the Doctor. "The child expired in my arms on these very stairs."

The Doctor sighed, "So it was dead when…when you buried it?"

"Damn it! I've just told you so!"

The Doctor looked as though he was about to say something then placed the poker back on the hearth. "A drink I think. By God, I need a drink." He returned to the armchair and sat down before he poured two large tumblers of whiskey.

Mr Delacherois sat on the other armchair and picked up the second glass. He looked the Doctor in the eye. "There's an end to it. Now you and Jane may look forward to a long and happy life here." He raised the glass. "Your health."

The Doctor and Mr Delacherois were sitting in the Doctor's study taking tea when Mr Delacherois reached over to his greatcoat, folded on a chair, and drew out a thick envelope. He held it out to the Doctor. "Here now. Take this."

The Doctor took the envelope in his hand and turned it over. "What's this then?"

"This my dear Doctor is Jane's dowry."

The Doctor hesitated and then opened the package. "Good God. These are the title deeds to half the property in the town!"

"They are properties attached to the estate. All rented with steady tenants, all in good repair." Mr Delacherois took a sip of his tea. "You made a good catch Doctor. Jane will be a wealthy woman when I'm gone."

"Oh now come on. You're as healthy as…as…as an ox. I'm your Doctor so I should know."

"Nevertheless." Mr Delacherois patted the Doctor's knee. "Of course, the rents remain with the estate until it all passes to Jane."

Slightly taken aback the Doctor pursed his lips. "Of

course…I would not wish it otherwise." He stood up and walked to the back of the room where, withdrawing a key from his watch chain he opened the safe that stood against the wall.

Mr Delacherois started at the sight. "Good Lord man. How much do you keep there?"

The Doctor chortled as he placed the package in the safe. "I'm afraid I inherited the Admiral's mistrust of banks."

"But still…really."

The Doctor closed the safe and locked it. "Should I now start calling you Father?"

Mr Delacherois laughed, "I'll call you out if you do."

The Doctor rang the bell. "Too early for something to celebrate?"

The Doctor and Miss Delacherois had taken to going on long rides when the weather was clement. Mrs McKee had noticed that when they returned Miss Delacherois' dress was wet with grass, and the knees of his britches were often muddy but she held her peace.

One day as they lay in one another's arms, beside a small copse of trees, Miss Delacherois spoke, "One thing my love. I have a favour to ask."

"For you anything."

"Mrs Hawthorne…she doesn't like me."

"Och, I'm sure that's not true! How could —"

"It doesn't matter. I don't like her."

"I'm sure if you got to know her you'd be great friends."

"Doctor…my dear. When we are wed she will not remain under our roof for one day more."

Chapter 23

Time passed and Emma got used to the loss of the infant child; on which she had pinned so much hope. The Doctor and Mrs McKee assured her that the child had been baptised, and then buried in the corner of the kirk-yard reserved for the graves of infants, whilst she had been lying in bed with a fever that would not leave her. Still weak Emma spent most of her time sleeping but came downstairs to eat with the others in the kitchen.

One day, on knocking on the study door and receiving an invitation to enter, Emma carried in a tray of sandwiches and small ale for the Doctor's lunch into his study. "Sarah sent this up Doctor."

The Doctor put down the book he had been studying in the window light and took the tray from her before sitting at his desk. "Ah good. Thank you, Emma. Very nice...em, I think we, do sit down, I think we should have a little talk now you're feeling better."

Emma sat and folded her hands on her lap. Without meeting the Doctor's eye she asked, "What about Doctor?"

The Doctor picked up his pipe and turned it over in his hands. "Well, I was wondering what your plans might be? Now...with losing the baby and all, and Charlie, a big boy, out there making his own way in the world?"

Emma looked up at the Doctor who dropped his eyes to his pipe. "I wasn't really planning on going anywhere, Doctor. Is my presence so distasteful to you?"

"Well no Emma, of course not. It's just...well dash it, the truth be told Miss Delacherois feels that..."

"Yes Doctor?"

"Well that she...it's not appropriate to have a young, why would you stay here? There's nothing for you here?"

"Nor anywhere else Doctor."

The Doctor sat back in his chair. "Oh, Emma. For your own sake, you need to get away from here. A fresh start. Find a man to marry."

"That's very kind of you Doctor. I do admit I had high hopes," she looked at the Doctor, "that I had found such a man here."

"What nonsense. If it's money that's worrying you I can give you six months' wages, and pay your rent somewhere 'til you get on your feet. Maybe somewhere in Belfast?"

"But your...our child. Does that mean nothing to you?"

The Doctor looked away. He put down his pipe and walked to the window. Standing there with his hands behind his back he said, "Thank you. That will be all Mrs Hawthorne. Consider this your three months' notice."

That evening was Halloween night and a small gathering was being held by Miss Delacherois, at the Manor House, at which the Doctor was attending. Left to her own devices Emma decided on a walk down to the Lighthouse. As she weaved her way down the High Street towards the town she watched the people going about their business: the shopkeepers, the carters, the porters, and above them all the Gentry. *In which of those classes did she belong?*

Passing Grace Neill's public house she hesitated. She may find Charlie there, may hear news of him, may convince him to come back with her. *No! She had no home to bring him to. Maybe when, if, she had she could bring him back from whatever path he had strayed down — but not yet!* Past the loafers smoking outside the front door and down the New Street towards the harbour. It was busy now with ships being loaded and unloaded ready to catch the next high tide. Over the noise, she could hear the bellow of cattle and the barking of the drovers' dogs as the beasts were driven onto luggers to be transported across the sea to Montgomery's other harbour in Portpatrick. Every beast that walked aboard was another penny in his pockets.

As Emma approached the lighthouse she looked up at the top deck to see if she could spy her - what, friend? fiend? She knocked on the door and after a few seconds, Willie opened it. He'd obviously been napping and didn't look too happy at the thought of visitors. When he saw Emma he stood unspeaking for a while before he said, "Mrs

Hawthorne? What brings you here? I didn't…please," he stood aside, "come in."

The fire in the little snug at the bottom of the lighthouse was burning fiercely and a comfortable armchair was pulled up close to it. A kettle and some cups sat on a tray on the floor beside it, and pipe and its accoutrements on a small table beside it. Emma gasped at the heat. "Oh Mr McKee! How can you stand it?" taking off her hat and fanning herself with it.

Willie gave a tight smile and gestured to a spare chair by the table. "These old bones feel the chill. Please take a seat. What can I do for you?"

Emma sat. "I just wanted to offer my condolences to you on Henry."

"Aye well. Thank you."

"I didn't get a chance to talk to you at the funeral and say how sorry I was."

"No matter. There was enough talking for the likes of me that day. You've done me a kindness by leaving it a while."

I do miss him. He was a good-hearted boy. Always kind and helpful."

"Lord it's hard to think over forty-odd years have passed since me and Betsy got married."

"Was..Henry your only child?"

Willie threw out another cloud. "Aye well…" Willie creased his brow. "Aye that'd be right. Och, she was a pretty wee thing in her day. She was apprenticed to the old Midwife, a scary old wan named…McBride something; half-mad, half-witch she was. Then the Doctor's father up and died and didn't he come back from Dublin and set up here."

"And Betsy went to work for him?"

"She did. I'd just got a berth as a Master's Mate running from Calcutta to Rangoon…too good a chance to miss for a young sailor." Willie tapped the ash out of his pipe and inspected the contents as though it was the most interesting and important thing he had ever witnessed. He looked up. "It was hard on her, me being away for nigh eight years you understand. Anyway, Henry was waiting for me when I got back."

Emma sat up. "But —"

"There's some questions with no answer, and there's some questions best not asked. I was a good father to the boy, and I loved him but that's all by the bye now." Willie finished his inspection of the pipe and placed it on the table. "Now would ye take a cup of tay?"

"That would be nice. Thank you."

Willie busied himself with the tea making filling the kettle and placing it on the stove.

Taking her opportunity Emma asked, "Willie would it be possible for me to see the town from the top deck?"

"For why? There's naught to see really."

"It just seems interesting to look down on the town from a great height."

"Well if that's what you want you'd be better going up the motte. Still…" he paused. "Maybe what you're looking for is closer than that. G'on aloft if you wish. The tay'll be brewed when ye come down."

Emma pushed the door in the lamp room open and stepped outside onto the upper deck into a bitter Easterly wind. It was colder up here and the smell of the salt water was stronger. Looking out to the East she was overlooking the Harbour with its collection of ships. This vantage point allowed Emma to study them in a way she had never been able to before. The intricate webs of ropes and pulleys traced a fantastic path in her eyes. *Oh! Charlie should have gone for the Navy! He would have loved all this with his quick mind.*

Slowly Emma became aware she was not alone. As she rounded a corner she saw her friend standing there, in his rough clothes and seaboots. Hands gripping the railing, as he looked out towards a row of cottages across the bay. Slowly she came closer until she was almost in touching distance. She turned to look out to sea, to see what was holding his attention. Taking hold of the rail she allowed her hand to come closer and closer to his…until she found that her hand covered his. He glanced over at her for a moment then renewed his gaze towards the horizon. His hand felt cool with calluses from years of hauling on wet ropes. *Not a Gentleman, a working man's hands.* Emma moved closer and, taking hold of his upper arm, she rested her head against his shoulder. His voice seemed to be in her head…inside more than outside. *'I wish I could be back at sea. That all this never happened, out there still. I found nothing but grief on this land,'* he was thinking. The town became less…clear. Her problems receded and for the first time in ages, she felt safe. Then he seemed to become less substantial, to fade, and then he was no longer there.

Emma retraced her steps down to the snug at the bottom of the lighthouse. Willie was sitting there reading a paper; his lips slowly moving. He looked up. "Yer back then? I'd near given up on you. Sit down."

Emma took her place at the table.

Picking up the kettle Willie put it back on the stove which had burnt down. "That pot'll be stewed now. I'll make us a fresh one. You look as you could do with it."

Emma was surprised when she looked out the window. *It's pitch dark! How long have I been up there?* "Willie, what time is it?"

"I just heard three bells strike on the old *Maid of Down*."

Emma looked puzzled. "What?"

Willie smiled as he handed Emma a fresh cup of tea. "About half past nine o'clock."

"But…how long was I up there?"

"Nigh on three hours I'd say. What kept you?"

Emma sipped warily at the strong tea. "Willie, what happened to the man who was here before?"

Willie looked at her. "What did you see up there?"

Emma stared into the fire. "Willie, he spoke to me. I touched him."

The next evening Mrs McKee was very much back in charge of the household; she and Sarah sat gossiping by the stove whilst Emma was relegated to a kitchen chair by the table. Mrs McKee muttered something to Sarah who giggled then covered her mouth and looked guiltily at Emma.

Emma bridled. "I didn't quite catch that Mrs McKee."

"I said you're like a bad smell round here, and the quicker the Doctor throws you out on the street where you belong the better."

"Mrs McKee! I'm still the Housekeeper in this house! I

insist —"

"Ye'll insist on nothing. You threw yersel at the Doctor and now he's finished with you and yer out!"

"Jealous are you? And did he throw you out when you cheated on your husband and then presented him with Henry?"

Sarah's jaw dropped and her eyes opened wide at the sally.

Mrs McKee flew into a towering rage. "I'll see the end of you! And that little harbour rat of a son! The Sergeant is after him now and when he catches him he'll hang!"

Emma choked back the shock. "Sarah I'll bid you Goodnight," and left the room.

Chapter 24

A stiff Easterly was whipping up the white horses and throwing sea spray over Mr Kerr and Mr Delacherois when they met on the beach one morning.

Wiping the spray off his face Mr Kerr said, "I have one hundred and twenty barrels of the best French Brandy arriving on tonight's tide Mr Delacherois, twenty with your name on them. Where d'ye want me to send them?"

"The Castle I think."

"That folly?"

"Why d'ye think I built it?"

"Was it not that Rennie had somewhere to store his gunpowder?"

"The harbour is finished and Rennie has no longer any need for it. Now it can start working for it's keep."

"You're a deep one indeed."

"You're welcome to store your share there as well if you wish…for a…consideration of course."

"A consideration you say? And what would that be?"

"Say twenty shillings a barrel?"

"Say what ye like. I'll pay ten shillings a barrel for your storage."

"Ridiculous! The expense I've gone to."

Mr Kerr shrugged. "Not much use to you without a share in my cargoes is it?"

Mr Delacherois looked sharply at Mr Kerr. "You'd cut me out, would you? B'God Sir if you dare I'll —"

"Be careful now Sir what you say next. We Kerrs don't take well to being threatened."

Mr Delacherois sucked his teeth. "Twelve shillings."

Mr Kerr broke into a wide smile and put his hand out. "Twelve it is then." They shook on the bargain but Mr Kerr held onto his grasp. "Including insurance."

"Insurance?"

"I…we'll hold you responsible for every barrel in your store." Mr Kerr shook Mr Delacherois' hand. "It's a fair deal."

"But —"

"That's the terms." Mr Kerr swiped his stick at some whins. "I'll have the whole load brought there tonight. Mind there's someone there to open the place up…and mind they shield those lanterns from view."

Emma had given up all hope of making a place for herself in the town and had resigned herself to taking up the Doctor's offer to help establish a new life elsewhere. But how could she leave whilst Charlie was in danger; she had to find a way to get him to leave with her. Her household duties seemed to have melted away and she tried to absent herself from the house as much as possible. During the day she took long walks along the dunes, or to the harbour where she often visited Willie, while all the time seeking news of Charlie. In the evenings she would keep to herself in her bedroom, only venturing downstairs when she knew Mrs McKee was out or had gone home for the night.

Emma made a point of walking into the town, past Grace Neill's public house then down the old Murder Lane route to the seafront rather than by the more respectable New Street that had become the main thoroughfare. The lane was lined with cottages with a mixture of the poorest sort, and those who made their living in various illegal, if not immoral, ways. Emma called often upon Mr McGowan on her travels, and it was from him she heard that Charlie was rumoured to have made his home in one of these hovels.

Normally if Emma met the Sergeant, or one of his Constables, on patrol they were happy to stop and report any gossip from about the town. From them she learnt, with some sympathy, that Charlie was suspected of taking up with a gang that made a precarious living stealing from unattended cargo at the quayside, and, more seriously, aiding smugglers that operated from the nearby Copeland Islands under the protection of Mr Kerr of Portavoe, much to the chagrin of Mr Montgomery, the Magistrate.

One morning, before the dawn broke, the Doctor's front door was subject to a furious assault. Such an occurrence rarely heralded good news and the house awoke and lay awake listening, praying it was not news for them, as the Doctor answered the door. "Wait, wait," as he drew open the bolts and opened the door sufficiently as to allow him to look outside. It was one of Sergeant Restrick's men and the Doctor opened the door further. "Boston, what's the matter?"

The Constable gathered his breath for he had been running and was not built for such an activity. "Doctor Leslie I'm sorry but the Sergeant sent me ahead. There's someone been shot by the Coastguard and they're bringing him here."

Pulling his dressing gown closer around him, for the mornings were getting colder, the Doctor ordered the Constable, "Go back then and wait for them. Direct them to the back door. I'll be waiting for them!"

The Constable puffed out his cheeks and hesitated. "Go on now Boston you lazy creature. You're too fond of the porter for your own good. Now go!" commanded the Doctor.

Looking as though he had been ordered into the very cannon's mouth the reluctant Constable staggered off from whence he came.

A cart clattered into the yard accompanied by shouts from the jubilant crowd. The Doctor, dressed now and wearing his rubber apron strode into the kitchen. "Sarah, run across and rouse Cob then boil me some water please."

Sarah curtseyed then dashed out leaving the back door open. "Cob, Cob! The Doctor wants ye!"

Sergeant Restrick entered. "Where do you want him, Doctor?"

The Doctor indicated the kitchen table. "Best in here I

think. It's still too dark outside."

The Sergeant nodded then left as Mr Montgomery came in. "Morning Doctor. Sorry to drag you up at this time." He pulled his gloves off, undid his cloak and then stood close to the stove. "If I'd know we were going to get such sport I'd have brought you, and your fowling piece, along with us."

The Doctor laughed. "I was far too snug for that. What happened?"

"I decided to take Kerr down a peg or two. Too damn cheeky by half." He chortled. "Where's Sarah?"

"She's just rousing Cob."

"She could rouse me any morn. Lucky Cob. D'ye think she'd make us a hot toddy when she gets back?"

"I'm sure if you —"

Mr Montgomery rubbed his hands in glee. "Oh, you should have been there! I haven't had so much fun in years. We came through Kerr's Demesne and bagged the bird showing the light then we —"

Two Constables entered, carrying a limp figure, followed by the Sergeant and Sarah.

The Doctor frowned and then indicated the kitchen table. "Up there with him lads!" He stepped forward and pulled off the cap covering the victim's face. "Good God Montgomery! This is young Charlie, Mrs Hawthorne's son."

Mr Montgomery broke away from negotiating hot toddies with Sarah. "Who?"

"Mrs Hawthorne, my housekeeper. Remember the young lad accused of stealing at the party here? You held court in this —"

"Oh yes! Such a party. I was telling —"

Cob entered.

"Cob my boy, please go and get Mrs Hawthorne." Cob stood and stared at Charlie on the kitchen table. "Fly boy, fly," and Cob dashed upstairs.

The Doctor indicated Charlie. "Mrs Hawthorne. My Housekeeper." The Doctor turned to the Sergeant. "John, would you have one of your men run and get Mrs McKee?"

Sarah placed a tray of hot toddies on a side table prompting the police party to crowd around jostling for a glass. "Boston!" said the Sergeant, "Put that back and go and fetch Mrs McKee." The Constable protested. "At the double Constable, or I'll have you rowing a beat around the islands for a month." The Constable looked as though he was going to burst into tears but replaced the toddy untouched and left. Raising his glass to Sarah the Sergeant toasted her. "To Sarah…and the cup that cheers!"

"Ah thank you Sarah," Mr Montgomery accepted his toddy from Sarah's own hand. He sniffed and looked down at Charlie. "Yes By God! I recall the young rogue." He took a draft and raised his glass to Sarah. "Your health Sarah. Told you he'd come to a bad end."

Glumly the Sergeant remarked, "They don't hang 'em no more."

"More's the pity!" Mr Montgomery replied.

"Nor even transport 'em. That's going too."

Mr Montgomery poked Charlie with his walking stick. "Well, hard labour then. From the beef on this one, it'd do him no end of good."

The Sergeant sniggered, "Maybe Constable Boston could do with some hard labour?" and the company laughed again.

Cob returned. "She's on her way down."

"Thank you Cob." The Doctor started cutting away Charlie's shirt and breeches. "I'll need you round here...no by his head. I may need you to hold him down."

Emma rushed in. She stopped dead and looked at Charlie. "My Charlie!" She grasped his hand and looked at the company. "What have you done? What have you done to him?"

The Doctor paused in his examination. "Emma. Emma! Let me work. The boy's been shot and —"

Emma gasped. "Shot?" She glanced around the company. "Which one of you has shot my baby? My Charlie? He's only a child, no more."

Mr Montgomery looked at his drink. "That was good." He looked at Constable Boston's portion still steaming on the tray. He looked around. "He's not touched that has he?" A few of the party shook their heads.

"Didn't have time," the Sergeant assured him.

"Oh well, best not waste it then," said Mr Montgomery replacing his own toddy with Constable Boston's. Mr Montgomery turned to Emma. "He was shot by one of the Coastguard, damn fine shot too, as he was coming ashore with a boatload of smugglers."

Emma protested, "But he's but a child."

"He took to his heels, and failed to stop when called upon to do so." Mr Montgomery turned to the Sergeant. "Fifty yards at a moving target in the dark By God."

The Doctor looked up from his work. He held a ball in a set of forceps. "Straight through the spine. He'll not be running anywhere again."

Emma grabbed the Doctor by the arm. "But he'll live Doctor? Tell me he'll live!"

Charlie had been put to bed upstairs and the Magistrate, the Sergeant, and the Doctor were comfortably ensconced in the study. The Doctor himself had lit the fire, and the smell of ham and eggs filled the house as Sarah prepared a celebration breakfast for the party.

"Like a little fat partridge! Low and fast I tell you!" wheezed Mr Montgomery to the company as Mrs McKee entered. The Sergeant and Mr Montgomery mumbled some greetings then fell silent as she looked past them to the patient on the table. She was a woman both feared and respected and who could make your passing either soft or very, very hard.

The Doctor struggled to his feet, as he'd kicked his boots off and they'd become entangled at his feet. "Betsy! Have you —"

"I spoke to Sarah. Is he upstairs?"

The Doctor nodded. "Indeed." He turned to his guests. "If you'd excuse us Betsy and I have some issues to discuss." He nodded to the side table. "There's a decanter there, and if you need a refill ring the bell." He bowed and then indicated the back room. "Betsy?"

The Doctor drew aside the curtain before he opened the door and followed Mrs McKee through closing it behind him. "Well, Betsy what do you think?"

Mrs McKee turned to face him. "I think that little rat killed my Henry, and," indicating the room, "knows too much about your research."

"Nobody would listen to a word," protested the Doctor.

"That's how rumours start…and you nor Mr Delacherois don't want that at all."

"To be honest I doubt he'll live. His backbone is shot through and I couldn't find the wadding."

"That's as may be," replied Mrs McKee as she went through the range of medicines on the shelf. She picked one and gave it a shake before holding it up to the light."

The Doctor shuddered. "Dear God remind me not to get on the wrong side of you."

Chapter 25

Sarah and Cob were sitting by the kitchen table holding hands. The table had been scrubbed down, and there was no trace of Charlie to be seen. Mrs McKee nodded approvingly "Well done Sarah. It's easy to see who'll be taking over from me here when I retire."

Sarah blushed and Cob squeezed her hand.

Mrs McKee handed Sarah the vial of medicine. "Sarah dear. Take this up to Emma, it's for Charlie...and mind he's to drain every last drop of it."

Sarah nodded. "I'll do it meself."

"No!" Mrs McKee interjected. "Emma should give it to him. She's his mother. At least that's what she claims."

Sarah bridled at this. "She's not as bad as you sometimes make out. She's just...I don't know...unlucky."

Mrs McKee smiled. "You've a good heart girl. Maybe take her up a cup of tea while you're at it?"

Emma sat on the bed holding Charlie's hand. Her eyes were red from weeping and she was pressing a cold compress to his forehead. "Charlie, Charlie, my love, my sweet. I'm here. I'm so sorry. I brought you to this place. It's all my fault."

Charlie was slipping in and out of delirium, writhing in pain. He gripped her hand tightly. "Mum, Mum! Are you there? It hurts so much." Blood was leaking from the bandages that swaddled his middle. "Mum, am I going to die?" then he lapsed into a fevered silence.

There was a knock at the door and Sarah entered. *That bedspread's ruined. I'll never get the blood out of that.* "How is the wee thing Emma? Is he sleeping?"

Emma turned her red-rimmed eyes to Sarah. "He's just gone over. Oh Sarah —"

"Hush now. I've some medicine for you to give him," she handed Emma the vial Mrs McKee had given her. "You're to make sure he takes the lot. And I've brought up a cup of tea for you."

"Oh thank you Sarah dear. You're the only friend Charlie and I have!"

Sarah looked uncomfortable. *Ye've brought most of it on yourselves.* "I'll just put your cup down here, shall I? And make sure he takes it all."

"Thank you."

"It was Mrs McKee suggested you could do with a cup... you know she's not as bad as all that."

Emma looked at the tea doubtfully. "Did you make this

210

tea yourself?"

"Indeed I did. Aren't Cob and I sitting downstairs having a cup and didn't she suggest that I brought one up for yourself as soon as she saw it?"

Emma smiled. "Thank you." She reached for the vial and took the top off before smelling it and recoiled. "Dear God, the smell. What is it?"

Sarah picked up some of Charlie's clothes that had been dropped on the floor in the effort to get him into bed. "I wouldn't have a notion. You'd have to ask the Doctor."

Emma put her hand behind Charlie's head and placed it in between his lips. "Drink this dear. It's from the Doctor." Charlie started to move his mouth away but Emma held him firmly. "Come on dear. Drink it all up. Drink up for Mummy...there all done."

Emma put the vial on the bedside table and picked up a cloth to mop his lips when Charlie suddenly sat bolt upright, looked wide-eyed at Emma, and then vomited blood.

Charlie's screams echoed throughout the house drawing the Doctor and his guests out from the study into the hall, where they stood looking up in horror towards Charlie's bedroom.

Mrs McKee appeared on the landing carrying fresh linen for the Doctor's bed and paused joining in with the listeners. The screaming abruptly stopped. "It's done." She wiped some dust off the bannister rail and tutted, before carrying on to change the Doctor's bed.

Later that day, when Emma had been sedated and put to bed in her own room, the Doctor and Mrs McKee stood at

Charlie's bedside surveying the corpse.

"It was a hard way to go, Betsy," the Doctor remarked.

"Not as bad as my Henry, burnt alive by that little rat."

The Doctor was unhappy; he was neither a cruel nor a vindictive man. "Is she…is Emma asleep?"

"What Sarah gave her will keep her quiet for a while."

"I've sent to the Undertaker to measure him up. We'll keep the coffin in the cellar, and I'll get Cob to help me carry the remains downstairs later. We might as well keep him there for now."

"When d'ye plan to pass him through?"

The Doctor considered the matter. "Well we'd best strike while he's fresh I suppose. I'll send Mr Delacherois a note and see if he's free this evening."

"We've never had a baptised one afore." Mrs McKee observed.

"That's true, well I suppose he's baptised. Isn't he?"

Mrs McKee shrugged. "He's English so Lord only knows. I'll tell Shields to bring the coffin here and box him up. He can arrange the funeral for the day after tomorrow. If the passing doesn't work you can just pop him back in the coffin and none's the wiser."

"Have faith, Betsy. If we can use this young man to teach us how to conquer death the world won't quibble over a few shortcuts."

"He was a cowardly dishonest viscous wee shite when he died." Mrs McKee looked at the body. "And I don't expect him to be anything other than a cowardly dishonest wee viscous shite if you do happen to bring him back."

It was evening and Mrs McKee carried a tray into the Doctor's study. She nodded to Mr Delacherois who was sitting opposite the Doctor. "Good Evening Sir. I've brought a few sandwiches for afore you start."

The Doctor rose and cleared some space for Mrs McKee to set the tray down. "Very kind, very…Oh these look very good. And Sarah?"

"I've given her the night off. Cob and her are away to a dance out the Cottown direction."

Mr Delacherois spoke through a mouthful of sandwich, "Ah! To be young again. Eh Betsy? And Emma?"

"Once was enough for me. Anyway, I've got her full of a sleeping draft and she'll no bother the pair of you."

"Well, will you not be joining us, Betsy? To see history being made."

"Somebody has to keep an eye on the house whilst you pair are at your doings. I'll be upstairs in the kitchen if you need me."

Mrs McKee left.

The Doctor sat silently and then turned to Mr Delacherois. "Well Sir, shall we begin?"

Chapter 26

The Doctor and Mr Delacherois descended the back steps down to the cellar. "Mind here! These steps are slippery. I really must get Cob to swab them. The girls won't go down here, and I don't like to ask Mrs McKee in case she falls."

They entered the cellar behind the font. It was dark outside already, and little light came through the windows above. The cellar smelt of damp, and the sand beneath their feet revealed dark trails when they scuffed it.

The Doctor paused at a small table by the door and used a brimstone and flint to light two lanterns before handing one to Mr Delacherois. They held the lamps up to throw the light further into the recesses. A plain coffin stood on two trestles by the double doors where Mr Shields had left it.

"Is it in there?" Mr Delacherois asked.

"Indeed so. Cob and I placed the remains in there this afternoon after we prised Emma away."

"I hope you'll be rid of her soon. Jane doesn't like the idea of you being in the house with her at all."

The Doctor looked embarrassed. "You may assure Miss Delacherois that I have given Emma her marching orders... but I can't just throw her out can I?"

"You've been warned that's all I can say. Jane is not Mrs Hawthorne's greatest admirer. Leave your lantern by the font and I'll hang mine up," he indicated a hook near the double doors, "here." Mr Delacherois stood back. "There. That should give us enough light to work."

Both men removed their coats and rolled up their sleeves, then the Doctor removed the coffin lid.

"I'll take the feet," Mr Delacherois offered. The Doctor moved to the head of the coffin and took a firm grasp under the cadaver's arms. "Up!" and both men heaved the body and lifted it across to the font. "He's heavier than he looks," said Mr Delacherois, "and down."

The men stood back and looked at Charlie's remains balanced on the edge of the font.

"Nearly ate me out of house and home this one did" offered the Doctor.

The Doctor opened a large book then dipped his finger in the font water and traced some symbols onto Charlie's forehead, his breast, and his navel. He nodded to Mr Delacherois and they both lowered Charlie into the still water.

"How long?" asked Mr Delacherois. He looked into the font. "I can't see anything."

The Doctor thumbed through the book. "The sources aren't clear on that." He shrugged. "The infants took minutes. But…"

The men waited. After a while, Mr Delacherois trailed his hand across the surface of the water. "Do you know I think the water's getting warmer?"

The Doctor gingerly dipped a finger in. "This has been most unscientific of me. I should have been recording temperatures all along."

They watched for about ten minutes. "I wonder if Mrs McKee would make us a cup of tea?" suggested Mr Delacherois.

The Doctor allowed the question to go unanswered for a while, then he glanced at the door to the kitchen stairs. "I suppose we could just nip up?"

"Exactly. We could even carry the cups down here again."

"And it is still quite cold in here." The Doctor lifted up his lantern, moved to the kitchen stairs and slid the bolt open. "I'll ask her to —"

Mr Delacherois withdrew his hand from the water with a yelp. "Good Lord man! The water's boiling!"

Putting the lantern on the ground by the open door the Doctor hurried back. Now the surface of the water was roiling, with great clouds of steam rising from the surface up to the stone ceiling, where it fell back down as a warm rain. "What on earth!" The Doctor tentatively touched the surface of the water and then quickly withdrew his digit. "He'll be cooked!" He leafed through the book again. "This…it doesn't…this seems to be unusual."

With a great splash, Charlie sat up throwing boiling water over both spectators. His eyes opened wide and he let out a great unending scream, as his hands grabbed each side of the font. The scream continued as he remained sitting bolt upright staring straight ahead. The scream ended, and he turned his head around as though seeking the source of the sounds. Spectral shapes rose translucent out of the water, then fell back in with shrieks of anger and pain.

Holding the book across his chest like a shield the Doctor spoke, "Ah…Charlie old man. How're you feeling?"

Charlie swivelled his head in the Doctor's direction.

"Probably not the best eh?"

Mr Delacherois stood there with his mouth open. "My God his eyes! What's wrong with his eyes? They're black!"

Charlie levered himself from the font and then lowered himself onto the stone plinth. Unsteadily he stood upright and took a few tentative steps holding tight to the side of the trough.

The Doctor put the book down. "That's it Charlie lad. You get your bearings eh?"

"It's impossible! His back was broken! He can't be walking!" said Mr Delacherois. "The spine's still shot through."

Charlie fell silent and turned his head to face him. His eyes stared sightlessly at Mr Delacherois, his jaw opened, then shut, wide open, and then tight shut, snapping. Like some monstrous creature, Charlie staggered towards Mr Delacherois - teeth furiously working.

Mr Delacherois started backwards and then edged himself around the font keeping it between Charlie and himself. "Damnit. It's coming after me! How the hell can it see?" The Charlie thing left a trail in the sand behind it; feet dragging, and two plump little fists shredding the empty air before him - searching. Mr Delacherois backed away and Charlie stalked after him, making little mewling noises as he did so.

"Damnit George! Do something!"

The Doctor looked around uncertainly but nothing sprang to hand. Gathering up his courage he moved towards Charlie. "Steady Charlie now, steady. Good Charlie." He held out his hand.

Charlie stopped and inclined his face towards him, his jaw opening, closing ceaselessly, head darting from side to side.

Nervously the Doctor advanced still holding out his hand as though approaching an uncertain dog. "Now Charlie old man. I can see why you feel somewhat put upon…it's blind! It's reacting to my voice. Call him!"

Mr Delacherois cleared his throat, "Charlie! Hey Charlie!" and the creature shuffled round, rotating its head as though to pinpoint the source of the sound.

The Doctor picked up Mr Delacherois's lantern from the font. "I wonder if we could guide it into the cage?" He opened up the shield and cast the light upon Charlie. "Here Charlie, here."

Charlie twisted back again searching for the source. The Doctor stepped forward clicking his fingers, and Charlie crept closer as though scenting his prey. The Doctor backed away towards the open cage Charlie followed snapping at the air.

"It also seems to be attracted to light!"

"I'll get the other lantern and help you draw it in." Mr Delacherois gingerly skirted along the wall to the kitchen door where he picked up the lamp left by the Doctor. As he did the movement of the light attracted Charlie. He shrieked as he darted towards Mr Delacherois, who stumbled and fell backwards, the light landed between him and the open door to the kitchen steps.

With a dreadful gibbering sound, the creature disappeared up the steps. "Betsy!" cried the Doctor and, leaping over Mr Delacherois, followed the creature up towards the kitchen.

After a few minutes, the Doctor returned. He found Mr Delacherois shaken and nursing his hand. "Straight out the back door. Thank God Betsy was dozing by the fire and didn't attract its attention; didn't even wake. Show me your hand."

Mr Delacherois offered the Doctor his hand. "Bit me on the way past by God."

The Doctor frowned. "I don't like bites at the best of times. But a bite from that." He bound Mr Delacherois' hand up in his handkerchief. "Best get that upstairs. I want to wash the wound and get some leeches on it to draw any poison out."

"John, what happened?"

The Doctor shrugged. "I don't know. We're in deep waters here. We have learnt that maybe a soul makes a difference and that the process does seem to repair wounds… the boiling water is interesting…"

"But where is it? Where did it go?"

"By the time I got up there I caught a glimpse of it just — "

"Imagine if it gets out…is seen by the townsfolk. They'll recognise him, and ask where it's come from. What happened."

" — going down the old well."

The following afternoon Charlie's funeral took place at the Parish Church on Mount Misery with the Reverend Hill presiding. Both the Doctor and Mr Delacherois attended, keeping a wary ear to the ground for rumours of Charlie; for no sight nor sound from him had been reported since he was seen going down the old well in the stable yard.

Still drugged by Mrs McKee, Emma, clung onto the arm of a reluctant Sarah and Cob; and a few onlookers who neither liked nor cared for Charlie, but who did enjoy a good funeral, made up the numbers.

Afterwards, Mr Delacherois heaved a sign of relief. "We're lucky that Mrs McKee kept the mother drugged. I wouldn't want to be there if she'd insisted on a last look at her only son and found the coffin empty, except for two sacks of McGilton's horse feed."

The Doctor swung his walking stick at a clump of grass, then looked out over the sea towards the islands. "Where is he though, that's the question. We can't expect him to remain invisible forever. That's when the questions will start."

"What if we sealed your well?"

"The trouble is that the well's supposed to be connected to the old river, and that — "

"Empties onto the beach." Mr Delacherois sucked his

teeth. "Well we either hope he never turns up, and that's probably too much to hope for, or…"

"Or?"

"Or we go looking for him."

"Where?" queried the Doctor.

"Do you fancy being lowered down the well on a rope?"

"No, God forbid!" muttered the Doctor, in some alarm.

Mr Delacherois sighed. "No, nor me. So how may we draw him out?"

"I have an idea. Come to my house after dark tonight, and bring a storm lantern and your pistols."

Chapter 27

That evening as night fell a waxing moon lit up the yard as if captured by a daguerreotype, and then a passing cloud plunged all back into darkness. Mr Delacherois and the Doctor sat in the kitchen. In front of both was a charged brace of pistols. The Doctor's father's old Sea Service Pattern 1824s sitting ready, as they had done so many times before when the Admiral had fought alongside Rajah Brooks in a more heroic age, and those belonging to Mr Delacherois, an elegant pair of French model 1822 percussion pistols, with which he practised on the foreshore, to the delight of the children, and the terror of the lady-folk.

Topping up his guest's glass with Cognac, and then his own the Doctor explained, "I've pulled the wooden cover over the well, and placed a tin bucket full of old horseshoes in it."

"Thankee…I wonder how long we'll have to wait."

The Doctor took a sip. "Mmm…we'd best go easy on this tonight." He lit the candles in the storm lanterns and then placed them beside the pistols. "Cheer up. Sunrise is about seven o'clock, so we may retire to our beds then."

Mr Delacherois indicated the two chairs by the stove. "We could sit there nice and snug."

The Doctor laughed. "We'd be fast asleep in no time. Best keep to the kitchen chairs I think. At least if we fade we'll fall off with a bump."

Mr Delacherois grumbled. "And this is why I've always detested hunting fowl. Too damn early for me."

"What do you think we should do if Charlie appears?"

Pointing to his pistols Mr Delacherois said, "I know what I'm going to do! I'll…wait a minute, you've not got some damn fool notion of capturing the creature have you?"

"It's a fascinating —"

"It bloody well bit me! No thank you very much, but it's a ball through the brain for that one."

"If we —"

"No! We can build a cage around the font next time, or chain the cadaver up first. But this one is out of control." Mr Delacherois tapped the butt of a pistol. "This one dies before the townsfolk hang the pair of us."

"I suppose you're right. It's such a waste, but it's probably for the best." The Doctor pulled out his pipe. "Normally Mrs McKee doesn't allow me to smoke in the kitchen but I think on this occasion."

Mr Delacherois pulled out a pouch and tossed it across

the table. "Try this."

The Doctor opened the pouch and sniffed. "Mr Kerr's I think. What would the Magistrate say?"

"As long as he doesn't hang me for smoking American tobacco I don't give a fig what he says."

The Doctor grinned. "And he never seems to say too much about it when he's guzzling down my brandy."

Mr Delacherois raised his glass. "To the Magistrate!"

"And confusion to the Excisemen!" They both toasted one another.

"So what are your thoughts about —"

A crash came from outside.

"The bucket!" exclaimed the Doctor.

"Your pistols!" Mr Delacherois pushed one pistol into his belt and took up the other, then, lantern in his spare hand, led the way into the yard.

The moon was hidden so they reluctantly approached the well holding up the lights before, and especially behind, them.

The wooden cover had been pushed to one side and the bucket was on the ground surrounded by horseshoes. Sultan and Sorrel wickered in their boxes and kicked the stall doors.

"Look here. The top's all wet." Mr Delacherois held the lamp up to show where something wet had been dragged over the parapet of the well. "There are tracks here!"

Footprints led through the wet grass towards the orchard. They both held up the lanterns. "We'd better follow," said the Doctor.

"You keep an eye to our left, and I'll do the right side." Mr Delacherois cocked his pistol. When the answering click indicated the Doctor had made his pistol ready they moved forward together, both scanning the moon-cast shadows on their flanks as though their very lives depended upon it.

Suddenly there was a sound of galloping from the orchard and Nero screamed. At that moment the clouds allowed the moon through to shine upon the scene. The Charlie creature was atop Nero and was attempting to savage the poor animal's neck with its teeth.   Both Mr Delacherois and the Doctor discharged their pistols at once, then the moon disappeared again cloaking the horror in darkness.

"Did you get him?" asked Mr Delacherois.

"I can't be sure."

They both set their empty pistols on the ground and then drew the other from their belts. "Ready?" asked the Doctor.

Mr Delacherois armed his pistol. "Ready!"

The Doctor also cocked his pistol, then opened the gate into the orchard. Their lights quickly sought out and found Nero; he was standing quivering in fear in front of them. The Doctor quickly examined the shaking animal. "He seems all right. No sign of a wound. I was half afeared I'd shot my own donkey."

Mr Delacherois had been examining the ground. He pointed to what appeared to be a black stain on the grass. "Here, bring your lamp here." Together they both examined the mark.

The Doctor put his finger on it and then held the finger up to the light. He rubbed his fingers together. "Blood by God. One of us has hit something, and it's not Nero."

"The tracks led down there." Mr Delacherois pointed to

the kitchen garden with a stand of trees behind it.

The Doctor stood still for a moment then turned. "We'd better charge the other pistols afore we go after it."

Mr Delacherois looked into the dark. "I expect we'd better."

The wind was getting up as the Doctor and Mr Delacherois approached the kitchen garden. Cob, at Mrs McKee's direction, had planted plots of vegetables. At the back rows of beans and other legumes supported by canes, marked the demarcation with a steep bank of whin bushes and rough pasture that ran down towards the harbour.

The smell of crushed greenery rose up from their footsteps, mingled with something sour.

The Doctor pointed to where some canes had been broken. "Look here, and here. Something has pushed through this!"

Gathering their courage they shouldered their way between the rows and stood at the beginning of the whins listening and looking.

Mr Delacherois spoke quietly. "We'll not pick up a trail through that."

"Nevertheless we'll have to try. If we don't stop him now, he'll be amongst the cottages at the old Salt-works, and God knows who'll see him down there."

With a pause that signposted their reluctance both men stepped out together into the pasture. The whin bushes threw insane shapes when the clouds allowed the moon to shine through, then disappeared as though they had slipped back into the darkness to wait in ambush.

Mr Delacherois put his hand on the Doctor's arm. "Hist! Over there. There's something moving." Both men stood stock still attempting to discern a shape in the silhouette that changed in the gusting wind. After a while, a dark shape emerged from the shadows and stood in the open unmoving.

The Doctor signalled to Mr Delacherois and they both separated to stalk their quarry from either side. Another shape, much larger, manifested itself and took position alongside the former, as though it also was standing in challenge…waiting.

A light appeared illuminating both the Doctor and Mr Delacherois, and in front of them, a small black cow with its calf at foot.

"Gentlemen," said Constable Boston adjusting the beam of his bull's-eye lantern. "Are you drunk?" He watched the strange pair as a man confronted by a pair of escaped lunatics. "Do you seek to hunt poor old Mother McKeown's milk cow for sport?"

Embarrassed Mr Delacherois and the Doctor uncocked their pistols and thrust them into their belts.

The Doctor shielded his eyes from the light. "Indeed not. We were seeking to ah."

Mr Delacherois moved close to the lantern holding his own up. "Ah Constable Boston. No indeed. We were at Doctor Leslie's and we…heard a commotion in the yard and we…ah"

The Doctor jumped in. "Constable Boston stout fellow. We sought to apprehend an intruder…a prowler and…"

The Constable held his peace for a moment then

remarked. "I heard shots. Was that you?"

Mr Delacherois spoke hastily, "It…he tried to steal the Doctor's donkey."

"Poor old Nero. The brute was upon his back when…"

"You shot at him? For sitting upon the beast's back?"

"He ran Constable…we're in hot pursuit."

Constable Boston dimmed his lantern, then took out a handkerchief and blew his nose. "Fortunate indeed that you each had your pistols to hand. I think you gentlemen should go to your beds. I'll keep an eye out for…donkey rustlers on my beat."

Chapter 28

The Doctor and Mr Delacherois stood aside the Castle on top of the motte and looked out to sea. A blustery easterly gale was piling the waves up on the shore and filling the air with the tang of salt.

Leaning on his stick Mr Delacherois shrugged deeper into his greatcoat, then said, "Well I don't know where else to look."

His voice raised in the wind the Doctor scanned the dunes below. "Those rabbits have been dead a good while."

"Indeed if it wasn't foxes that took them anyway."

The Doctor shrugged. "Maybe the creature has fled...or even..."

"We'd better hope so....for all our sake."

"I just can't get the thought of the creature stumbling

across that wee girl out of my head."

"Patterson's lassie Florence? God help us if it has. The townspeople will hold us responsible," responded Mr Delacherois.

"The Sergeant's been bending Montgomery's ear over the other night with us a-hunting milk cows."

"The wee lassie's brother claimed that it was Charlie who called her over."

"Boston's a babbling fool. I'm more worried about Kerr going about stirring up the townsfolk against the authorities." The Doctor set his cap against the gusts. "There's a search party over by the warrens. We'd better try there next."

As the Doctor and Mr Delacherois approached the Warren they saw a crowd gathered and increased their pace pushing their way through the throng to the centre.

The Sergeant looked up. "Doctor, Mr Delacherois...well we've found her the poor wee thing."

The remains of a young girl was lying on the cold sand. Her hair was wet and tangled covering her face. The Doctor stooped down to examine her and as he did a growl erupted from the crowd. Startled the Doctor looked up at the Sergeant who paused then nodded.

"Quieten down you lot. If you would Doctor?"

The Doctor glanced uncertainly around then gently rolled the body to one side. "The sand beneath is dry." He manipulated Flory's arm. "She was killed yesterday evening by my estimate. It rained last night but the ground is dry, and the body is starting to loosen up now."

The Sergeant nodded. "That fits. Tell me, gentlemen. Flory's brother tells me they were out looking for a lost hen yesterday when they heard someone calling to them from behind a hedge. Whoever it was said he had the hen there and for Florry to come and get it."

The Doctor and Mr Delacherois looked at each other, and then Mr Delacherois offered, "Tinkers maybe? There been a few seen about recently I believe."

"Constable Boston tells me you were troubled yourselves the other night. Someone was on Nero's back he said?"

"True, true. We met the Constable when we were searching for the intruder," said the Doctor.

The Sergeant paused for a moment looking at the girl. "With pistols drawn?" He gestured to one of the crowd. "Cover the wee thing up, and take her home to her Mammy."

The Doctor and Mr Delacherois turned to go.

"The girl's brother said it was Charlie who called her over. He recognised him from school," said the Sergeant addressing their backs as they departed.

The next morning, just as the sun was starting to appear pale and watery from over the lighthouse, the Magistrate and the Reverend Hill stood on Mount Misery while the Sergeant supervised two gravediggers hard at work.

Pulling his old army greatcoat tighter against the chill the Magistrate offered the Reverend a snuff box. "A pinch Hill? Against the cold."

Distracted the Reverend watched the diggers. "Thank you, no. You can't seriously expect —"

"I expect nothing Reverend." He sneezed.

"But the child's mother. How could such a thing be true? The Hawthorne boy was dead. Mr Shields was quite certain and he should know."

The Magistrate shuffled his feet on the cold ground. "Mr Shields is a fine Undertaker and tells me he boxed the boy himself."

"Well then?"

"Well, then we wait." The Magistrate nodded towards the grave. "Not long now I expect."

The Sergeant looked over towards the Magistrate "That's it, Sir. We're down."

The Magistrate walked over to the graveside. "Good men. Now place the box out here...to the side."

This was done and Charlie's plain wooden coffin lay on the grass beside the pile of dark earth that had been excavated.

The Magistrate removed a leather case from the folds of his coat and offered the contents around. "Cheroot?" The Sergeant and the gravediggers accepted with thanks, but the Reverend looked askance. "In case corruption has set in Reverend."

Hastily the Reverend accepted and they all lit the small black cigars from a lantern. The Magistrate examined the coffin. "Right lads open it up."

One of the gravediggers picked up a small crowbar and prised the lid free. With a glance and a nod from the Magistrate, he lifted it to reveal two sacks of horse feed.

"Bless my soul!" exclaimed the Reverend.

The Magistrate threw his cheroot into the open grave. "Sergeant send those sacks to the barracks if you please. And have one of your Constables tell Mr Shields I want a word with him as soon as is convenient; now would be the best time I think. He may find me in the Downshire having breakfast."

Rumour spread fast and by the time the Sergeant and Mr Shields had joined Mr Montgomery, the Magistrate in the Downshire Arms the news of the empty coffin had spread far and wide.

The Magistrate addressed Mr Shields, the Undertaker. "Are you certain the boy was dead?"

Nodding Mr Shields assured the company. "As dead as can be. I've worked in this business nigh forty years, as did my father before me, and I can assure you I've never buried a live one." He shifted uncomfortably in his seat. "At least I don't think I have."

The Magistrate sat back in his chair and looked at the smoke from his pipe curling upwards. He poured a little more coffee into his cup and offered the pot around. "Gentlemen?"

Turning back to Mr Shields the Magistrate asked, "And did you box the remains yourself?"

"I did. That very night."

The Sergeant leaned across the table. "So the coffin was closed? There was no wake for the boy?"

"I expect the mother didn't want one, them being English. They don't do they?"

Stuffing his pipe the Sergeant asked, "So you drove the coffin out to the grave the next morning?"

"I did. As soon as picked it up I —"

Drawing himself upright the Magistrate furrowed his brow. "Picked him up you say. So you didn't keep the body in the mortuary yard overnight?"

"Oh, no sir. I took the coffin to the Doctor's the previous night, and boxed him up there and then."

The Magistrate turned to the Sergeant. "You've spoken to the girl's brother?"

"Indeed I have."

"And what do you think of him."

"A sensible lad sir."

The Magistrate drew on his pipe. "D'ye know I'd like to meet him. Is the house far?"

Chapter 29

After the Magistrate and the Sergeant had spoken to Flory's brother they walked together towards New Street.

They paused to study the horizon then the Sergeant spoke. "So Charlie's not dead? I saw him die myself - shot through the backbone."

"It would seem not if we are to believe the boy."

"Mr Shields won't be happy thinking he buried a live one...no, I don't believe that! My money is still on Kerr making some sort of mischief about the place."

"For what end Sergeant, for what end?" murmured the Magistrate. He paused and touched the Sergeant's arm. "McGilton's horse feed?"

"Fraid not sir. They supply half the town."

"Surely since the Anatomy Act was passed there is no

shortage of cadavers."

"He had more than you could count from the Workhouse during the Famine years. Rosebank must have been a veritable charnel house."

The Magistrate eased himself into the chair opposite the Doctor. "It's been too early a start for these old bones. I don't suppose Mrs McKee is making a pot of tea eh?"

Uncertain as to the findings of this morning's disinterment the Doctor smiled weakly and rang the bell. "So how did this morning go?"

"Well we opened up the —"

Lizzie entered the Doctor's study and dropped a curtsy. "You rang Sir?"

"Ah, Lizzie. Would you serve us some tea and," looking at the Magistrate, "some sandwiches?"

The Magistrate shook his head. "My thanks but I have breakfasted already."

"Just tea then please Lizzie." As Lizzie left the room the Doctor turned back to the Magistrate. "I'm sorry. You were saying."

"Well as you know we opened young Hawthorne's grave this morning…"

"And?"

"And it was empty. Not a trace of the body. Just some sacks of grain…for weight I expect."

"Good Lord! And what will you do now?"

"I'll question those involved.

Lizzie entered and placed a tray on the table. The Doctor busied himself with pouring. "And your thoughts to date?"

"I'm confident that the remains were delivered intact to this house on the evening before the funeral."

The Doctor passed a cup of tea to the Magistrate. "Dear, dear what a confusion."

"Why did you insist the body was to be held here overnight? As I understand it there was no wake."

"Well, the mother…Mrs Hawthorne. We —"

"We?"

"Mr Delacherois and myself felt that Mrs Hawthorne would feel happier that the boy was near her."

"Did either Mr Delacherois or yourself cause the coffin to be opened that evening?"

"No, no indeed. There was no need. Mrs Hawthorne was indisposed and in no state to view the remains."

"So as far as you are concerned the body was in the coffin when it was held here overnight?"

"I have… have no reason to think otherwise...yet."

It was a dreich day as Mr Delacherois and the Doctor were walking towards the harbour, and the smell from the cattle being loaded on the beach drifted across to the harbour.

Pulling the folds of his boat cloak tighter around him as he avoided the piles of dung outside the Downshire Hotel the Doctor continued. "I simply told him that I couldn't be held responsible for what happened between the mortuary chamber and my house."

"How did he reply to that?"

"Oh not best pleased but as long as we stick to our guns and deny ever having opened the coffin he may huff and puff all he wishes."

Exasperated Mr Delacherois swiped his cane at a stack of lobster pots. "So where the Devil is the wretched creature?"

"I don't know…but I believe someone may."

"Damnit Doctor pray stop talking in riddles!" A grey-faced Mr Delacherois stopped and looked up at the lighthouse. "I've other things to worry about! I've not slept for days." He turned to face the Doctor. "I may have to apply to you for a sleeping draft."

The Doctor touched Mr Delacherois' arm. "Steady on old man. We'll see ourselves clear of this yet. And think about what we've achieved."

Mr Delacherois looked towards a seal swimming between the ships. "Pray then who is this mysterious person?"

"Mrs Hawthorne herself."

"The boy's mother! Why… how would —"

"I believe the creature has been in contact with her… tapped a window…who knows but Mrs McKee was talking to Mr Devonport the butcher and he —"

"George! I'm at my wit's end here."

"And he passed remark that he hoped the house was happy with all the fowl we'd purchased."

"And?"

"And we've had nary a bird in the house this fortnight past."

Mr Delacherois' nose wrinkled at this. "So you're putting two and two together and —"

"Mrs Hawthorne has been purchasing fowl for the benefit of another."

"By God, she's feeding the brute!"

"That is my conclusion also."

"Well then, we need to interrogate her immediately!"

The Doctor held up a cautionary hand. "I wouldn't expect a mother to give up her son."

Exasperated Mr Delacherois stopped again and looked at the Doctor. "Her son! He…it's a monster!"

"Nevertheless her son."

"Well, then we must force her!"

"Or we may lie in wait tonight and follow her."

About seven of the evening, when a weak moon was barely discernible through the clouds in the night sky, Mr Delacherois and the Doctor sat in the hay barn. About eight o'clock they saw Emma, wrapped in her shawl, emerge from the back door into the stable yard and retrieve a bundle from the bushes lining the drive before continuing towards the town.

Keeping to the shadows they silently stalked her along the High Street as she weaved her way between late shoppers, and early pot-house crowds. The sound of shutters being closed, blinds being drawn, and locks turned, as shops shut for the night, echoed in her wake as she made her way along the lane-way to the bottom of the motte.

The Doctor pulled Mr Delacherois into a porch and they watched as Emma climbed the spiral path that led up to the Castle itself.

"By God, the brute's there right enough!" exclaimed Mr Delacherois.

The Doctor strained to see Emma in the gloom. "The tower-house would seem most likely. Now the harbour is completed it remains merely as a folly."

"And I don't want people poking around in there, they have no business!" Mr Delacherois stepped back into the road and drew a pistol. "Come now. Let's be after it."

"Steady now. I want to see if she still carries the parcel when she leaves."

Replacing the pistol in the folds of his greatcoat Mr Delacherois stepped back into the shadows. "Damn it but you're right. Best not to have her present when we dispose of the brute. We'll wait."

The Doctor withdrew his pipe from a pocket and stuck a brimstone against the wall. "We'll wait."

In turn, Mr Delacherois lit his pipe and they stood there watching for Emma to descend again.

After a while, the Doctor nudged Mr Delacherois. "There…see…she comes."

"Good, I'm floundered. Can you see…has she the parcel?"

"Wait…wait until she passes that house…wait…wait… no it's gone! That's our cue!"

Both men tapped their pipes out on their boot heels, then drew their pistols. Stepping out of the shadows they watched until Emma was well out of sight.

"Let us hope we don't bump into Constable Boston again this night," chuckled the Doctor.

Mr Delacherois cocked his pistols and scowled. "For his sake, I hope not."

Chapter 30

His head was full of images swirling in and out of existence. Pain from untended injuries was driving the Charlie-thing mad with rage. *Mama-thing!* He'd detected Emma approaching accompanied by a crave-churning scent of raw meat long ago. Guiding himself from the Tower and through the tunnel to the outer door of the Castle yard he waited, salivating, tasting the flesh.

The door opened and Emma entered - "Maaa maaa." She threw the chicken carcass into the yard then retreated pulling the door closed behind her. "Maaa maaa," Charlie moaned, then the thoughts of Mama-thing had been replaced with visions of hunts long ago under strange skies, of meat being torn from the living body of his prey, of hot blood spurting into his mouth and sating the hunger. The Charlie-thing started to devour the offering, pulling great gobs of flesh off the remains, with the ecstatic, life-giving fluids — *Bad-things!* He smelt the air; underneath the lingering, diminishing scent of Mama-thing, new aromas were growing stronger.

Clutching the remains of the meal Charlie-thing shuffled back into the Tower. The smooth stone floor was cooler here, and he lingered allowing the heat from his wounds to be soothed by the cold until he suddenly sensed the *Bad-things* coming approaching.

At the summit of the motte, both men stood at the Castle yard's outer door. Mr Delacherois pushed it with the barrel of his pistol and it moved silently inwards revealing the southern yard.

The Doctor held up his hand. "Hold hard now…a… minute…till I catch my breath."

"I told them to bloody lock this!" Ignoring the Doctor's protests Mr Delacherois pushed the door fully open. "Come on man. While the creature is still here."

The Doctor struggled back to his feet and, puffing and blowing like a beached Manatee, followed Mr Delacherois.

They found themselves in a square yard which fully enclosed a windowless stone building, which had been rumoured to have stored the gun-powder during the construction of the harbour below. To their left was a narrow covered walkway which led northwards to another square courtyard which contained a high tower with a door opposite the walkway; everything constructed of stone blocks shipped all the way from Anglesey.

Mr Delacherois opened the window on his lantern

enough to view the doors into the gun-powder store - it was chained and secured by a heavy lock. "Good," he whispered to the Doctor, "Not here." Indicating the curtilage of the store. "We must examine the perimeter. You remain here and if I flush the beast out then kill it." That said Mr Delacherois squared his shoulders and started to follow the dim light on his lonely patrol.

Miserable the Doctor looked around as best he could then closed the Castle door exiting to the outside world, set his back to it, and waited. It was even darker now but he did not dare expose his own light for revealing his position to the Charlie-beast. Little noise from the town below reached his ears, bar the occasional shout carried across the water from the hostelries on the other side of the bay. The regular sweep of the lighthouse lamp over the building reflected enough light from the walls as to disturb the Doctor's night vision, with every rotation necessitating him to momentarily close his eyes. He stood there watching the place where Mr Delacherois would emerge, sometimes closing his eyes to guard them from the sweeps of the lighthouse, whilst praying that he would not open them to the Charlie beast springing upon him with those grasping hands, that terrible hungry mouth agape.

There was a scratching noise, then a pebble was kicked into the yard and Mr Delacherois emerged. A shake of the head, then both men turned to look into the darkness of the covered walkway that led into the yard containing the Tower; the door of which stood ajar.

The Doctor was the first to speak, "Did that door stand open when we first entered?"

Mr Delacherois shrugged. "The same as before. You stand at the far end of this walkway and guard the door at the base. I shall examine the outside of the building."

They advanced into the tunnel examining the passage, and the roof above, until they reached the end where both realised that they had not drawn a breath between them and exhaled together. They glanced at one another then Mr Delacherois turned to carry out his patrol.

The Doctor touched his arm. "Pray wait a moment." He stepped across the gravelled yard and placed his lantern by the Tower door, then opened a window on it to fully illuminate the threshold, before he returned to the Tunnel exit and withdrew a second pistol from his coat and cocked it. "Ready."

Mr Delacherois nodded, then started to circumnavigate the base of the Tower. Unlike the gun-powder Store in the south yard the Tower was penetrated by large arched windows at every floor which meant that Mr Delacherois was obliged to walk, one pistol in hand and his lantern in the other, with his back to the outer wall in case of ambush. As he circled the Tower the Lighthouse would throw light onto the upper windows which would reflect down the Tower itself.

There! There was something in the upper window! Then the light from the Lighthouse disappeared and the courtyard was plunged into darkness. Mr Delacherois could hardly see as he first searched his immediate surroundings, before directing the beam towards the window. *No, nothing.* He held his breath *One! Two! Three! Four!* The light reappeared. The Charlie-beast was looking down at him; it hissed then vanished, as did the light. *One! Two! Three! Four!* Nothing. *One! Two! Three! Four!* Nothing. *One! Two! Three! Four!* Mr Delacherois's hands shook as he searched his immediate vicinity. *It could be upon him in a heartbeat!* Quickly he retraced his steps to the Doctor his feet crunching over the gravel.

"I saw it! It's in the Tower!" No need for silence now.

"It hasn't passed this door. By God we have it trapped".

Both men advanced to the Tower entrance and stepped through the door. The Doctor allowed his light to play over the room revealing a black and white tiled floor with half a dozen barrels, from which a strong smell of raw spirits emanated, in the far corner, and a curved stone stairway leading upstairs. Mr Delacherois crossed the floor to examine the casks. "What the hell are these doing out here? By God, I'll —"

A terrible clucking chittering noise echoed down the building and bounced off the walls.

The Doctor allowed his light to play over the room and stairway. "Damnit look. Whatever fool that built this had enough knowledge to build the stairs curving clockwise."

Mr Delacherois kept his lantern searching the corners around them. "And?"

"Whomsoever leads will likely lose his pistol hand before he may bring it to bear.

Both men stood reluctant to ascend the steps.

"Wait," The Doctor uttered. "Guard the stairway a moment!"

"What are you doing?" cried Mr Delacherois, but the Doctor was already manhandling the barrels into the centre of the room. Pushing a barrel over the sharp stink of brandy filled the room. "I'll burn the bugger out!"

"No, wait!" Mr Delacherois skipped back from the flood. "You can't —"

"Too late!" as the Doctor flung his lantern onto the pile. "Quickly we must go!"

Parts of the Tower were now collapsing inwards as the Doctor and Mr Delacherois stood on the gravel surrounding it. Driving back by the heat they watched through the open door into the oven where the monster was trapped.

A floor collapsed. "By God Sir, nothing will survive that!" exclaimed the Doctor.

Mr Delacherois lowered his pistol. "Damn it man! You'll draw the whole town upon us!" He held up a hand. "You've ruined me!"

The Doctor cocked an ear. "What d'ye mean man! We've killed the beast!"

Mr Delacherois shook his head. "You've ruined me. All gone."

The two men stood awhile in silence as the Doctor digested his neighbour's remark, and Mr Delacherois contemplated his ruin. Then the bell from the Parish Church rang out from atop Mount Misery, and was quickly joined by the church bells from the other, lesser, denominations; all united, for once, in mutual alarm.

The Doctor was still watching the door into the Tower. He took Mr Delacherois by the arm. "I think this would be a good time to leave."

A shadow, a noise, a sense caused the Doctor and Mr

Delacherois to look up together.

"It's escaping!" they cried together as they spied Charlie above them scrambling for a hold on the walkway. As one they fired their pistols.

Bad-thing! The parapet of the walkway roof had been edged with shards of broken glass which sliced into his hands as he scrambled for a handhold. He didn't feel the balls which struck his legs, puncturing veins and arteries that no longer coursed with blood. At last, he dragged himself up onto the roof, the glass carving strips of dead flesh from his lower body.

"Did you hit it?" cried Mr Delacherois.

The Doctor stood playing his lamp over the gravel. "Aha!" he laid his pistol on the ground and bent to pick something up.

"What do you have?"

The Doctor held the item up for Mr Delacherois to examine. "A piece of flesh, and look there!" he pointed to something on the ground.

Mr Delacherois wrinkled his nose in distaste. "What is it?"

"A finger." The Doctor picked it up and sniffed it. "As I thought…rather hoped…the flesh is corrupted. The creature is rotting from within." He smiled at Mr Delacherois. "We shall soon be rid of it; it deliquesces."

"How long?"

The Doctor frowned. "At this rate…a week…ten days at the most then it will no longer hang together.

The sound of a mob could be detected outside.

Mr Delacherois seized the Doctor. "Quickly. We must not

be found here. They think the place is stuffed with gun-powder. We can slide down the side of the motte and join them."

The Sergeant pushed his way through the crowd to where Constable Boston was standing. "Report Constable!"

The Constable looked surprised. "I'm organising a party to fight the fire, Sergeant."

"Stand down man. Just keep the crowd back as best you can."

"But the fire Sergeant?"

"Do you know if there's any gun-powder in that store? Stake your life on it?"

The Constable hesitated. "Well someone said —"

"Not good enough lad. Keep them clear and let the fire burn itself out." The Sergeant walked a little up the motte and turned to face the crowd. "Now listen to me, listen to me, everybody. We don't know if there's gun-powder in that store or not." He glanced up the hill. "Anyway, we couldn't carry enough water up there to make any difference. Stay here lads and let the fire burn itself out."

The Doctor and Mr Delacherois were making their way back into the town against a growing stream of townsfolk eager to view the conflagration.

"That bloody man as good as accused us of setting fire to the place!" complained the Doctor.

Mr Delacherois shook his head. "You've ruined me man. All gone…everything."

The Doctor stopped in his tracks. "What are you talking

about? How are you ruined?"

"I had stored…some considerable merchandise there."

"Merchandise? What merchandise?"

Mr Delacherois faced the Doctor. "The proceeds of a joint venture with Mr Kerr."

The Doctor laughed and then stopped. "Merchandise! By God the Brandy? D'ye mean you've stored smuggled goods in there? In the Castle?"

Mr Delacherois looked at the Doctor. "Why do you think I built it? A folly…give me strength."

The Doctor looked uneasy. "I…I'd no idea. Look old man things will work out d'ye see." They'd reached the Manor House. The Doctor put his hand on Mr Delacherois's arm. "Well goodnight…we'll talk in the morning. Remind me to Miss Delacherois if you would. I have been somewhat neglectful of her of late."

Bad-thing! Bad-thing! As the Charlie-creature hesitated then crept from shadow to shadow following the Doctor up the hill towards Rosebank and into the stable yard. The Doctor called across to Cob wishing him a goodnight then disappeared in the back door. The Charlie creature remained in the darkness watching and listening and smelling. *Mama-thing!* Emma's scent was stronger here! Comforted by the thought the Charlie-thing spied the old well across the yard. Quickly he pulled himself across and pushed the cover aside and allowed himself to fall into the dark still water below; where he could sleep, could dream, could gather his strength.

Chapter 31

Bad-thing! Bad-thing! As the Charlie-creature hesitated then crept from shadow to shadow following the Doctor up the hill towards Rosebank and into the stable yard. The Doctor called across to Cob wishing him a goodnight then disappeared in the back door. The Charlie creature remained in the darkness watching and listening and smelling. *Mama-thing!* Emma's scent was stronger here! Comforted by the thought the Charlie-thing spied the old well across the yard.

In retrospect, the Doctor had thoroughly enjoyed that evening and was in fine fettle when he entered the house by the back door where he found Emma and Sarah sitting by the stove.

Taking off his hat and coat the Doctor greeted them with, "What aren't you out watching all the excitement?"

Sarah looked up from her sewing, "Excitement? What's happening out there?"

Grinning the Doctor did a little dance. "The Castle is aflame. The whole town's wagering if there's gun-powder in the store or not."

Emma and Sarah rushed into the yard where they were joined by the Doctor. A jet of orange sparks lit up the night sky and the smell of tar drifted to their nostrils.

"See," he pointed.

Sarah gasped, "Oh Lord!"

Emma stood rooted to the spot the she span round to confront the Doctor. "You! What have you done?"

Startled the Doctor replied, "Done? Emma, I've done nothing."

"You did something to my Charlie!" Emma sobbed, "What did you do to my boy?"

The Doctor took her hand in his. "Emma my dear. Charlie's dead. You were at the funeral. Do you not remember?"

Furious Emma snatched her hand away. "I saw him! I saw him tonight! What have you done to him!"

"You're upset. That's silly talk." The Doctor extracted a small vial from his waistcoat pocket. "I want you to take a few drops of this, to help you sleep."

Emma stepped back. "No! I don't want to take any of your medicines. I want you to tell me the truth."

The Doctor advanced holding the small bottle. "Now Emma you're upset." He nodded to Sarah. "If you could hold Emma for a moment."

Sarah looked at Emma. "I can't Doctor! I'm sorry I just

can't. The poor —"

The Doctor hesitated. "Sarah I need your help here. If you, and Cob, wish to remain part of my household then you have to be prepared to assist me in my duties, all my duties."

Sarah looked back at Emma. "I'm sorry. Please just take your medicine. It's for your own good."

"That's better. Now just hold her arms." The Doctor eased the stopper. "A few drops my dear. To ease your pain awhile." The Doctor advanced.

Emma retreated again. "No, I will not! Not until you tell me what you did to Charlie."

Sarah stepped behind Emma and put her arms around her. "Emma please don't. The Doctor is —"

"Is going to kill me! Like he did for Charlie! Please help me."

Expertly the Doctor forced the contents between Emma's lips then covered her mouth and massaged her throat. "That's it, Emma. Don't fight now. Swallow it down."

Emma gagged for breath and then sagged in Sarah's arms crying.

The Doctor spoke, "Just a few drops of laudanum. To ease your pain." He caught Emma as she collapsed. "Now Sarah, well done. Now help me put Emma upstairs to bed."

"But Doctor what —"

"Sarah you heard her. Either you help us look after Emma here or it'll have to be the madhouse."

Mr Delacherois and the Doctor were sitting in the Doctor's study. It was evening and the drapes were pulled against the evening chill and a fire was burning in the grate. A decanter with two glasses, a small china jar of tapers, and a small spirit burner, were on the table between the two men who were engaged with charging their pipes.

The Doctor waved a taper and deposited it back in the china pot, before taking a deep draw, and then slowly exhaling it. "That's better.   I've been riding halfway round the country today. Watch out now, there's a bad cold going around."

"A hot Toddy at bedtime has always done for me." Said Mr Delacherois.

The Doctor took a sip of his wine. "Anyway, to what do I owe the pleasure of this visit? You said you had some business to discuss?"

Mr Delacherois put his pipe down. "Indeed Sir…I have been offered the opportunity to join in a small business venture and —"

"Is this connected with the fire at the Castle?"

"Well it —"

"I feel bad about that though I feel we had no other choice…still."

"Hopefully the brute is finished. Nevertheless, I had a share in the contents stored."

The Doctor chuckled. "I'd no idea I was marrying into such an…adventurous milieu."

"Yes well…I do find myself…I'm not enjoying this y'know."

The Doctor sat up in his chair. "I do apologise. But you shouldn't feel…we're kin now…well almost. How may I help?"

"I have a chance to recoup my losses…another venture.

Unfortunately, I find myself somewhat short of ready cash."

"And I take it that this isn't the sort of venture you want to take to the bank? No, enough. How much d'ye need?"

"I was hoping to…five hundred guineas would — on this." Mr Delacherois handed the Doctor a sealed document.

"M'Father never put more than two hundred into Kerr's father's little ventures." The Doctor broke the seal and studied the documents. "Here, these are the titles to the home farm. I can't —"

"You can…you must leave me some dignity. Unfortunately, Mr Kerr also requires compensation for his losses," said Mr Delacherois.

The Doctor moved to his safe and, extracting the key from his watch chain, opened the heavy door and placed the document in the strong box. "Well if you insist. I suppose… look you I'll just pop them in here with the rest for safety. B'God he's got his claws into you rightly." He handed a leather pouch to Mr Delacherois. "D'ye think the Admiral built his fortune on prize money alone? Here that should be five hundred in Gold."

Mrs McKee and the Doctor were sitting at the kitchen table sharing a pot of tea. A few biscuit crumbs remained on a plate that the Doctor had idly snacked upon. "Pity you didn't kill the little brute when you had the chance."

"It can't last much longer out there Betsy. Then things will get back to normal."

Mrs McKee looked out the window. "Where d'ye think it's the now?"

The Doctor considered. "My best guess…somewhere on

the dunes would be where I'd suggest. Plenty of rabbits."

Mrs McKee turned back to look at the Doctor. "Rabbits!" she scoffed. "D'ye no think it's got the taste for bigger game?"

"That's as may be but soon it'll be dead. You didn't see the creature, Betsy. It's rotting alive from the inside, if I can use that word for it. Soon we'll see the crows over the dunes and Mr Delacherois and I will go out and retrieve the carcass."

"Before the police?"

"Maybe…it doesn't matter. I'll certify the creature dead and the whole thing will be written off as a bad-taste prank."

"And the Sergeant?"

"He doesn't know what to think between smugglers and dead bodies walking. He can't go to the District Inspector or the Magistrate with anything because even he wouldn't believe it."

"Speak of the Devil."

"What?"

"The Sergeant. He's standing outside in the yard talking to Cob. Maybe he's going to come in?"

The Doctor extracted a small vial from his waistcoat pocket and placed it on the table. "That should be enough to keep her quiet for the next week or so. Will you make sure she keeps to her bed?"

Mrs McKee nodded.

"We'll get through this Betsy. Great things await us in our investigations…mark my word. Now where's my hat? I'll go and see my betrothed and Mr Delacherois and say hello to the Sergeant on the way past."

The Sergeant saluted the Doctor as he left Rosebank by the backdoor and crossed the stableyard to meet him. "Sleep well, Doctor?"

"Like a top. That was quite a show the other night. Is there much left of the Castle?"

"The Tower is gutted but thankfully the gun-powder store had been emptied of powder."

The Doctor smiled ruefully. "I thought as much or I expect I'd have heard the bang."

"It wasn't gun-powder that would have would have blown us all sky high."

"John?"

"We forced open the store once the fire had burned down. What do you think we found?"

"gun-powder?"

"I wish. That would be too simple. No the place was stacked high with brandy and the likes."

"Brandy! Good God!"

"That surprises you Doctor?"

"Indeed it does. I had no idea. I say d'ye know who owns it?"

"The Magistrate now. Before that…my money's on Mr Kerr."

"Ach John you've a bee in your bonnet about Kerr."

"Mark my words Doctor he's at the root of most wickedness here. The murder of Johnston, the Custom's man. The theft of the body of that wee lad, and now this."

"Stuff! I mean why would he?"

"Johnston must have been onto him —"

"And Charlie?"

"All I can think of is that he wanted to send a message."

"To whom? Damn all point in sending a message if no one understands it."

"What does the Magistrate say?"

"He says find who stored the contraband in the Castle and all will be revealed."

The next morning Mr Delacherois rode out to Mr Kerr's seat at Portavoe House. As he halted in front of the house a gang of ruffians was loading a cart with crates and cast an uneasy eye towards him.

A surly-looking specimen detached himself from the others and took hold of Mr Delacherois' horses' bridle. "He's not seeing no visitors today."

Mr Delacherois tried to jerk his horse free. "Damn you! Take your cap off when you address me! Unhand my horse!"

Several other of the rogues surrounded Mr Delacherois and grabbed at his horse while shouting *Come down o'that*. Mr Delacherois laid about with his whip with as much gusto as he had with his sabre, as a young Cornet, against Marshal Soult's men at the Battle of Talavera.

The front door of the house was thrown open and Mr Kerr emerged. "Let him go, let him go at once damn you!"

Mr Delacherois' attackers fell back scowling with several nursing bloody wheals where his whip had made its mark.

"Come in man. They'll not touch you now." Mr Kerr grinned at the gang. "At least not with me here."

Somewhat unsettled Mr Delacherois dismounted, handed his horse to a stable hand that had appeared to see what the noise was, and followed Mr Kerr into the house, pushing through the grumbling crowd who parted reluctantly before him.

"Welcome," said Mr Kerr. "I wasn't expecting you or I'd have arranged a fairer welcome." Mr Kerr led them into a Sitting Room and indicated a battered leather chair. "I'd be careful down the town for a few weeks in case you take a knife in the kidney."

Standing Mr Delacherois withdrew the leather pouch the Doctor had given him, and tossed it to Mr Kerr.

"Payment in full," said Mr Delacherois.

Weighing the purse in his hands Mr Kerr replied, "More than that I'd say."

"Two hundred Guineas to cover your losses and three hundred more for the next voyage."

Mr Kerr looked at Mr Delacherois. "I don't remember inviting you to invest in future ventures?"

"Damnit man you've ruined me!" Mr Delacherois stamped his foot.

"How's that pretty wee daughter of yours then?"

"You leave Jane out of this! I warn you I'll —"

"Still betrothed to that fat wee Doctor then?"

"Doctor Leslie is —"

"I've watched that creature hunting. He should be riding sidesaddle." Mr Kerr laughed. "I'm only teasing now. Your money's good here. Now see yourself out like a good fellow will you?"

Sarah entered the darkened bedroom. "Are you feeling better Emma?" She pulled the curtains open allowing light to fill the room. "Let's get this bed straight then." Sarah tucked the bed in and straightened the blankets. "Are you feeling better today now?"

Emma struggled to sit up. "What day is it? How long have I been here?"

"Three days. Are you feeling more yourself now?"

"I dreamt that Charlie was calling me. He was at the window."

"Well now you know you're not yourself. Poor wee Charlie's dead and buried and you've got to stop torturing yourself."

"But I saw him and —"

"Emma you've got to stop this! Mrs McKee wants you sent over to the madhouse in The Ards. The Doctor talked her out of it, for now, but you've got to stop it!"

"I can't! I can't! I saw him in the Tower the night of —"

"Now stop that talk!" Sarah sat on the edge of the bed. "Emma if I was to miss tonight's laudanum is there anybody you could write to…for help?"

"Henry's parents have made clear that they want nothing to do with me."

"But what about your own parents? Could you write to them? Would they take you in?"

"Oh Sarah! I'd be ashamed. I was so cruel to them. My Dad didn't want me to marry Henry. Said no good would come of marrying above myself."

"Emma they're your parents. No matter what they love you."

"But what —"

"I'll bring you pen and paper upstairs now and you write

to them...before Mrs McKee gives you your evening medicine and I'll post it tomorrow."

"But Sarah I can hardly think straight. To write such a letter."

"Emma, I'm afraid what'll happen to you if you don't." Sarah stood up and smoothed the counterpane. "The Doctor and Mr Delacherois had such a row yesterday over what was to become of you. You need to leave here as soon as you're able."

Rosebank House,
    Donaghadee,
    County Down.

11th November 1855
    My Dear Parents,

I am afraid I write to you with sorrow in my heart. I pray you steel yourselves for Charlie, your Grandson, has been lost to us in the most horrible of circumstances. He passed last week and his body was committed to the ground, in this most inhospitable country, without friend or family other than your poor, grieving daughter, humbled before you.

Charlie and me came here, after the loss of Henry in the recent war, in the hope of finding a new life for ourselves, but it has been a great disappointment and source of much sorrow and regret.

I have summoned up the courage to write to you and beg your forgiveness. When you forbade me to wed above my station I was too much the child to heed your wise words. Words that I now realise came only from your concern for my welfare.

Since Henry's loss, I have been adrift in a hostile world, and I

only ever sought security for myself and your Grandson. My pride,
the pride that led me to marry against your wishes, has brought me
alone to this place: friendless, without means, and shortly to be
reduced to the most wretched of positions.

    I beg of you, if you can, find forgiveness in your heart for your
only child; that you fold the prodigal back into your hearts.

    Please reply soonest, as I am at the end of my tether here.

    Your disobedient but always loving daughter,

    Emma

Chapter 32

It was bitter cold, with horizontal sleet blowing from the East, when Mr Delacherois approached Mr Kerr at the harbour where he was supervising the unloading of one of his legitimate cargoes.

Half walking, half running Mr Delacherois drew the curiosity of the discreet party of Excisemen watching the proceedings from a distance.

Panting with his exertions, Mr Delacherois elbowed his way through the hostile jostling of the gang and seized Kerr by the sleeve. "God man tell me it's not true! Tell me —"

Mr Kerr glanced around in alarm and shook himself free. "Watch your mouth damn you!"

"Damn you!" retorted Mr Delacherois. "Tell me what happened!"

Glancing around Mr Kerr drew his interrogator to one side. "A Coastguard cutter was hidden 'ween the islands. As soon as our brig appeared they sprang out from the mist and on her."

A frantic Mr Delacherois grasped at Mr Kerr's arm. "But tell me! What —"

"Everything. The Brig's been seized and taken to Belfast - whole damn cargo!"

"This can't be! I gave you that money to —"

Mr Kerr shook Mr Delacherois' hand off. "You knew the risks." Mr Kerr turned back to face Mr Delacherois. "There'll be a dead Excise agent floating in Douglas harbour by week's end if that's any consolation?"

Mr Delacherois stamped his foot. "I don't give a damn for dead agents! I want my money back!"

"For that, both of us may whistle."

"I insist I —"

"Complain to the Magistrate why don't ye?" said Mr Kerr over his shoulder as he walked away.

That evening Mrs McKee arrived at Emma's bedroom carrying her medicine on a tray. She placed it on the side table and then poured some laudanum into a large spoon. "Right open wide," she commanded.

Emma turned her head away. "No! I don't want it! You can't make me!"

Mrs McKee stood over Emma. "No more nonsense from you. If you don't take your medicine then I'll get Cob up here to pour it down your throat."

Reluctantly Emma opened her mouth and swallowed the

laudanum. She looked blearily at Mrs McKee. "Why do you hate me so much?"

Mrs McKee lifted the tray from the side table and looked back at Emma. "Because you killed my son. My only son, and you and your boy killed him."

Emma's brain couldn't master this. *Who was Mrs McKee's son? How had she, or Charlie, killed him?* "I don't... understand," Emma slurred.

Mrs McKee put the tray back on the side table and bent over Emma. "You don't understand. Tell me what is it you don't understand?" She pulled a pillow from under Emma's head. "I'll explain," then placed the pillow over Emma's face and held it there.

Emma struggled for breath. *I'm underwater! I'm with Charlie!* As the pain in her chest increased she saw figures coming into view and looking at her closely, before moving away. She tried to ask them if they had seen Charlie but they ignored her questions. She started to swim deeper in pursuit when she suddenly found herself dragged back and found herself gasping for breath and floundering back where she started.

Sarah slapped her face. "Emma wake up now, wake up."

Mrs McKee stood by the window where Sarah had thrust her when she had entered the room. "You should have let me finish her Sarah. I warn you she hasn't done with us yet."

Sarah stood up and turned to face Mrs McKee. "What are you talking about? Have you taken leave of your senses? Henry —"

The door opened and the Doctor walked in. "Hello, what's all the noise in here?"

Mrs McKee started to answer but Sarah cut her short. "You'd best ask her Doctor." She indicated Mrs McKee. "I came in here and she was holding a pillow over Emma's face. She nearly had the poor thing choked."

"Betsy is this true?"

"Aye and if Sarah hadn't stuck her nose in all this would be over." Mrs McKee swung round to face Emma. "She's evil I tell you. We've had nothing but grief and sadness in this house since she and her brat showed up!"

The Doctor raised a hand. "Now Betsy I'm not sure —"

Mrs McKee spun round. Spittle flecked her mouth. "He was your son too! Or had you forgotten?"

The Doctor's mouth tightened. "That'll do Betsy!"

Sarah had been watching all of this. "She's not safe here. If anything happens to her…well you'll be sorry."

The Doctor glared at Sarah. "I thought we'd talked about your and Cob's future here had we not?"

"I'll not be a party to murder! Neither will my Cob! And I don't see how her parents would let you get away with it either."

The Doctor's forehead frowned, "Her parents…but —"

"Aye, she's wrote to them," Sarah exaggerated. "So they'll know everything now."

"What…when?" demanded the Doctor.

Sarah stood up straight. "Today. Sure I posted the letter meself."

"When?"

"In time for the post boat. I just caught this afternoon's mail."

The Doctor looked shocked. "You shouldn't have done

that Sarah. Consider yourself and Cob dismissed immediately."

"I'll consider myself dismissed when she walks out this door on her own two feet. Until then we'll be staying." Sarah dropped a curtsy to the Doctor. "Will there be anything else Sir?"

There was a pause then the Doctor replied, "No that will be all. Thank you, Sarah."

The Doctor and Mr Delacherois were sitting in a snug in the Downshire Hotel with a bottle of wine between them.

"You're restless this evening," observed the Doctor.

Mr Delacherois fixed the Doctor with a steady gaze. "You get about. Have you heard…have you heard of a boat being seized hereabouts recently?"

"Not a word. I was talking to the Magistrate only this morning and he never mentioned anything. Why?"

Mr Delacherois slammed his fist on the table. "I knew it. The rogue has ruined me and…damn it!" He gestured to a pot boy. "Bring us a bottle of whiskey." He suddenly sprang to his feet. "Damn your eyes! Don't dawdle!" and the pot-boy fled.

The Doctor reached out and put a restraining hand on Mr Delacherois' arm. "What ails you, old friend? Who has done you ill?"

"Kerr! Kerr damn him! He has ruined me. He tells me —"

"Kerr? You're a damn fool to trow in with him!"

"That devil! I made an investment in a business venture with him and now he tells me it has failed and my money lost!"

The Doctor furrowed his brow. "And it isn't the sort of business arrangement that you may take to the law?"

A frightened pot-boy entered the snug and placed the bottle of whiskey and two glasses on the table before fleeing.

Mr Delacherois seized the bottle and tore the cork out before pouring two large measures, slopping whiskey over the table in his haste. "No! Damn it! He has me over a barrel!" Mr Delacherois drained his glass and then poured another one. "It was your damned money he lost."

The Doctor stiffened. "I don't remember making such an investment?"

Ignoring him Mr Delacherois ploughed on. "I mortgaged the lot with the banks in Belfast…to build that damn pier… and the castle. Now…I've lost the lot and —"

The Doctor bridled. "I'm sorry for your loss of course, but I don't see how it involves me?"

Mr Delacherois drained his glass and refilled it. "It's all Jane's of course. I'm ruined…not a penny to my name."

"Jane's? But the Manor House, Home Farm, the tenant farms, the town? Why you still own the rent roll from the town? That must —"

"All Jane's…all gone. The whole estate was left in trust to Jane by her mother and I've lost it." He laughed, "She was the money I was merely a penniless subaltern when I married her." Mr Delacherois took a large draft of whiskey the refilled his glass, spilling most of it on the desk. "Now you've gone and got yourself a penniless wife, and a ruined Father-In-Law."

"But the documents you pledged. What —"

"Worthless!" Mr Delacherois shook his head. "Worthless! All mortgaged." He looked straight at the Doctor. "What do you care anyway? You've plenty of money tucked away. I know you have!"

"Nevertheless I —"

Mr Delacherois suddenly sat up straight. "I say you couldn't see your way to extending the loan. Maybe Kerr's right about…if he's making another voyage I could —"

"Not with my money! You made your bed and now you'll lie in it!"

"You've forgotten I've seen what you have in your safe. You'd hardly —"

The Doctor stood up and threw some coins on the table. "And that's where it'll remain!"

Mr Delacherois sat on and called for another bottle of whiskey. Several acquaintances approached but it quickly became apparent that he was in no mood for company. Mr Lemon himself looked in and then instructed his staff to keep visitors away from Mr Delacherois's snug and the man himself supplied with all that he asked for.

Time passed and the evening drew in with no sound from Mr Delacherois, with the customers at the bar casting uneasy glances over towards the snug, for Mr Delacherois was popular around the town and had done great service to the people therein. The door from outside opened and a tall man blocked what little light the setting sun cast then Mr Kerr, accompanied by several of his men, entered.

Mr Kerr nodded to the house. "Good evening gentlemen, good evening. A grand night it is." Amid the subdued responses, several customers hastily finished their drinks and, muttering excuses, made discreet exits gingerly skirting the new arrivals.

"Get yourselves a drink boys," Mr Kerr said. "And send me a fresh glass into the snug." Mr Lemon sought to protest but it was too late.

The snug door opened and Mr Delacherois snarled "I told you to —" Then he recognised the intruder. "Oh, it's you. What the Devil do you want?"

"And a good evening to you as well." Mr Kerr sat down and filled his glass from Mr Delacherois's bottle. He raised the glass. "Your health!" and sank the whiskey in one before refilling it and Mr Delacherois's glasses.

Mr Delacherois pushed the glass away and stood up. He swayed and held the table top to steady himself. "I'm not in the mood for your antics tonight Kerr."

"Really? I think you'd be interested in these." Mr Kerr placed a leather wallet on the table.

Mr Delacherois tried to focus. "What is it? What nonsense are —"

"Sit down old man before you fall down."

Mr Delacherois sat down heavily. "What is it that you want?" He prodded the wallet. "What's this?"

Mr Kerr opened the wallet and extracted some papers. "Don't you recognise them?" He spread out the top document. "Here, look. That's your signature ain't it?"

Mr Delacherois patted his pockets for a pair of eyeglasses. He reached for one of the papers and examined it. "What's this? What are you doing with those?" He spread the other papers across the table. "These are…how did you get —"

"Your mortgages? Is that what you mean?" Mr Kerr swept up the papers and carefully replaced them in the wallet which he restored to his pocket. "I bought 'em. The banks in Belfast don't rate your credit too much anymore."

Mr Delacherois sat there blinking. "But…those were for the harbour. I —"

"Borrowed to the hilt on Jane's estate. It's a grand harbour thank ye. But now it's time to pay the piper."

"But…" Mr Delacherois slumped down.

Mr Kerr ploughed onwards. "You gambled with your daughter's money and now you've lost. Cheer up old man, nobody could have foreseen those damn stink pots —"

"Jane doesn't—""

"Steaming up and down with no heed to tide nor wind —"

"The mails. I didn't —"

"None of us did but that's the way of it. You lost the mail contract when they moved it to Belfast and now you're stuck with a useless harbour and a handful of sailing ships on their last legs." Mr Kerr touched the breast of his coat where he has stowed the wallet. "Between these and what you already owe me," he sipped at his glass and looked at Mr Delacherois. "D'ye know I rather think I may move into the Manor House myself." He sat upright. "There's a thought. Have you paid that wee fat Doctor Jane's dowry yet? Ye have, haven't ye? Well you'll not be getting that back in a hurry."

Mr Delacherois world was spinning. "You…you leave my Jane —"

"Unless…here's an idea. Maybe I'll marry Jane myself? What do you think of that? Better than you pair being put out on the street eh?" He grinned, reached across the table, and poked Mr Delacherois in the midriff. "What would you think on that then?"

Sarah lifted a steaming pot of potatoes off the stove and spooned them onto Cob's plate then put the empty pot in the sink. "There's a pot for you Lizzie." Then sat down and looked at Cob. "The cheeky auld mare had the neck, the bloody neck, to threaten us! And her trying to smother Emma in front of me as bold as brass!"

Cob considered the potato in front of him for a moment, then applied some salt and a dab of butter to it. "I think maybe we need to start looking for somewhere else." He carefully fitted the portion into his mouth and swallowed.

"Not that Mr Delacherois one mind!"

Cob took a gulp of tea and nodded. "Aye, he's as bad." He looked around. "Pity though…we had some good times here before…"

Sarah shifted uncomfortably in her seat. "Maybe Emma brought bad luck but she can't be blamed for all that."

"Well, she didn't do herself any good carrying on like that with the Doctor."

"Maybe, maybe not but he's as much to blame there."

"She was a fool getting involved with the likes of him. Thinking she was going to be Lady Muck around here. Wee Janie Delacherois put that nonsense out of her head quick enough."

Sarah chortled, "She did that. Mind you —"

The kitchen door from the house opened and Mrs McKee entered followed by the Doctor who stood behind her looking embarrassed. "Are you pair still here? Did you not hear me? You're both dismissed and —"

"Steady on Betsy," the Doctor intervened.

Sarah looked at Mrs McKee. "And I told you we're going nowhere until Emma's safe out of this house."

Her face reddened Mrs McKee turned to the Doctor. "Are you going to allow them to talk to me like that?"

"What's happened to us?" The Doctor turned to Cob. "Can't we all just go back to the way things were before…?"

"That'd be nice. I was just —"

Sarah intervened, "Before yon started trying to kill people d'ye mean?"

Mrs McKee turned puce. "Ye cheeky wee besom. I'll —"

"I suppose I could go to the Sergeant and tell him what I seen in the house."

The Doctor turned pale. "Steady on Sarah. No need to involve the police. Tell you what when Emma's back on her feet we'll get her sorted out, then we'll all sit down and have a talk…eh? Get things back to normal?"

Sarah stood and turned to Cob. "Come on you. We need to talk." She looked at Mrs McKee and the Doctor. "But not here. Get your coat."

Mrs McKee stood there for a moment then pushed past the Doctor and left through the back door into the stable yard.

Breathing heavily Mrs McKee stood in the evening damp. "I'll sort you out m'girl." Pulling her shawl around her shoulders against the evening chill she made her way across the yard to the old well. Grasping the edge of the wooden cover she managed to dislodge it exposing the well itself. Looking down into the darkness she muttered, "I sorted you out and I'll sort your mother out next." Withdrawing a straw dolly from her apron pocket she pushed the handle of the spoon, she had used to dose Emma with, deep into the body then, with a few dark words, she spat on the doll and thrust it into the well.

A faint splash then she smiled. "Murder my Henry you creature you. I'll see you burn afore you leave here."

Chapter 33

It was dark when Emma awoke in her bedroom from a tapping at her window. Sarah hadn't drawn the curtains and, in the confusion earlier, her evening draft had been overlooked. The moonlight flooded through the window showing the room in black and white, up and down, good and bad.

Where am I? Where is this place? were her first thoughts as she looked around her bedroom. *There must be a wind outside,* as the tapping repeated. Emma sat up in the bed and, after a few moments, managed to recover her thoughts, *How long have I been like this?* The fire had died down long ago and the room was cold with her breath clouding as she exhaled. She drew her shawl closer and made her way to the window to view this strange outside world. A young couple were conversing arm-in-arm as they walked across the yard. *I should know these people* Emma thought as they turned towards the main street and the town.

Again the tapping *A branch knocking on the window? There wasn't a trace of a breeze in the branches of the trees surrounding the stable yard.* Sarah rubbed the window pane where her breath had frosted. She staggered back. *Charlie!*

Emma felt the bed push against her legs and sat down on it. *But this couldn't be right. She thought she'd dreamt the scene in the tower. She couldn't think straight with the daily doses of laudanum. What had the Doctor done to her, to Charlie? How long had she been here?*

Again the sound at the window; tap, tap, tap. Unsteadily Emma rose to her feet and, terrified, approached the sound. There he was a small, drawn, helpless figure clinging to the ivy outside. Behind him, she saw the cover was off the old well again. *He must be so cold. So hungry. So dangerous!* Emma thrust that thought aside. She opened the window a crack.

Charlie was looking at her in desperation, "Ma ma, Ma ma, Mama."

Emma pushed the window fully open and reached out, "Charlie, it's Mama. Come to Mama."

There was a rustle in the ivy then Charlie was in her arms. *Flesh and bones so light, and eyes burning so very bright.* Easily lifting him over the sill Emma bore the small bundle to the bed. In her heart, Emma knew that Charlie was no longer of this world, *should not be in this world, had no part in this world.*

Charlie had his arms around her, his face buried in her neck, "Ma ma."

Stroking his hair, caressing his head, "There baby, mummy's here now. Hush." Her nostrils filled with the stick of corruption. *This must be what the grave stinks like.*

Her head was spinning. *What would she do, what would become of him?* He couldn't stay here. Even she could see that he had deteriorated badly since she had last seen him in the tower. He was dying, if that was the right word, even she could see that.

"What have they done to us Charlie my love," she moaned. "What did you do to them that you would deserve this?" *We're not dirt, we're not his playthings to dispose of us as he wishes.* The resentments of the last year rose to the surface in Emma as a big black bubble of fear and anger. *The Doctor has done this thing, the Doctor deserves to pay.*

Cradling Charlie Emma hushed him. *She'd seen Sarah and Cob go out, Mrs McKee would have gone home by now, and, unless he'd gone out, the Doctor would be locked in his study with his books or with his cronies in some pothouse.*

Emma rose from the bed and, still holding Charlie in her arms soothed him, "Come baby, come with Mummy."

Light as a feather Emma held Charlie in one arm as she opened the door to the landing. Outside the bedroom, it was dark and cold with only a little light filtering up from a candle in the hallway below.

Emma stood listening for a few moments then holding the banister in her spare hand slowly made her way down the stairs. Again Emma paused at the foot of the stairs; all was quiet, with a small gleam of light from under the door of the Doctor's study as the only sign of life.

In her bare feet, Emma padded silently to the stairs

leading down to the kitchen and made her way down. The door at the bottom was closed and Emma put her ear to it; silence. Slowly Emma opened the door and then peeped into the kitchen. A glow from the stove was enough to show it was unoccupied.

Emma shifted Charlie in her arm, "We're nearly there baby. Not long," then quickly made her way to the cellar door.

The door at the bottom of the cellar stairs was bolted from the inside. Emma slid the bolt open and stepped into the cellar. It was dark apart from a little light through the small windows at ground height; enough to see.

Feeling her way, still carrying Charlie, Emma crossed the cellar to the door that led up to the doctor's study. Putting Charlie down she slid the bolt on the door open and slightly opened it. He had changed, now since they had entered the cellar; more alert, smelling the air.

Emma bent down and caressed his cheek. She kissed his head, "Goodbye baby, goodbye until we see each other in heaven." Then Emma retraced her way to the kitchen steps and thence to her bedroom.

The fever was raging in Charlie's body as he explored the cellar. Dreams, or maybe memories filled his mind with visions of past lives; some his, some from people or beings he did not recognise.

Charlie moaned and twitched. *Bad-things! Bad-things! Keep away!* He was hungry now. Mama had not brought him food and he was growing restless alone in the dark. He yearned to be back outside in the dunes hunting for small animals. Tearing the quivering flesh apart and allowing the hot blood to pour down his throat *The taste of life, the giver of life!*

Cautiously he shuffled out into the middle of the cellar and scented the air; the sharp tangy smell of urine flooded his nostrils; *food!* Eagerly Charlie made his way over to a corner where a heap of old feed sacks had been placed and forgotten. The smell was strong here and Charlie started pulling the pile apart as he burrowed deeper into the stack. He could feel, he could hear the sounds of three, four, five maybe more, little hearts beating together; faster, faster as he got closer.

There! Two rats, and a nest of pups cowering in the corner. Charlie struck with one hand and the big male rat jumped over his shoulder and scurried away. Frantically Charlie scrabbled deeper into the corner and emerged with a fat female rat, already gravid with the next generation, clasped tight in his hand. She squealed and writhed as Charlie bit deep into her belly tearing flesh and guts in great gobbing quivering chunks. His appetite sated for now Charlie sat, back against the wall, and surveyed the cellar. Absent-mindedly he pulled a back leg from the rat then stripped the sweet thigh muscle off with his front teeth.

The stone trough sat at the far end of the cellar on a stepped plinth. It stirred memories up to the surface of his mind. Something had happened there. Something bad. Charlie discarded the remains of his meal and approached it. The stone felt cool to the touch. He pulled himself up onto the edge so that he could look down into it. The still cool dark water reflected the moonlight outside. He could hide there, rest there, submerge himself in the cool of its depths; extinguish the fires that tormented his body and his mind.

Charlie was about to let himself topple into the water, to sleep, to ease the pain when the sound of quarrelling voices from the door behind the font attracted his attention. *Bad-man! Bad-man was back. To hurt Charlie, to hurt Mama!* Raising his face Charlie sniffed the air *New, new bad-man.* Someone else had joined them in the house.

Charlie lowered himself back to the floor and started to creep towards the stairs that led up to the Doctor's study. Step by pain-filled step Charlie levered himself up the staircase towards the Doctor's inner sanctum. He pushed the door open at the top of the stairs and crept into the back room. The eyes of the infants entombed in the glass jars silently followed his actions.

The Doctor was sitting at his desk with his back to a fire nursing a glass of claret and brooding over the loss of his son when his study door opened and Mr Delacherois entered. "I need to speak to you?" Without waiting on an invitation he closed the door behind him and collapsed into an armchair with his head in his hands. "I'm…Jane's ruined."

The Doctor quickly tidied his documents into his strongbox, leaving the door pushed closed but not locked, before sitting in the other armchair.

"What's amiss? Has something happened?"

Mr Delacherois looked up. "I've just had that rogue Kerr threaten me…in public before the whole town. With Lemon standing behind the bar taking in every word."

The Doctor stood up. "Threaten you? We should call the police then!"

"No, you don't understand." Mr Delacherois grasped the Doctor's arm and pulled him back into the seat. "He holds my debts. He bought them from the banks in Belfast."

The Doctor frowned. "I know you have some debts…to Kerr and myself. But they're not that much, not the end of the world."

"It was all Jane's—all of it.   I merely managed it for her…until her majority…or until she was married. And I mortgaged the lot to build that damn harbour." Mr Delacherois waved his hand at the town. "And now I've lost that as well. I'm…we're penniless now. Kerr holds me in the palm of his hand. I live…Jane lives by his sufferance."

"What everything?"

"Every the very house we're sitting in now. Kerr's your new landlord." Mr Delacherois took a large pull at his glass and then unsteadily refilled it

Thinking furiously the Doctor poured himself some wine. "You'll always have a home with Jane and myself."

Step by pain-filled step Charlie levered himself up the staircase towards the Doctor's inner sanctum. He pushed the door open at the top of the stairs and crept into the back room. The eyes of the infants entombed in the glass jars silently followed his actions. Charlie crept across the floor to the door into the Doctor's study and peered through the gap in the curtain.

"A pensioner in my own daughter's house." Mr Delacherois groaned. "What will…I know!" Mr Delacherois leapt to his feet and the Doctor rose after him. "You! You've got the riches of Croesus in there." He pointed to the strongbox. "You could make everything all right!"

Alarmed the Doctor interjected, "Steady on. I ain't about to lend you any more of my money."

Mr Delacherois darted over to the Doctor's safe where he fell to his knees and started pulling out leather purses. Some fell open and spilt gold coins across the floor. "Look at it! Look at it! We're saved! This'll be —"

The Doctor bent over trying to retrieve the pouches and restore them to his strongbox. "Stop! This isn't yours to —"

Mr Delacherois swept his arm back to push the Doctor away. "Damn it no! I need this for Jane!" The Doctor, caught off balance tripped over his feet and fell backwards into the hearth striking his temple an almighty blow as he did so.

Casting around Mr Delacherois spied the Doctor's bag sitting by the safe. Discarding its contents he threw bag after bag of gold into the case. Then he stood up stuffing a few loose coins into his pockets. "What's up with you?" he addressed the Doctor. "Get up you fool."

The Doctor lay there on his back. His eyes unfocused and unable to move he merely groaned, "Arrumph."

Mr Delacherois bent over the Doctor. "What's that you said? Get up man and stop horsing about!"

The Doctor remained on the floor with the fingers of his left hand fluttering ineffectually.

Uncertain Mr Delacherois stood watching the Doctor. Quietly he muttered, "You brought this upon yourself now. Don't be blaming me." He shouldered the bag, gasping slightly at its weight, then let himself out closing the study door into the hall quietly behind him.

"Arrgump," groaned the Doctor staring at the ceiling with fishy eyes.

As the study door shut Charlie crept into the room and looked at the Doctor then knelt and pressed his ear to the Doctor's chest. The Doctor made a series of small squeaking noises and his fingers wriggled frantically. The fire had burnt down but still threw out enough of a glow that Charlie could make out a drizzle of saliva that hung from the Doctor's mouth and was pooling on his chin.

Through the madness that now lived in Charlie's brain a memory of pain surfaced. *bad-man! Hurt!* Carefully Charlie drew closer and stared into the Doctor's eyes. The Doctor's breathing was shallow, shuddering, and interspersed with long silent pauses; the reek of alcohol was strong now. Suddenly the Doctor gave a great snuffling gasp, sat upright and fixed his gaze on Charlie.

Bad-man! Danger! Charlie jumped up. His eye fell on the paper knife sitting on the Doctor's desk. Charlie picked it up and drove it into the Doctor's eye; his body convulsed, the legs shot out, and a great shuddering quiver passed down his body from head to toe. Blood oozed from the wound and meandered down his cheek until it merged with the drool, and carried on to its final destination on Doctor's shirt.

Reassured by the stillness Charlie moved closer. Reaching out he dipped a finger in the blood and then tasted it. The coals in the grate shifted startling him. He poked the Doctor's leg; no reaction. *Bad-man gone! Can't hurt Charlie!*

Charlie pulled himself onto the Doctor's lap and studied the *familiar not familiar* face. He knew it meant something. He stroked the cheek pleased with the feeling of the stubble *Father! Da-da!* and rested his head on the Doctor's breast. *Safe! Sleep now. Twinkle little stars.*

After a while Charlie stirred, the hunger pangs growing. He knew where the choicest samples were hidden, and how to access the blood-rich, life-giving morsels secreted away. He withdrew the knife and pulled down the Doctor's jaw then looked in.

Chapter 34

It was a fine Autumn day with dust mites dancing in the sunbeams as Sarah readied the tray with the Doctor's breakfast when Mrs McKee arrived.

Sarah turned to see who it was before she resumed her work.

Mrs McKee removed her hat and coat. "Is that for the Doctor?"

Without looking at her Sarah replied, "It is."

"Well quick about it. Don't keep him waiting."

Sarah bit her lip, picked up the tray and carried it up the kitchen stairs. On the landing she paused outside the Doctor's bedroom and knocked; no reply. Sarah waited for a few moments then knocked again before opening the bedroom door; the bed had not been slept in.

Sarah muttered to herself, "He'll not be feeling well this morning," and carried the tray back down the stairs to the Doctor's study. She rapped the door. "Doctor…Doctor…are you up? Here's your breakfast." There was no reply so Sarah elbowed the door handle and, using her hip, backed the door open.

The room was dark with the drapes still closed. The fire was dead in the grate. "Morning Doctor. Here's your breakfast." Sarah could make out the side table in the gloom and slid the tray on, gently displacing a glass and an empty bottle. "I'll just pull the curtains open, shall I? Let some light in?"

Sarah pulled the drapes open and the daylight flooded in to reveal the Doctor lying on the floor with his paper knife driven into his right eye; Sarah screamed.

Mrs McKee entered, "What is all that   —" and staggered back against the door. "What on earth girl…oh my God. What happened?"

"He's dead! He wasn't in his bed so I brought his breakfast here and —"

Mrs McKee straightened up. "We must send for Mr Delacherois."

"Mr Delacherois! Are you mad? I'm fetching the police this instant."

Mrs McKee stood in the doorway. "No wait girl —"

Sarah walked to the door. "Get out of my way this instant or I'll put you out of my way."

Mrs McKee hesitated and then stood to one side. "You're being hasty now Sarah. If —" but Sarah had gone.

It wasn't long before Sergeant Restrick and a Constable arrived at the front door which was lying open.

Boots clattering on the hall tiles the Sergeant framed the door. "Mrs McKee, Sarah what's —" Then he noticed the Doctor's body on the floor "Constable back to the barracks and rouse the Night duty men. Tell 'em to get down here immediately, then you get down to Mr Lemon's and get him to send for the Magistrate."

As the Constable took to his heels the Sergeant called him back, "Wait." He scribbled a quick note in his notepad before tearing off the page and handing it to the Constable. "Give that to Mr Lemon for the Magistrate. We'll need him to bring a Doctor."

As the Constable departed the Sergeant addressed Mrs McKee, "Is it just yourselves in the house?"

Mrs McKee remained silent. Sarah gave her a glance the answered, "There's Cob, he's out in the yard still I expect, oh and Emma, Mrs Hawthorne. She'll be in her room still."

The Sergeant looked puzzled. "She slept through all of this?"

Hurriedly Mrs McKee interjected, "She's not been well. The Doctor sent her to bed and —"

Sarah stamped her foot. "She's drugged. These pair have been feeding her enough laudanum to kill a horse these last days."

The Sergeant stood awhile taking in the scene. "Does this door lock?"

Sarah pointed to Mrs McKee. "She has the key."

The Sergeant held out his hand. "The key please."

Slowly Mrs McKee unhooked the bunch of keys from her

belt. "Mr Delacherois doesn't like me sharing the keys with anybody."

The Sergeant drew himself up to his full height. "I am not anybody. The keys please…now."

After clearing the room and locking the door the Sergeant turned to Sarah and Mrs McKee. "Where's Mrs Hawthorne?"

Sarah pointed to the stairs. "Straight up and in front of you."

At that moment three Constables arrived. The first one reported, "I left Boston in the barracks in case we need to pass messages, and Mr Lemon has sent a boy riding to the Ards to fetch the Magistrate, and another to Millisle to fetch Doctor Miskelly."

"Good man. You come with me and you stay here and," pointing to the study door, "let no one enter here. I have the keys." He turned to Sarah. "We need to check on Mrs Hawthorne. Will you accompany us?"

Sarah nodded.

The Sergeant turned to Mrs McKee. "Please wait for us downstairs in the kitchen." He turned to a Constable. "Fetch Cob in from the yard, and then you stay with him and Mrs McKee in the kitchen until the Magistrate arrives."

Mrs McKee objected, "I have to fetch Mr Delacherois."

The Sergeant paused on the way up the stairs. "Mr Delacherois may wait. Constable escort Mrs McKee to the kitchen."

At the top of the stairs, Sarah pointed to Emma's room. The Sergeant knocked on the door, "Mrs Hawthorne, Mrs

Hawthorne? Are you in there? It's the police. We need to speak to you." There was no answer and when he tried the handle it was locked. He turned to Sarah. "Is this door always locked?"

"Only in the last few days. I'm not allowed in."

The Sergeant raised the bunch of keys. "Here?"

Sarah nodded and then looked closely. She pointed at one. "There! That's the one I think."

The Sergeant nodded, selected the key, and unlocked the door. He knocked on the door again. "Mrs Hawthorne, Mrs Hawthorne?" then pushed it open.

The room was dark and fetid as they entered. "Mrs Hawthorne, Mrs Hawthorne? It's the police. No need to be afraid."

Light burst over the scene as Sarah and the Constable pulled open the drapes revealing a crumpled unmade bed with the figure of a woman propped up on some pillows.

The Sergeant moved to Emma's side and put his ear to her mouth. "I think she's breathing." He looked to the Constable. "When Doctor Miskelly arrives she's his first patient." He looked at a glass and a small medicine vial on the side table. Picking up the glass he smelt it and held it up to the light. "Water I think." And placed it back on the table. "Is this the medicine Sarah?" She nodded and he checked the cork before putting it in his pocket.

There was a clatter of boots and raised voices from the hall below. "Constable you stay here with Mrs Hawthorne. Sarah, you come with me."

The Magistrate was standing in the hallway with Doctor

Miskelly as the Sergeant descended the stairs. "Ah! Sergeant," he indicated the door, "These men tell me you have the key."

The Sergeant held up the bunch of keys. "Indeed I do Sir. But may I first ask Doctor Miskelly to attend to Mrs Hawthorne upstairs?"

Doctor Miskelly nodded then began to ascend.

The Sergeant pointed to Emma's room, "Straight through there Doctor. Constable Maguire is in attendance."

"Is she hurt?" asked the Magistrate.

"I'd rather leave that to the Doctor to decide Sir." He placed the key in the lock on the Doctor's study and turned it. "Sarah, perhaps you'd go downstairs and make some tea, eh? I'll talk to the Magistrate first." He pushed open the door. "After you Sir."

"Pull those drapes open that we may examine properly," ordered the Magistrate and one of the Constables hurried to obey. Weak grey winter sun was admitted both the Magistrate and the Sergeant stood back to examine things in their entirety.

Both men looked quite pale. "So John tell me what I am looking at here if you please?"

The Sergeant withdrew his notebook. "On the nineteenth of —"

The Magistrate placed his hand on the Sergeant's arm. "No, John. It's too early for all that. Just what's happened please."

The Sergeant nodded and replaced his notebook. "Sarah found him this morning lying here when she brought his breakfast tray in. From the stink of him, he'd been drinking all last night." The Sergeant pointed to the safe. "The Admiral's strongbox was lying open and empty." The Sergeant pointed to the contents of the Doctor's bag scattered around the floor. "And look here I think he's taken the Doctor's bag to carry away whatever was in the safe."

The Magistrate moved to the safe and opened the door fully. "D'ye know if he kept much in it?"

"A King's, or rather an Admiral's, ransom according to rumour."

There was a knock at the door and both men turned to see Doctor Miskelly on the threshold.

The Magistrate waved him in. "First things first Doctor. How is Mrs Hawthorne?"

"She'll live. As bad a case of laudanum poisoning as I've seen, but she should recover given time."

"Well, that's some good news at least. Perhaps you would examine poor Doctor Leslie and share your thoughts?" The Magistrate snorted, "Such a pity. The Doctor always used to enjoy this so much."

The Sergeant nodded. "Aye, he was a great one at looking over the dead bodies he was. D'ye remember the dead Exciseman on the beach?"

Doctor Miskelly looked up from his examination and grinned. "I heard there was a great party that day."

The Magistrate glanced at the Sergeant and then back to Doctor Miskelly. "I'll admit that a terrible contagion of sore heads ran amok for several days. Well then to business. What are your thoughts?"

Doctor Miskelly started tidying his instruments back into

his bag. "Well, he died maybe six or eight hours ago from a blow to the head." He pointed to the Doctor's temple. "Here. I can't give you a better estimate than that. He's been lying too close to the fire for that. Makes my estimate more difficult."

The Magistrate pointed to the paper-knife protruding from the Doctor's eye, "A blow then, not that?"

He pulled up the Doctor's left eyelid. "The knife would have been fatal but the blow killed him first, but either would have done." Doctor Miskelly pointed to the paper-knife that remained in the Doctor's eye. "D'ye want this out or should I leave it where it is for now?"

The Magistrate sucked on his teeth. "Out, please. Well, thank you, Doctor. It's a start I suppose."

Doctor Miskelly stood and handed the knife to the Sergeant before picking up his bag. "There's more." He paused dramatically. "His tongue's missing."

Removing his hat the Sergeant wiped his brow. "Missing?"

"Well it has been cut out, crudely I may add, and I can't see it," he indicated the desk, "here. So if you find a spare about the place it's probably his. I'll have the body brought to the mortuary yard and let you know if I find anything else." Doctor Miskelly shrugged on his Inverness coat and replaced his hat. "Good day to you gentlemen."

The Magistrate and the Sergeant watched Doctor Miskelly leave, then the Magistrate nodded towards the deceased. "We'll miss him. His postmortems were much more fun."

The Sergeant sighed, "Happy days Sir, happy days

indeed."

"Mark my words this is Kerr's work. First the Exciseman and now the Doctor, both with their tongues out," said the Magistrate. "He's warning people to keep silent."

The Sergeant looked uncomfortable. "Don't forget stealing young Charlie's body."

The Magistrate sucked on his teeth. "We'd better start by searching the house."

The Magistrate examined a corner by the door for any clues then removed his greatcoat and folded it, placing it on an empty chair with his hat on top. Turning to the Sergeant he said, "Now John I suppose we'd best get on with examining the scene. I'll check here. Would you have your men start in the rest of the house?"

The Sergeant nodded his acquiescence and left the Magistrate alone in the room. Ignoring the desk with the body behind it he circled the study checking window locks, pausing at the door behind the curtain that led to the Doctor's private room, before moving on to the shelves that held the Doctor's library. Running his fingers along the spines he paused at a set of large leather-bound tomes. Selecting one at random he pulled it off the shelf and opened the cover to be greeted by page after page of handwritten notes. After a while, he closed the book and returned it before looking over at the remains of the Doctor. "Well well old man. I always thought you were a rum sort."

Pausing to scan the Doctor's desk the Magistrate drew aside the curtain and entered the Doctor's private room. It was bright and airy with the drapes already opened. His attention was drawn to the sample shelf to his right. Puzzled the Magistrate moved closer, then stared in horror at what he saw. "Dear God man. What have you done!" he murmured to himself. He reached out a finger and tapped the glass and the small figure within twitched, causing him to jump back. "Sweet Jesus!" then he quickly looked around to make sure no one had witnessed his loss of composure.

Moving to the back of the room the Magistrate heard voices as he descended the stairs to the cellar. Lit now by lanterns and candles throwing shadows over them the Magistrate espied several policemen in their shirtsleeves digging in the corner beside a set of iron cages. The Sergeant was standing watching.

"Anything to report John?"

The Sergeant drew on his pipe. "Babies, one no more than a day or two old, but the most of them are near skeletons. Here! If ye'd credit it."

"You'd be surprised at what I would credit after what I found upstairs." He looked over at the font. "What's a horse trough doing down here?"

"I think it's a well."

"In a cellar?"

The Sergeant shrugged. "All I know is one of the lads tried to measure the depth with his spade and couldn't find it."

The Magistrate walked over and peered in. "John."

"Sir."

"Don't let any of the men drink from this."

The Sergeant joined him and looked at the water. "Do

you think it's bad then?"

"Not in that sense. Are the men happy to carry on by themselves?" said the Magistrate.

"They are. Constable Donnell, you're in charge. If you want us we'll —"

"Be upstairs in the study," said the Magistrate, as he and the Sergeant left.

The Sergeant and the Magistrate entered the Doctor's private study by the cellar stairs.

The Sergeant looked around at the comfortable snug. "Nice little place."

The Magistrate pointed. "Look on those shelves."

The Sergeant peered closely. He moved between several examining the contents then said, "These are wee babbies here."

"They are indeed. John, would you be so kind as to tap at one or two?"

"Why? What do you expect me to see?"

"I will not answer that until you have complied with my request, for I fear for my sanity."

"Well we can't have that." The Sergeant smiled and tapped the glass. He frowned and looking more closely he tapped again. In a sudden movement, the homunculus swirled around in its glass tomb and bared tiny teeth causing the Sergeant to take a step back. "My God! What is it?"

"I'm glad you saw that also. I think we need to see Mr Delacherois now. Can you arrange it?"

Both the Magistrate and the Sergeant were sitting in the

Doctor's study reading the Doctor's records of his experiments when Mr Delacherois entered. "John! What do you mean summoning me." He noticed the body behind the desk. "My God, what has happened here?"

Both men rose and the Magistrate stood forward. "I summoned you Mr Delacherois." He put one of the volumes on the table and tapped it. "I require you to give me an explanation for these."

"I have nothing to say, Sir." Mr Delacherois indicated the Doctor. "What has passed here? I insist you tell me."

The Magistrate looked dubiously at Mr Delacherois. "He was found dead at his desk this morning and —"

"But we were in the Downshire till late!"

"No matter. He was stabbed through each eye," the Magistrate pointed to the paper knife on the desk, "With this."

"Each eye!" Mr Delacherois glanced at the remains. "And you think I did this?"

"No Sir. But in the course of our investigations, we have come across a most foul matter." He tapped the laboratory notes. "A matter in which you are named as a participant."

Mr Delacherois stiffened. "And what law am I suspected of having broken."

"Of that, I am not yet sure Sir. But something evil has been happening here. Mr Delacherois will you throw no light on this?"

"I would remind you I am a lawyer Sir. Good and evil are not my concern, the law has no business with such matters. Now if you excuse me I will have to have arrangements made to close the house until I find a new tenant."

Mr Delacherois entered the kitchen where he found the staff gathered under the watchful eye of a Constable. Mr Delacherois glared around the room. "Well here's a fine mess. Did no one hear a thing?"

Heads shook as Mrs McKee replied, "Sure there was nobody in the house at all." She paused. "Except for thon Hawthorne woman."

Mr Delacherois looked around. "And where is she?"

There was a silence and then Sarah said, "She's upstairs in her room. The police are with her."

"Ah!" He glanced at the Constable. "In view of this tragedy, I'll have to close the house. So I'm afraid I have to give you all your notice. Mrs McKee, I expect you'll be alright?"

"Oh, don't you mind about me? Willie and I will be fine."

Sarah said, "An' Cob and me had given our notice anyway."

"Really? I didn't know that. I'm sure that Cob would be welcome in my stables and we could fit you in somewhere."

Sarah made as to reply but Cob placed his hand over hers. "I…we thank you for the offer Sir, but we'll have to have a wee chat about our plans first."

"Well, I'll pay you your notice if you call down to the Manor House later. Mrs McKee, would you arrange for the house to be shut?"

"I will indeed sir."

Sarah interjected, "What about Mrs Hawthorne sir? She's nowhere to go."

"Well there's no place for her here…but I suppose she's entitled to stay until she works out her notice." Mr Delacherois turned back to Mrs McKee. "Tell her she can stay on half-pay until after the New Year. After that, it's no longer my concern. She can act as a custodian for the house until then."

That night Emma slept alone in an empty house.

Chapter 35

There had been mutterings about the goings on at Rosebank, and even a debate between Mr Delacherois and the Reverend Hill, about the propriety of burying the Doctor in consecrated ground however Mr Delacherois had quickly stamped that out, reminding the town who owned the very ground they lived on, and who had repaired the old church tower which had threatened collapse last winter.

The Doctor was buried on Mount Misery when a bitterly cold Easterly wind guaranteed that more than one attendant would catch their death. Black clouds promised rain and the Reverend Hill, still bruised from his disagreement with Mr Delacherois, sped through the service as fast as decency would permit.

Standing beside the grave Mr and Miss Delacherois had

assumed the position as chief mourners with Mrs McKee at their side. Sarah and Cob, who was buttoned uncomfortably into one of the Doctor's old suits, stood slightly behind but there was little in the way of congress between the parties beyond the stiffest inclination of heads.

Emma had attended but had stood at the very back speaking to no one through her veil. The coffin lowered and the ceremony complete, the mourners started to break up in anticipation of the funeral lunch that had been laid on at the Downshire Arms. Mr Delacherois handed Miss Delacherois up into his jarvey, and after a few muttered words, she took up the reins and started down the hill.

Emma had remained behind and moved closer to the grave watching as the sextons shovelled the raw earth over the Doctor.

Mr Delacherois approached Emma from behind and removed his hat. "I thought it was you."

Emma made a brief curtsy. "Pray replace your hat, Sir," Emma indicated the grave, "before you join him."

"Indeed…will you be joining us for luncheon?" He replaced his hat, then paused. "You would be most welcome."

Mr Delacherois's foot toyed with a clod of earth then pushed it into the grave. "He wasn't a bad man you know… just driven."

"For all the grief he has brought upon me and my son I still find it difficult in my heart to hate him."

"What will you do?"

"I'm hoping to go back to England, to my parents."

He nodded. "It's for the best I think, for everybody, if

you leave after the New Year." Mr Delacherois stared across the town towards the harbour where the packet was just putting out to sea. He started. "Have you enough? I mean have you sufficient —"

"I do Sir. The Doctor had given me enough for a few months. To help me to start a new life somewhere else."

Mr Delacherois raised his hat. "Goodbye, Mrs Hawthorne. It's unlikely we'll meet again."

14 Lexington Street,
  Teddington,
  London
  20th December 1855

Dear Mrs Hawthorne,

I hope you will forgive me writing to you, however, Mr Pettigrew the postman was at a loss as to what to do with your recent letter and passed it to me as he knew I was great chums with your Mother.

It's with a heavy heart that I have to tell you that your parents have both passed over in last year's outbreak of the flux. Your poor Mother was taken first followed closely by your Father, who was in attendance to her at the last.

I know that you were much in their thoughts at the end and both frequently called out to you.

Due to the press of bodies, they were both taken to the Crossbones graveyard over in Southwark and we had a whip around for a clergyman to say a few words and place some flowers at their final resting place.

The costs were five shillings and six pennies so if you would

like to make a small contribution it would be very gratefully
received.

Your obt. Servant,
Mrs James Dunn

With the house closed up and empty Emma wept as she went for long lonely walks through the dunes. Several times she approached the lighthouse but did not knock on the door. Seemingly content to stare up at the lighthouse as the rain ran down her cheeks.

Once or twice she saw Mrs McKee and, occasionally Sarah, but neither party acknowledged the other.

The town was lit and decorated for Christmas with even the rain falling to earth with a cheery note. Emma walked amongst the townsfolk ungreeted and, seemingly, unseen. She was regarded as the author of her own misfortunes and responsible for the loss of their pride and joy, Doctor Leslie.

Chapter 36

A small crowd had gathered by the pier surrounding Constable Boston when the Sergeant arrived. A fishing boat was tied to the foot of the steps with the remains of a body in it.

"Report Constable," the Sergeant ordered.

"We was out crabbing," interrupted the Skipper. "Out by the island when we saw a lot of gulls going at something on the rocks and —"

"We thought it was a seal but —" interrupted his Mate.

"You mind yer own business now! I'm talking to the Sergeant on official business." The Skipper turned back to the Sergeant. "But seals don't wear trousers see!"

The Sergeant looked down at the boat. "Bring him up here now."

The Skipper looked at the Sergeant. "Well see now we've lost a days fishing here. Would there be anything in the way of compensation?"

The Sergeant glanced at Constable Boston and raised his eyebrows. "I doubt it. Go on and hoist him up."

The Skipper looked down into the boat. "By rights he's salvage."

"Or bait," said the Mate.

"Oh for Christ's sake." The Sergeant took out a florin. "Here two bob to wet your whistles. Now bring him up!"

With much grumbling the body was recovered to the quayside.

"Oh God!" cried Constable Boston as he vomited.

Glaring at the Constable the Sergeant said, "Mind my boots Boston! Look at the state of them now!" He gestured to the fishermen. "Roll him over so we can get a look!" he ordered.

The Sergeant stepped closer to the body and stared at the face. "Jesus the gulls have given him a going over...still the face, the...By God, I know this one. This here is wee Charlie Hawthorne...the one Kerr's gang robbed out from his grave."

The Sergeant and the Magistrate were standing on Mount Misery watching gravediggers refilling Charlie's grave.

"Why do you think they took the body in the first place Sir?"

The Magistrate shook his head. "Your guess is as good as mine John. Maybe they thought to teach us a lesson?"

"Rum sort of lesson Sir."

The Magistrate snorted. "Rum! Oh very good. I'd say

more a Brandy sort of a lesson though wouldn't you?"

The Sergeant nodded towards Emma who was standing a little way away. "It's broken her."

"Aye well. She hasn't had much luck here poor thing," said the Magistrate.

That Christmas Eve night Emma couldn't sleep. She remembered the hope she had when they first arrived in this place. Emma had dreamed that Charlie and herself would find some safety and security in this new place. Of bettering herself, and giving Charlie a start in life, making his father proud. *Was that so wrong, to seek, to try, to hope?* Emma wandered from room to room in the darkened house with the crying of babies and the patter of tiny feet ahead, behind, all around her now.

As the pale sun rose over the town Emma walked to the harbour in a bitter East wind. Chilled to the bone and shivering she cast about the quayside until she found a heavy shackle, *that'll do.* Clutching it tight to her chest she staggered to the pier's edge. There Emma stood for a moment gathering her courage. Then taking a deep breath she stepped backwards into the grave-cold sea.

Instantly the shock drove the breath from her body. Emma gasped for air but only salt water answered. Panicking she released the shackle and tried to claw her way back to the surface but her wet clothes were now heavy enough to pull her down. As Emma looked up in desperation at the surface for assistance she thought that she could see Caleb and Charlie on the top deck of the lighthouse looking down at her then all faded to darkness.

I hope you enjoyed this book. If you did please leave a review on the Amazon website.

These reviews are very valuable and help support independent authors.

Thank you again,
JC

Thanks to Tom, Blair, and Di for all the support, gentle encouragement, and feedback.

Printed in Great Britain
by Amazon